# COLD-BLOODED BEAUTIFUL

By

Christine Zolendz

© 2014

*Again, this is dedicated to the ones that are*
*bruised and broken*
*Take my hand*
*It's scarred and stained*
*I'll pull you up and help you stand*
*You have the strength to ride the storm*
*I promise you*
*Don't look into the darkness*
*Don't look back*
*Don't even wave goodbye*
*Just find that courage*
*There is strength inside all of us*

# PROLOGUE

*Samantha*

I had just finished my trauma ICU rounds. The overhead call came through for an incoming trauma, while I was sneaking in a Snickers candy bar and leaning with my back against the cool wall of the staff lounge. "Trauma One. Trauma One. ETA five minutes." Savoring the sweetness of my first mouth-watering bite, I learned that the paramedics were en route and they were transporting a fifteen-year-old girl. She had been ejected from her family's car after a head-on collision *with an 18-wheeler* on the Henry Hudson Parkway. *God,* that made my stomach plunge, while burning bits of chocolate-nougat-caramel bile teased the back of my throat. In this job, you never knew what was going to come through those emergency room doors: gunshot wounds, stabbings, motor vehicle collisions, but the worst, was when any of them had anything to do with kids.

Shoving one more bite of candy into my mouth, I tossed the rest of the unfinished chocolate bar into the trash, rushed out, and sprinted down the corridor. Icy blasts of sterilized air mingled with the dark bitter smells of disinfectant and hospital food, permeated around me— through me.

I was running through a crowd of people toward the trauma bay to scrub up, when a stunningly gorgeous woman stepped in front of me, tripping me and almost hurling me into the wall. She grabbed my arm with icy cold hands and yanked me to a stop just before I landed.

"You know," she whispered in my ear, digging her perfectly manicured fingers into my skin, "he says my pussy is *perfect*. He calls me his 'Triple P.' *Perfect Piece of Pussy.*"

*Oh, crap. Did the Freud Squad lose another patient?*

"Excuse me?" I laughed, a bit out of breath, thinking she must have me confused with someone else. Either that, or someone left a bag of *nympho-crazy-women* open on the wrong floor of the hospital.

"Your husband," she explains, "after I ride him hard and fast. It's what he says. 'Triple P is what he calls me." She smiled triumphantly through blood red lipstick, and sashayed away on a pair of loud, deep-red clicking heels that were the exact shade that was smeared heavily across her lips.

"I believe you have the wrong person, Miss," I called after her, standing straighter, one hand dropping over my stomach.

The stunning woman pivoted on the balls of her feet, flinging a handful of golden bouncy curls over a shoulder as if she was starring in one of those perfect hair dye commercials. The hospital corridors spiraled out behind her; bright florescent lights casting blurs of bleeding rainbows inside my tired eyes. "Oh, I don't think so, Doctor *Samantha* Matthews. No, I don't think so at all. He, *David*, even showed me a picture of you."

She knew my name. *And my husband's.*

*Was my I.D. badge showing?*

*No, it was inside my scrubs.*

Behind the woman at the other end of the hall, over the loud hiss and clink of the emergency room doors, chaos erupted with the incoming rush of EMTs rolling in the injured girl, and for a moment, a brief one that *I am still so ashamed of*, I froze in complete and utter anguish. Rusty metallic smells hit my senses so forcefully that I stumbled back a step, caught off guard. The blonde haired woman smiled widely, winked, and then my vision caught the body of the fifteen-year-old trauma patient rolling towards me. I was on the move, trying my best to detach and store the hurt and anger for later. *This bleeding fifteen-year-old needed me more.* I barely had time to snap on a pair of latex gloves.

My stomach twisted, tightening every organ on its way up to my throat, filling it with a pool of vomit. I had to gag before swallowing it back down. *Detach. Just do your job. Focus, before your knees buckle.*

The patient flailed about on the gurney, covered from head to toe with blood, as panting paramedics screamed the rundown of what had happened. Deep crimson gauze was wrapped around the patient's thigh, head, and midsection, and I had to work fast and stay sharp if I was going to save the child's life. *Dear God, please, please help me save this child. Let me forget about David for a minute. Let me do my job.*

Removing the dressings, I started going through my checklist and barking out orders. Thankfully, *Samantha Matthews, the sideswiped wife,* disappeared, and Doctor Samantha Matthews, head trauma surgeon, took over.

Despite the thousands of hours of surgical training, horrifying years as a military surgeon overseas, and even all the brainwashing I endured in my early medical career, I still struggled with all of the human emotions that go along with harsh trauma. You don't get desensitized to it, not when it's a kid lying on the table, fighting for her life. Anyone who tells you otherwise is lying. Yet, as I always do, I try my hardest to project confidence, grace, strength, and complete control in front of my trauma team. Mentally, as my hands crawled along the poorly bandaged girl, I felt all of her injuries with the tips of my fingers.

*Holy shit, under the bandages, the kid was ripped to shreds.* It was as if her skin, the entirety of it, split down her center on impact. The stark white of her bones stood out against the angry red of her torn flesh. The deafening sound of my pulse rushed through my ears, engulfing my entire universe into one focal pinpoint. Exact. Simple. Save the life.

Immediately, I shoved my index finger into the bloodiest laceration on her thigh, plugging up the source of the most lethal area of the hemorrhage.

"Let's secure an airway!" I turned my attention to one of the trauma nurses. "I need an IV, an operating room...and get me two units of O-negative."

"Vitals!"

"Eighty-two over fifty-two! Heart rate one twenty!"

"Let's go. Let's go," I barked, and within minutes, my trauma team flew into the operating room, rolling in the patient with my fingers still deep inside her leg. The child's femoral artery was completely severed. In a matter of minutes, she could be dead, so I needed to work fast.

My team worked like one fluid person, perfect, and precise. No one noticed my bones were warring with gravity to move, or that my muscles were braided with thousand pound weights that were trying to pull me through the floor.

Within a few hours, I meticulously repaired whatever damage I could, dressed her wounds, and in my head, said a tiny prayer for the girl. Praising my flawless operating staff, I trudged out of the operating room, and headed straight to the sink to scrub the mess of blood and fluids from my body.

Emotionally exhausted, I made my way back to my office where I'd left the small lamp on, and the door wide open. The outside sky had turned almost black with the moonless night, and only one street lamp shone through my small window.

I'd done my best to save that girl's life. She was finally in stable condition in ICU, after four hours of intense surgery, and piecing her back together. But there was no family for her to be comforted by, because they were all down in the morgue. There wasn't any family to inform of the surgery or condition of the patient, because they all perished in the crash.

With my adrenaline rush depleted, my body crashed, and I collapsed heavily into the chair behind my desk. I was beyond exhausted, and I still had two hours left of my shift. Dropping my gaze, I noticed a stark white envelope lying in the middle of the desktop, with my name written in bold red letters across the top. I could've left it there, unopened and untouched, and then my story would have been so very different, but I didn't. The tiny slip of a paper, a small tear in the flap, and life could change completely. Endings and beginnings were meshed together, and formed circles like the little hamster wheels I never knew I ran in. My bones turned rubbery as I opened it, hesitantly, and fumbling. Unfolding the letter that was hidden inside, written on elegant pale pink stationary, I leaned my head back against the cold leather of the chair and read the words that would change my entire *fucking* life. Decorated and scented with roses was this *shit*:

*Dear Samantha Matthews,*

*You don't know me, and you may not believe anything in this letter. You may even think of it as a cruel prank, but please read it in its entirety and try to believe every word. I'm writing because you need to know the truth. We both need to know where each of us stands on this issue.*

*We have a lot in common, you and I. For one, we are both fucking your husband. Yes, you're the wife of my lover. A lover who has told me that he and I need to take some time away from each other, because he says that you are pregnant. That's why I came to the hospital today, to see for myself. To see with my own eyes all that should have been mine.*

*I've hated you for so long. I've hated everything you were. You have taken everything that was supposed to be mine and kept it for yourself. Now you need to know the truth, the truth about David and me, and let us be. I only hope that you have the brains to understand that I'm the one he's supposed to be with. He doesn't love you. He can't, because he's too in love with me. I'm the one he craves, and I'm the one he sneaks out to, because you're just not enough for him. Truth be told, he never loved you. Yours was a marriage of convenience, a business deal.*

*I'm not sorry for anything I have done. I'm not sorry for hurting you, because everything you have, should have been mine. And I'm not sorry for telling you this, because you need to leave and let us be together. Everything I have done with David has been out of pure love and zero regret. My heart, my body, my mind, and my soul, belong to him; not yours. I belong with him and to him; you are not the right one for his needs. Maybe in the medical world that you both live in, but not in David's real world. A world you know nothing about. You're not what he wants or needs, I am.*

*I love him too much to be without him.*

*Every single time he came home late, it was because of me. Every single time he came into your bed, smelling a little different, it was because of me. Every minute he is away from you, he is with me.*

*I don't even know if you're really pregnant, nor do I care. Just realize that you will never know the real David, the one who loves me more than he could ever love someone like you.*

*Please show this letter to him, and listen to what he says. I'm sure he'll lie to you and leave the punishments for me. I will take anything he will give me.*

*Aurora*

My heart raced. *What the hell kind of crap did I just step in? What kind of delusional freak writes a letter to her lover's wife?* Not that I believed it. I needed my shift to end. I needed to get home. I needed to show this to David. None of this could be true, right?

*Right?*

*I mean, I would know if he...I would be able to tell... Right?*

*I feel sick.*

He says my pussy is *perfect.* He calls me his Triple P. *Perfect Piece of Pussy. He showed me a picture of you,* she'd said. Those were the exact words. I couldn't unhear them, and they wouldn't get the hell out of my head.

I counted the minutes in heartbeats, because that was all I felt, all I heard. The thick pounding thumps of my pulse slammed against my chest, until I could leave the hospital and go home.

In the stark white hallways, people spoke to me. I might have smiled some sort of zombified smile back at them, but I'll never be sure. You're never sure how other people experience you. The only thing I knew, was that I was just walking through corridors and waiting. Waiting until I could get home. Waiting to see my husband.

My husband.

The one who might be fucking a perfect piece of pussy.

Which apparently, was *not* mine.

David, the man that stood next to me in his sharp Armani suit, in my excruciatingly expensive antique framed wedding picture, which hung on tiny silver hooks against the soft cream-colored walls of our home.

I don't even remember leaving the hospital. My brain could not wrap around the thought of the person I was married to, being with someone else. The front door to our apartment just sort of appeared in front of me, and I walked right through it. Sick to my stomach and so freaking nervous, I thought that I might shit myself.

I found him in the kitchen drinking his morning coffee, New York Times in hand, a glint of early morning light reflecting rainbows off his Rolex watch. He'd be leaving in ten minutes, following my rounds in the hospital. We were a well-oiled machine, at least that's what I had thought. Until that woman grabbed my arm and whispered those words in my ear.

*Perfect Piece of Pussy.* His *Triple P.*

He never called me that. He usually never spoke while having sex with me.

This bullshit couldn't be true.

*But she knew I was pregnant. Not many people knew, and I sure as shit didn't look almost twenty weeks into my pregnancy. I really feel sick.*

I laid the letter out flat on the kitchen island where he sat, sliding it silently across the granite top, until it passed underneath the newsprint paper he grasped in his fingers.

He took a few seconds to skim over it. A small downward dip of his lip was all the expression he gave. "You aren't entertaining the writings of some psychotic, are you?" He asked casually, after dropping the paper quickly. Picking up his coffee cup gingerly, he sipped silently at his fancy homemade vanilla cream latte. The stench of its sweetness made me gag.

"I thought it warranted a peek from you, since your name was implicated in the affair."

"Where does it say my name?" He asked, turning the letter this way and that. "My *full* name? How do I know she's writing this about me and not David Resner over in gynecology. He's faced with cunts all day long. It's probably him."

"She spoke it, when she came to visit me at the hospital, and don't be vulgar." *Yes, I was bluffing.* She never mentioned his last name, only mine. Look, I usually trusted my husband explicitly, but something just didn't feel right about this. It felt too *real*. For the first time, I questioned him, because really, it could very well be true. Maybe being pregnant was giving me a sixth sense. Paranoia.

He stood up and pecked a chaste kiss against my temple, leaving the letter on the table, disregarding it completely. "Don't be fooled by childish high school drama. I have no time for affairs. I'm lucky if I get to make love to my wife." He smiled, grabbed my chin hard, and told me he loved me.

It was the first time I knew, without a doubt, he was lying to me. *The first of many times.*

It wouldn't be one rash moment of infidelity, it was tens, it was hundreds, *hell,* it was probably more like thousands. I thought David was the love of my life. I was wrong. He was the love of many women's lives. I found out that little tidbit of information fifteen minutes after that bastard left, and I tore through his piece of shit computer, armed with his password and printer.

What the *hell?*

Images, so many of them, *file folders of them,* of the most disturbing sexual nature I'd ever seen. Videos of rape fantasies, and OH MY GOD! *WAS THAT A HORSE?* Emails and exchanged pictures with other women, so many other women. There was an account on the popular *AshleyMadison website,* the number one dating site to find someone to cheat on your spouse with, beyond disturbing correspondence with private *punishment clubs.*

I know what all you marriage-believing-you-could-work-through-anything-if-you-just-believe-people,     are thinking right now. *Oh, she shouldn't throw away a good marriage just because of a little infidelity.* If only it were that easy.

Although, I would give you a slow applause for whatever *you* would choose in *your* own situation, I was not a person who believed a *slew of infidelities* could be forgiven. It couldn't. Not in my eyes. Not in my heart. My marriage was over. There were no accidental slips and falls into various different vaginas. There were only distinct planned out *choices* to have affairs and go through with them. Repeatedly. Unfortunately, his affairs were the least of my problems.

One particular file folder glowed on his desktop as if it were radioactive. *SamMatt Pharmaceuticals.*

*SamMatt Pharmaceuticals? As in Samantha Matthew Pharmaceuticals? What the hell was in there?* With steady and precise fingers, I clicked it open.

SamMatt Pharmaceuticals was a multi-million dollar company almost as big as Johnson & Johnson and Pfizer. Its labs were outsourced to other countries, and there was a list of top hospitals and doctors who spoke in their favor. Why was my name at the top of this list? Why was this company, SamMatt, named after me?

I had no clue. I couldn't think straight. I had no...I mean...David was cheating on me and I had no idea what to do. For the first time in my life, I was clueless.

I was damn sure to print out everything I found.

And copy all his files onto my flash drives.

Both of my flash drives.

It was like signing my own death certificate.

Three hours later, I walked out of his office, sick to my stomach, feeling the very first fluttery butterflies of the small life that had been growing inside me for the last four and a half months. I hid everything in my computer bag, emailed everything to myself, and walked out into the brilliant light of the August summer sun. Moist heat melted over my body, instantly sticking my clothes to my skin. My stomach rolled and fluttered. Placing a free hand over it, I hummed a small lullaby to the child within. With trembling legs and a feverish mind, I completed a couple of errands that were on the criminally insane side of the law. I would not let David get away with what I found, not with cheating on me, and not with whatever pharmaceutical hood he was pulling over the hospital's eyes. I mean, this was my father's hospital. *My father* was the president and those papers were falsified. God only knew what that was all about. Then I vomited for the rest of the day, hovering over my bathroom sink, wishing I had the physical strength to pack my bags. *Maybe after a little nap.* I had plenty of time to pack a bag and leave.

But all that wasn't the bad part. No, not yet. That was just the beginning of my nightmares. I should have left then. Through the stomach rolling, vomiting, and exhaustion, I should have just gotten up and hailed a cab to a hotel. I should have just disappeared and never turned back.

Nobody would have died then.

# CHAPTER 1

## Kade

It was a humbling experience to know and love her. She made everything I'd ever thought as my truth, something that I could transform into, and something better that I could live with on the inside.

Samantha was still asleep. Loose cinnamon colored hair splayed out across the feathered pillows as she curled herself around my body. She lay bare, save for the thick gray comforter she'd tangled her body in. I wanted to wake her and talk. I wanted her to tell me the story of her past, the one she had run from, the one that led her to this desolate town, the one for whom I had the whole bloody Sherriff's department and hospital fake her death. It was terror that stopped me from waking her and demanding more answers. Not my terror, not my fear; hers. For all the strength and courage she possessed, I knew that whatever had happened between her husband, David and her, was some sort of darkness that had slowly spread inside her, completely paralyzing her.

I knew everyone had a past. I knew she wasn't some bright-eyed virgin when I met her. She was a thirty-two year old woman who was one of New York City's most renowned trauma surgeons, who spent six years overseas putting back the pieces of our broken soldiers. This woman was tough, brave, and I just wanted, *no...fuck*, I needed to know how one piece of shit of a man, made her give up everything and run. I mean, the man made her give up her career. She was a *surgeon*, and I knew she loved it. I saw her save my brother's life when he was gunned down in his bar. I watched her eyes light up when her trained fingertips slid over his broken flesh, and like some sort of magic, stopped his blood from flowing out of his body. Why would she leave all that behind?

She curled tighter beside me, nuzzling her face deeper into the soft folds of the blankets. A faint glint of light fell through the open curtains, as the sun began to break over the horizon. It landed softly along the smooth skin of her arm, making her ivory skin look as if she was cast in stone, and her beautiful skin that whispered her scent to me, the soft, smooth, ivory flesh that touched me like no other. Despite the gentle rays of sun brightening on her, she somehow radiated light from within. For months now, she'd been bloody illuminating my darkness, shedding light on my demons who lurked and hunkered down, drooling and growling in the corners of my messed up mind. I wanted to skim my fingers across her skin and wake her, make her tell me all her fears. I wanted to destroy them, rip them to small confetti sized pieces, send them out to sea, and feed my savage demons with them.

I knew everything else about her, except for those fears, and that heavy weight of horror she'd carried around. I knew the way she took her coffee was different for each flavor she chose. Regular coffee was black, but hazelnut, you add sugar. Her choice of favorite color changed each day with her mood. Gray was for when she was sad, purple when she was happy. I knew she loved her new job at the hospital where she'd been working for the last few months, but I questioned if it was challenging enough for her. I didn't get why she wasn't put on the trauma team.

I wanted to shake her awake and make her tell me everything.

I wanted to bloody know why she wasn't taken to be part of the trauma team at the hospital in town. I had the right to know too, since my damn money was what funded their psychiatric wing for the last 10 years, and again, my money that helped build their suicide prevention campaign. I wanted to know why, as the best trauma surgeon in New York City, she wasn't given the head trauma position at the hospital. Especially, since I specifically asked that she be interviewed for the position. She still held all her credentials, still held all her licenses, just under a different name.

*Annnd*, because I'm a mean dick, I poked her with my figures. What? Don't give me that face, she's used to my *Kade-ness*. *You should be too*. Come on, it's me, Mr. Dark and intriguing with a side of fucked up. *Yeah, I'm pretty much priceless.*

She shifted against me as her eyes fluttered open. "Hey," she sighed, lifting her head up off the pillows.

Her hair spilled around her shoulders, and the comforter slid beneath her breasts. Rose tipped nipples teased out at me, and immediately, I was lost in the thought of my mouth around one, nipping at it softly with my teeth. I watched, captivated, as they trembled when she giggled at the way I was looking at her. "You look hungry, Kade."

She was right. And all my questions vanished. The answers could wait. Tasting her flesh was more important.

"Starving," I whispered, lapping my tongue around a nipple, as it hardened and puckered tightly between my lips. Head tipping back, she arched her body closer to me and sighed. My mouth slipped slowly from her breasts and traveled along her silky neck up to her lips. Her hands quickly slipped my shorts off and wrapped tightly around my suddenly throbbing cock. *She was just as hungry as I was*.

I wanted her so desperately that moment, I could already hear the sounds of her moans when she's falling apart around me. I could smell her arousal, and it was fucking making me salivate. "You make me want to devour you." I shifted over to the side and flipped her onto her stomach, straddling her calves.

She giggled her laugh into the blankets, muting its music.

From the soft nape of her neck, to the dimples of her lower back, I trailed the tip of my tongue. Delicately, I bit into the flesh of her hip, as I slowly skimmed my fingertips down her back.

"That's just...Kade, oh, God," she squirmed underneath me. I ravaged her body with my tongue, my lips, and the rough pads of my fingers, not stopping until her thighs quivered with need, and her breathing panted with thick anticipation.

She arched her back and moaned when I slipped my fingers into the wet flesh between her thighs. With the other hand, I threaded my fingers through her hair, and gently pulled her head back to see her eyes. "Please, Kade. I need you," she whispered softly, through parted lips.

Lowering my mouth to her warmth, I ran my tongue along the edges where my fingers slowly pushed and pulled inside her. No one should taste that good. Sinful. Delicious. Someone needed to bottle that shit.

Muscles pulsed and wept against my fingers, as I took her to the edge, then stilled my efforts and withdrew, sliding wet fingers along her thighs and up her sides. Pressing myself against her, my hard tight skin to her damp wet flesh.

"Fuck me," her voice trembled.

*My favorite words.*

I sunk into her slowly, pulling the back of her thighs flush against the skin of my hips. "Fuck, Sam. Your body does wicked things to my cock." Her muscles fluttered and pulsed around me, as I moved inside her with slow, hard thrusts.

She whimpered and fisted the sheets above her head, as her muscles trembled and thickened around me. The sight of her, my Samantha, bent over in front of me, sheathing me in her warmth, was almost unbearably breathtaking, and every roll and plunge of my shaft, flooded me with a burning heat that coiled from somewhere deep in my darkness. Restraining myself to slow, steady thrusts, I let my eyes travel her perfection, taking in every detail that was only mine to see. The arch of her spine, the exquisite dimples over her lower back, and the scars I tried each day to erase with my kisses. Lowering my mouth to her skin and my hands around to the front, I let my fingers play a rhythm to match her breathing. She drove her back against me, slipping and sliding along the edge with me, over and over, until the pressure building became too much, until the intensity became too strong, and she whimpered, "Kade...don't stop...oh, God..." Her muscles twitched and tightened, convulsing around me so tightly that I could barely hold on to her hips. I thrust faster and harder to match the sound of her cries, and spilled myself inside her until both of us collapsed against the warm sheets beneath us. I would melt inside her if I could, fade into her flesh, asphyxiate in her bloodstream, and drown in her heat.

Yes, I know. You think I'm all foam, no beer. Certifiable. Hat-full-of-asshole-crazy.

You think I need some sort of bloody help, yeah? An intervention? Yes, I absolutely do, but don't bother with one, because I'd only end up killing you.

For the last few months, my life was full of everything, full of Samantha. It was good. My life consisted of:

1. Writing
2. Waking up to Sam
3. Laughing
4. Spending time with Dylan
5. Sex with Sam
6. Lots of fucking sex with Sam

7. Laughing and having lots of amazing fucking sex with Sam

It was pure heaven, and I wasn't leaving heaven any bloody time soon, I was getting a house built there and moving the fuck in. I mean, come on, go and reread 2, 5, 6 and 7. Samantha was now my primary coping mechanism. Her touch, her voice, *hell* just her smile, helped me to stave off turning in my house for four padded walls and a straightjacket. Until I met Sam, my life was tragic to say the least, with my demons always casting shadows over me, clawing and scratching at my door. In my youth I had been touched by violence, *that bloody shit changes you*. Violence destroys. After it strikes and runs, it continues to devour you. People touched by it spend the rest of their lives like a mouse in a maze, desperate for a bloody way out. Sam was my way out.

Months of shared glances and soft touches. Evading secrets and living in our little darkness, hot breaths and hungry furious caresses, frenzied kisses, ripping off one another's clothes with no words between us, just touches and teeth and tongues. Smells, tastes, and the sounds of warm wet skin, touching, kissing, and fucking each time like it would be our last. Never getting enough of each other, whispers and needs, sweat and filth; trying desperately to calm the demons that possessed us both. *And her demons, well, they played very well with mine*, and when we were together, neither of us had to babysit them, they went off on their own, leaving us be.

It's never been like this before, not for me, not with any other woman. The things I felt about Sam should probably be bloody illegal in most states, not that I'd care, because I couldn't stop. I couldn't stop how I felt, I can't stop how I feel; I won't. Ever.

I fought so hard to keep her out of my mind when we first met, but she slipped in like soft vapors of mist, and seeped into my skin, her soul burrowing into my chest, taking such a complete hold of it that I felt it would not work without her. My heart, the half-dead organ it was, was bruised from the bloody hand that she held it in. I had told her I was falling in love with her, a few moments before my body claimed hers for the first time months ago, the utmost bloody disgusting cliché for a writer, but I did it. It was pure deception. Because I wasn't falling, I had plummeted the minute I saw her, and have been lying at her feet ever since.

I left her to sleep, my beautiful sanity, my literal Doctor Frankenstein, who'd brought me back to life. Without her, I turn cold and harsh, mute and inhuman, like the stone sculptures that decorate the ancient world that's been long lost.

I got dressed in the shadows of my bedroom, our bedroom, since I refused to let her leave and find her own place. It was too dangerous anyway. I know that her ex thinks she's dead, but I couldn't concentrate or breathe right when I know she's alone, and the people whom I suspect have tried to kill her are still out there. I've even gone to the extreme of moving my brother, Dylan, and his girlfriend, Jennifer, here with me, with us. Jen and

Samantha were on the run together, but now they're safe, I've made sure of it. We had gone to the Sheriff's Department together, Samantha and I, and she gave all the evidence she found on her ex's computer over to them, who in turn handed it to the New York City Police Department.

Because of the severity of domestic abuse she told them about (and let's be honest, my exuberant donation to the department), they staged an accident and her death. They even sent a request for her dental records so we'd have them on hand for the accident, helping us with every little detail. For two months, she stayed in an undisclosed location, as she was questioned at length about what she knew. Me, I was told nothing, of course. I couldn't even see her. I could only write letters to her. But did that stop me from stalking the shit out of her, fuck no. I'd bump into her at different places, slipping notes in her pockets. Yeah, I even creeped myself out there for a bit, but Sam, she bloody loved it.

She filled out a New York State name change petition and a name change order, and she was now Samantha Tucseedo. She changed her social security number and had requested all the documents to be sealed, because of her fear of domestic violence, she didn't speak much about it, kept it all from me. For a while, before we faked the accident, she had to prove she needed protection from him to seal all the records. I was left out of it all. She didn't want me to know any of the details. Yet, they had been given all the details and were building their case against David and Samantha's father, for whatever part he was guilty for, but that was their job. My job was to keep her safe, and that's what I'd been doing for the last few months.

I knew I'd been extreme, I knew what I felt, the paranoia was irrational, but Samantha understood where I was coming from. She understood my distrust in people, my violent tendencies, and she accepted me without pause. She'd even let me install a cell tracker on her phone so I'd always know she was safe if I needed too. Don't get all your feminist panties in a twist yet; it was Samantha's idea. See what I mean? She bloody accepted me.

Look, I don't know how much you know about me, but I'm not...bloody right. I'm trying my best to be, but it's bloody hard with everything I've been through. So don't judge. Not unless you were ever on the receiving side of a barrel of a gun *with* the trigger pulled.

Leaving her a note about getting some errands done, I walked out into the icy winter morning and climbed into my truck. Sam didn't have to be at the clinic for another two hours, so I figured I'd let her sleep and get my chance to speak to the hospital's president about the trauma unit position, and see if there was some sort of misunderstanding. *Yes, I know, I'm pushy.* I'm also arrogant, selfish, mean, and pretty much clinically fucked in the head, so whatever. You try debating it with my demons. They usually don't let you get a word in edgewise.

For some odd reason, my truck smelled like some sort of citrusy sandalwood scent. For a fleeting second, I wondered what weird tasting coffee Sam might have found in town and brought back home in my truck, but I just opened the windows to the crisp cold air and started the twenty-five minute drive to the hospital. It was too citrusy to be a coffee anyway, sort of smelled like shitty perfume. It was probably Jen; she had horrible taste in things, just look at my brother.

Zipping through the roads, I drove as fast as I could get the truck to move, knowing Sam was probably just getting herself ready to make her own trek to the hospital for her shift. It took me less time to drive there, and double the time to find the head of the place. The one I'd been playing tag with for the last four weeks to talk to her about all this bloody shit.

Within the hour, I was literally cornering the president, Doctor Janet Luger, in her office, me standing there, arms crossed over my chest like a damn street thug. I'm bloody positive I wasn't a very friendly sight, but she looked worse for wear than I did. I hadn't seen a doctor wear a white lab coat in years, yet, there she stood, Doctor Luger with the coat buttoned tight up to her wrinkled neck, wearing a thick layered inch of caked on make-up that threatened to crack off in tiny crumbs down the front of her uniform. Her skin had a strange orange hue to it, like she'd just come from the Jersey Shore. With one tiny paper-thin skinned finger, she slowly pushed a pair of bright red-framed glasses up along the bridge of her nose.

"Kade Grayson, what do I owe this pleasure?" she chuckled, leaning her bottom on the edge of her desk.

Small delicate hands gestured for me to take a seat in front of her on one of the leather hospital chairs. They were vomit-green and made me cringe when my body touched down on them.

*She knew damn bloody well why I was here.*

"You know I'm here about Samantha. Janet, I thought she'd he a perfect shoe-in for the head of the trauma team. She *is* perfect for it. You and I have spoke about this numerous times, and I just don't understand why you would refuse to give her the position after everything I've told you. I don't get it, the best trauma surgeon you could ask for is working downstairs in your *family clinic.* It's a waste of good resources."

She leaned further back on her desk, slightly lifting her feet off the floor, and gave me a small nod of her ancient head. Then sighed.

I shifted forward, propping my elbows on the hard metal of the chairs. "What happened?"

"Kade, nothing happened, she just refused it. You have to understand her position here, we don't know if they'll ever go away, and they haven't gotten worse, but they would be a great liability to the hospital and she just doesn't want to take the chance."

"I'm bloody lost. What *they* are you speaking about? *Who* will go away, *who* hasn't gotten worse?" I stammered, as a thick knot of something formed tightly in my chest, and shifted itself up into the back of my throat, making the taste of anger real and tangible to my tongue.

"Not *who,* Kade. *What.* Her tremors."

"What tremors?"

Janet's expression stilled and only the smallest intake of a gasp met my ears. "She hasn't told you about her condition?"

"No," I could barely get the word out. Fuck. Fuck. Fuck.

"Oh, darling, I've known you for so many years. You've given so much to this hospital and have healed so much. You need to speak with Samantha, Kade. I think there are things she hasn't told you." Her faded-blue eyes moistened and her eyebrows lifted together.

Samantha had a *condition*. The thought of her being sick made my fists ball.

"Is...is this condition...life threatening?" I spit out.

*Please don't say something that will make me fucking lose my shit on your old wrinkled ass.*

"In my book, Samantha Tucseedo is a miracle. She shouldn't still be alive," she said, standing and slowly making her way past me. Her arm reached out to me, her hand neared my shoulder and paused. Frail fingertips brushed my skin. "Sorry," she whispered, "I know you don't like to be touched. She's a strong woman, Kade, just keep that ex-husband of hers away from her."

I was left standing in her office with more questions than answers about Samantha, *again*. "NO! You're not leaving this office. Not until I know more. Give me her bloody files then, let me see all her files. Janet, I need to know what's going on, and she won't tell me anything."

Spinning on her heels, she arched her brows at me. "You know very well that I uphold doctor-patient confidentiality to the highest degrees and..."

*Staunch-holier-than-thou-bitch. She'd probably freeze a dick right off a man with just a blow of a kiss.*

"I'm not asking you to go in front of a court of law and expel all her secrets, I'm asking you to give me something...fucking anything..." I wanted to wring her neck. Could just picture it, the way her eyes would bulge with thick bursting veins.

Janet just stared at me and blinked. "Ask yourself why she won't let you in, maybe you need to ask yourself why she can't tell you things, maybe she's not who you really think she is. Did that ever occur to you, Kade? That maybe she *is* a criminal? I don't know anything about her, Kade. All I know, is that she's here because of *you*. She's got sealed records of her entire career as a surgeon, what's that say to people? It says to me that she was in some kind of trouble, bigger than what she's telling everyone." She walked away stiffly, the sharp click of her heels bounced off the walls, piercing my ears. That bitch just tried to redirect my anger from her to Sam; *do I look like I'm five?*

To hell with that, I looked down at my watch. *Jen would still be at the hospital, so I'll go get answers from her.*

I stalked through the hallways, and stormed down four flights of stairs, because I was too impatient to wait for an elevator. Jen had been a nurse in the same hospital in New York City where Sam had worked, so it was easy to get her a job here in the hospital as well. It wasn't as fast paced as what they were both used to, but it beat working in my brother's strip club as waitresses.

I found her in the pediatrics wing at the nurse's station, a bit out of breath and fuming.

The minute she saw me, her face blanched and guilt tore through me. "Kade? What's wrong? Is Dylan okay?" A handful of loose papers slipped out of her fingers and fell like feathers to the ground. I should have realized she would have been bloody worried about seeing me, but I was never one to think about what other people might be going through, I was selfish that way. *And apparently classy and personable, like you wouldn't believe.*

"Dylan's fine. He's still at home, probably in bed playing that X-box thing I bought him," I said evenly. "Can I talk to you? Privately for a minute."

Bending down, she kept her narrowed eyes on mine and quickly scooped up the papers that had fallen. "Yeah, sure. Let's go into the lounge, okay?"

I walked ahead of her, as she explained to the other nurses at the station that she needed to speak with me for a few moments, and then she started texting on her phone. *Great, the twit was telling on me, as if we were bloody ten.* I slammed open the door to the lounge, making two orderlies jump and gasp.

"Your break is up. Get out of here," I hissed. I smiled when they left without questioning me, the pussies. They even answered me with a *yes sir.* I forgot sometimes that the townspeople here still think I'm more dangerous than the devil himself; it was good to know I still scared the crap out of people. *I'll save all the muscle flexing and gratuitous display of gun show until later; right now, I needed answers.*

Behind me, Jen rushed in with her hands deep in the front pockets of her uniform, eyes wide. "What's going on?"

Stepping really close to her, I tried to use my anger to show how very serious I was. I knew it was a douchebag move, but to hell with it. It's what I was known for. When I was about a foot from her face, staring down at her, I snapped. "I was just informed that Samantha refused the head trauma position." Jen opened her mouth to talk, but I shoved my hand up in the air to tell her I wasn't finished speaking. "That's not what I'm twisted about, so don't say anything until I'm bloody well finished. Luger told me that the reason she said no is because of some condition she has; something about tremors." I leaned my face in closer, "Start talking."

"You and Sam should try having a lot more discussions and a lot less sex. And stop being all threatening to me too, Kade. I just texted her when you asked me to talk. She's here at the hospital and she's on her way up now."

"Just fucking tell me if she's sick! Or so help me God, I will get her medical files myself!" I screamed.

"Oh, Kade, no. No, she's fine, she'll be fine," she whispered.

"Does this have to do with *him*?"

"Yes," she whispered, just as if death sighed into the wind.

"I should've fucking killed him. Scratch that, *I'm going to fucking kill him*," I roared, slamming my fists into the counter behind me.

*If I kill him I'll lose everything*, but if I don't, she'll never be free. I've changed so much in the last few months since her mock accident. I've been through intense therapy; I've psychoanalyzed the shit out of myself, yet I'm still obsessed with her and with possessing her, consuming her completely. I know it's not healthy, but seriously, from the dark reclusive corners I've reserved myself to, I find this to be a much more pleasant place. But, thinking that something is wrong with her and it has something to do with him is going to make me fucking go insane.

The lounge door opened and closed with a small bell-like sound. I didn't know who had come in or left; I was blinded with fury, but I could hear her soft fluid movements and smell the cinnamon and apple scent of her soap. "Kade? Kade what's wrong?" she whispered.

It took me a few minutes for my eyes to focus on her, for my head to clear itself of violent images, and for me to see her actually standing in front of me. We were alone in the room. I couldn't even tell you when Jen left, or how long I stood there.

"You're sick?" I whispered hoarsely. "You didn't take the position because you're sick." Visions of hospital beds and breathing tubes, blood and stapled skin filled my vision. The sounds that my brain offered me were worse;

gunshots, clicks, pleas, cries, and the never ending hiss and buzz of the ventilator. I hadn't had a flashback in so long that I had to grip the edge of the counter to stop myself from falling to my knees.

Instantly, her cool hands were around my neck, her small frame pressed against mine, and the only thing I could do, was grasp on to her. "I'm fine, Kade. Why did you come here? You should have just asked me."

"You're bloody sick, Sam, and you haven't told me."

"Stop, Kade. I'm fine. I swear, I'm fine."

"You're bloody fucking lying to me. You have some sort of condition and tremors. DON'T LIE TO ME!"

She backed away quickly. Of course, she would. Who in their right mind would step on a landmine? I was about to explode. I'm positive that in her head, she heard a metallic clink and felt the vacuum of air, as I self-destructed like a forgotten pressure mine buried just below the ground that she stood upon.

Shoving her hands into the front pockets of her sweater, she stared at me with red-rimmed eyes. Her chest started rising and falling heavily, panting as if she'd just finished a bloody marathon. Hell, we were both breathing hard. "This is a hospital," she hissed. "Control your emotions. This can wait until we get home. This is going too far, Kade. You DO NOT get to go through my private medical files because you have questions. And you don't get to scream at me like that. What do you want from me?"

"I WANT THE TRUTH!" I demanded, shoving one of the chairs over.

"Really, Kade? How are you going to handle that?" Her eyes were vicious and challenging. At least, I thought that's what it looked like. A definite blur of thick-knotted tension between us fogged up the room. She pivoted and reached to open the door, and before I could think straight, I was grasping at her waist and pushing her against the wall. Pressing my body against her, she was trapped, her hands pushing against my chest, but not nearly hard enough.

"Truth," I whispered into her ear, gripping her tighter. The tips of my fingers dug into her flesh.

She stood, eyes wide, and breathing heavy. One lone tear raged war against her eyelid and won, slipping down her cheek and dropping perfectly against the soft flesh of her chest. "He killed my baby, Kade. He killed my baby while it was still inside me. Then he killed me, *literally*, Kade. I *died*. He poisoned me over and over, until I died. Now, I live with the after effects. I'll never be a trauma surgeon again. I have neurological damage that make my hands tremble *all the time*. Would you want me to cut someone you love open with twitchy fingers?"

# CHAPTER 2

## Samantha

It had just passed midnight as I stood outside to wait for Kade on his flagstone porch, wondering where he'd gone, and what he'd done. A few hours before, when I finished my shift at the hospital, I had built a fire in the stone pit built into the middle of the porch. It was smoldering now, just a few small embers of wood left to help me stay warm. At eleven, it had started to hail. Icy cold cascades of marble sized sleet collided hard against the stones, creating a thunderous sound that drowned out even my most horrible thoughts with its echoes. I was certain that, as soon as he came home, things were going to escalate. I was positive that everything we had would go up in flames when his obsessive behaviors wouldn't accept my past. Kade wanted to go back and change everything, but he couldn't. He wanted to right every wrong done to me, and if I told him everything, and I gave him the chance, he'd kill David and my father. I couldn't let him, not after all the violence that he had to live through in his own life. For that reason, in the last two months we've lived together, I have deflected most of his questions, only giving him a little bit of answers at a time. I knew it wasn't going to last long, his patience, but his therapy was going so well and he'd changed so much. I just didn't want to cause him any more hurt; he didn't deserve it.

Fifteen minutes after the last embers of the fire died out, and there was nothing more than ashes, his figure emerged from the dense evergreen forest that surrounded the house. Slowly, with his dangerous eyes glaring their venom at me, he made his way up the path to the stone steps of the porch. Dark strands of wet hair were plastered to his face. His clothing was drenched, sticking icily to his body, and they made a theatrical sound as he moved.

"Where did you go?" my voice betrayed me, wavering and cracking with insecurity.

"I went for a run," he hissed through clenched teeth. His muscles were taut and granite-like under the wet material of his clothes. His shirt, completely see-through, with rippling tendons and tissue just underneath, made my mouth dry.

"You're going to end up with pneumonia, Kade..." I stood up to reach my hands out to him to try to warm him, but he stepped away.

"How would you feel, Sam, if everybody knew that fact *but you*? If I hid it from you, along with a whole closet full of bloody secrets. It makes me feel all bloody warm and cuddly inside when you lie to me, *said no one, ever*."

I opened the patio doors of the house for him to walk inside, and watched in fear, as the warmth wracked shivers up his body so violently that he needed to lean against the wall for help. "Take off your clothes, Kade."

Slumping against the wall, he stood watching me, his soaking clothes pooling a large lake of icy water around his sneakers. "You've gutted me with worry today, and you want to *fuck?*"

Idiot. I lunged at him, yanked the heavy wet material of his shirt over his head, and began pulling down his running pants, "Yeah, Kade. I cherish the idea of jabbing an icicle inside my body right now." I tried to calm myself by taking a deep breath, but my challenging rage got the better of me, as it seemed to always do when I'm with Kade. "In all your glorious-brilliant-idiocy, did you ever stop to think that maybe I'm stripping you of your clothing because I don't want you to freeze to death?" I finally got all of the sopping clothes off and dropped them heavily into the kitchen sink. I dragged him to the den where a fire was burning and wrapped him in whatever blankets I could find, and tossed a pair of warm flannel pants at him. I put on a pot of water for tea, and within a few minutes, placed a steaming cup of tea laced with a bit of his favorite brandy in front of him. "Drink it," I whispered.

The hard muscles of his jaw tightened and flexed beneath the skin, as he brought the cup to his lips. I watched his throat move as he swallowed, and found myself wanting to tangle my body with his and fuck this fight away. It's what we always did when our emotions became too intense. When the truth of our pasts became to heavy to bear, we slipped easily into each other and blocked out the world. *We couldn't keep doing this to each other, could we?* I felt the skin of my face burn when his eyes fixed unblinkingly on mine.

"Do you even understand how you make me feel when I see you blush like that? You need to tell me what's going on. Tell me *something*, babe. I can't do this anymore, this sick twisted worrying, I need more of the story." The sad smile he offered me pulled at my insides, "I don't want half of you, or bits and pieces, baby. I bloody want all of you."

In the reflection of his smoky grey eyes, I saw myself surrender. It was bittersweet. I cherished being able to tell him my problems, to find comfort in him. I knew with every truth I would tell, it would become an open festering wound on him that would never heal. Kade had enough of his own scars to deal with, but I had to give him something, he was right.

It was hard for me to begin, hard for me to repeat. It was hard for me to *believe*. I was ashamed, because I never thought anything like that could happen to someone like me. It made me feel weak. I didn't even know where to begin. There was no starting point, was there?

There was no point at all.

I could still feel the rope tightening around my neck. My husband David brought me to the gallows, carried me up and let the lynch mob have at me. He'd tied me to my own funeral pyre and set it aflame, all while laughing, as he watched the fire lick at my skin. He had signed my name to papers, and built *an entire corporation* that I would never have allowed to be in existence, setting up and framing me for something I'd never do. The bridal veil of my wedding day was a beautiful veil of illusions. He never loved me. Not ever. Not one ounce.

I tried to explain the experience of being married to David. It's easy to remember too, because all I have to do is close my eyes, and my nightmares play as if there's an IMAX theater behind my lids.

When I got home from my last deployment, my father pulled his puppet strings, and immediately, I was in the trauma unit at New York Presbyterian Hospital, where I met Doctor David Stanton. He was controlling, vicious, dangerous, sadistic, and extremely manipulative. Competitive with me and my career, but I didn't see any of these things until later, until after. Until after the blonde in the hospital, the one with the blood red heels.

That day, when I found the note, what she had written and the things I found on the computer, it turned me into a stalker. I'm sorry. You may think it immature or infantile, but if the words that woman whispered in my ear didn't suddenly make *you* an expert in reconnaissance on your husband and his mistress, you're a better person than I am. I knew my behavior wasn't normal. It wasn't something an intelligent woman with a medical degree would do, but it was something that a broken hearted woman did, one that wanted the truth. So, in my crowning moment of most awesomeness, I hid behind the steering wheel of my car, jacket wrapped over my head and eyes peeking out, watching and waiting.

The blonde woman was so easy to find too. All I had to do was step foot outside the hospital and there she was, smiling and swaying her ass at one of the new resident doctors. *Great, she's a medical groupie, one of those nutrient starved minds who try to hook a doctor for the prestige and money they could gain, instead of working for it.* Okay, maybe she wasn't nutrient deprived, but the fact was, she wasn't Mensa material, and that's for sure. What mistress in their right mind would go and tell the wife all of their secrets? How would *that* get him back? *Okay, let's be honest here. Of course, I'm going to call her stupid and nutrient deprived, because she was telling me she was sleeping with my husband, and that's not a person you're going to think lovely-yay-the-world-is-so-beautiful things about. No, you're going to rub their name around in the mud, sling it all over the place, and dirty it up to make you feel better about getting your heart broken. Truth. Right then in my head, she was an evil, sexual predator that sunk her gold-digging talons into my husband's cock, and was sucking him dry.*

Grasping my steering wheel as if I was strangling someone's freaking esophagus, I followed her home. I hated her instantly. From the stupid perfect way her salon-style hair blew in the wind, to the way her stilettos *didn't* tremble awkwardly as she walked like mine did if I tried to wear them. I hated that she looked so perfect, like a perfect porn star specimen, compared to the frump-styled bookworm nerd that I was.

I was never a violent person, but I *really* wanted to watch her being hit by a bus, and yes, I am ashamed of thinking that, but I did, and images of her flat on the ground instead of '*riding my husband with her Triple P status*', made me feel a lot better.

I followed her all the way to a tiny apartment on the Upper West Side of Manhattan, and sat outside in my car as if I was on an episode of a new reality TV show, *Whorehunters*. *I know I sound mean and petty, but it's a natural thought process to blame the mistress, and not the husband first. If you don't believe me, you're lucky to never have felt it, then good on you, go hug your significant other.* Mine is a devious, soul sucking, small dicked bastard, and his mistress is a whore. Period.

Then in a rash moment of morbid insanity, I rang her bell and invited myself in for some decaf coffee. Again, please remember, I was pregnant, emotional, hormonal, and hurt. There were no plans, no set thoughts. I just *went and did*, as if my life had gone on autopilot. I just went there and rang her bell, as if it was no big deal.

*Aurora* was more than happy to tell me all about their sordid affair, and completed the experience with a high definition video of her riding my husband like a fucking bronco bull, while someone else plugged up her various other orifices. She was also, somehow, hogtied. I knew David was occasionally into bondage and playing the dominant role *lightly*, but what I saw was pure sadistic. Not only did he enjoy hurting her (at one point, his entire arm was inserted *somewhere* up to his *elbow*), he ended the video by forcing the other man to excrete a bowel movement on her chest. *Yes, you just read that right.* It's okay to cringe, because it's definitely cringe-worthy. Gag a little if you have to. *I was a freaking trauma surgeon* and it was the most disgusting thing I'd ever seen. My face was in Aurora's bathroom sink, instantly purging anything and everything from my stomach, while my husband's mistress rubbed my aching back, trying somehow to soothe me.

The entire time, she smiled and giggled like what she just showed me brought back fond memories for her. Now, I'm not one to judge people on their sexual desires, and if that got Aurora off, then that's just awesome for her, but *my husband*? He was so controlled and soft with me, almost to the point of me feeling a bit bored with my sex life, but what I saw in that video was like another person.

Everything I had ever thought about my husband was a lie. Everything. We had been married for less than six months. We had one of those fast whirlwind courtships that lasted a year before we were married. I thought I knew him. I thought all wrong. I had been married to an extremely talented liar. Not once in our entire relationship, did I even have a glimmer of suspicion of him carrying on a secret affair. There wasn't even a speck of guilt I could remember, and no strange warnings or dubious actions that I was aware of.

I wasn't a naïve little idiot in denial, no, he was just that damn good at it.

That night, when his shift was over, he walked into our penthouse with all the televisions playing the video of them fucking. He laughed like it was a brilliant joke.

"Divorce," was the only word I could say.

"No, thank you," was his reply.

He sauntered into our bedroom and undressed, pulling this and that out of his drawers. I didn't pay attention. The pretty little sky in my world was crumbling, raining down fake blue shards of glass that pierced my heart and instantly made me hate him. *Fuck him and his no thank you.* I didn't need him. I didn't need any man.

And I certainly didn't want a man that had a whole secret life that had nothing to do with me.

So, while his ego filled the room and his peacock feathers spread out, I smiled to myself and pulled out my duffel bag and started packing *my* belongings. He could have the penthouse apartment and furniture, the knickknacks and photos, the towels and every other material thing that was there. I just wanted my dignity.

But that wasn't enough for him.

"Do you want to know who else I fucked?" He asked, walking closer to me. He stood over me, so close and menacingly. I immediately looked him dead in the eyes. I wasn't going to cower. Yeah, me, not the cowering type. "I fucked someone in the bathroom at our dinner party last week while you served our guests cocktails and hors d'oeuvres. I loved those little toasted shrimp things, by the way." He laughed, then leaned his head down and whispered into my ear, "You heard me grunting and moaning and asked if I was okay, didn't you?" He smiled. "It makes me hard as fucking hell to think that you're going to wonder who it was I was fucking up against your bathroom wall, while you were a few feet away. The next time we go out together, or maybe the next time we're at a hospital function, you'll wonder if the woman across from you whispering into another's ear is gossiping to her friends about how big your husband's cock is."

"Yeah, not going to happen. You see, I'm walking out that front door over there." I made sure to dramatically point to it, in case he didn't have the brain function to comprehend me. "And when I do, I will *never...* Let me say it clearer...*NEVER* give you another thought. *Oh, and your dick isn't big at all.*"

"I didn't even wash them off my skin before I sunk my dick inside you," he seethed.

I vomited. I vomited violently in front of him and he laughed. "You make me sick," I spit the words out with the last of the bile, and wiped my mouth clean with the edge of the bedspread that I would also be leaving to him.

Out of nowhere, the palm of his hand lay into my face like an oncoming freight train and left a wave of pain and fresh blood inside my mouth. "You don't get to speak to me like that," he barked, raising his hand to hit me again. Immediately, my fists were up ready to block another hit, one to protect my face, another to protect my unborn child.

"I'm not afraid of you, David. And, I'm not one of your little collared whores who will submit to you. If you want someone to heel to your will, buy a damn dog. I'm leaving." Leaning on the bed, I straightened up, fists clenched and itching to hit him, but I needed to protect my baby. I was pregnant. I needed to be in a safe place, away from that animal. "And if you ever hit me again, I *will* fight back."

Just as I reached the door, I heard *it*. The unmistakable sound of a magazine being pressed into its mag-well with a harsh metallic *clack*. The racking of the slide, as a bullet slid into the chamber. Metal glided against metal and clicked. It's a sound that makes you stop, makes you paralyzed with finality, as you wait for the shot. For me though, it's a sound that I turned my head towards, so I could look the ass-maggot in the eyes.

David's Glock was steady, aimed right for my head. The only thing I could think about was my baby inside of me, and protecting her. I needed to talk my way out of this. "David..."

"You are *my* wife. *I own you*. I know every little thing about you, your fears, your wants and needs. I know what makes you dripping wet, Samantha. You like it when I make you dripping wet, right, Sam? You can't go anywhere, Sam. If you do, I will fucking find you. I will hunt you down like a fucking deer and shoot you right between the eyes. Are you afraid of me now?"

*Oh, my God, he's crazy.* "Yes, David. I'm...I'm afraid," I stammered, blinking back tears as he touched the cold barrel of the gun to my throat. My pulse beat against the metal, moving his hand in small quick tremors. One small pull of the trigger, a mere six pounds of pressure, and my jugular would be blown to shit, and no one would find me, he'd be brilliant about it, I was sure. *Feed his ego, but don't let him see you cry*. I refused to give him the satisfaction of watching my tears fall.

Ominous whiskey colored eyes gleamed and danced with the sight of my fear. The sick fuck was reveling in it.

My husband, the man I once vowed to spend the rest of my life with, was a monster. I was shocked. And, don't ask those stupid condescending questions people always think when they hear about a husband abusing his wife – *Why didn't you just leave? Why were you so weak?*

*Didn't you see it coming?* There are no universal domestic violence guidelines. There aren't any fucking abuse checklists that us girls sit around and learn about in a high school class, or an orientation of relationships 101. I had a strong sense of self. I had decent self-esteem. I'd fought in fucking wars and I'd seen and done things not many women ever did. And, I sure as shit didn't see this coming.

It *did* happen all at once with David and me. I was in love with him, but I had a separate life than him. I had a career, an ambitious demanding career, and so did he. **He never hit me, never got jealous, and never showed me anything but complete adoration**. *Until he didn't...* Little things changed at first, and you don't see them at once, only in hindsight. Only then, when I stood with a gun to my throat and his finger on the trigger. Hindsight is a bitch isn't it? It loves to come back and fuck you from out of nowhere.

I've seen him belittle and demean the sweetest nurses and orderlies at the hospital. I've watched him once, *and only once,* get jealous and snap my cell phone in half, when a fellow soldier called me while on leave in the city wanting to get together for coffee. It was little things that became clear and pronounced that very minute. Just a handful of tiny things and the rest was a perfect husband, *or at least the facade of one*.

"Take off your clothes," he demanded, sliding the gun up my cheek to stop on my temple. A hundred panic filled scenarios filled my mind, the loudest one being him forcing himself on me, and I, *Lorena-Bobbitt* the motherfucker. *Yes, in a heartbeat, I would bite that dick right off.* The shock and sheer pain he'd be in would give me plenty of time to get to the door. I prayed like hell he'd put the gun down, Because other than the *Bobbitt* situation, I couldn't fight him. The gun was too close, and the life of my baby, too precious.

"Take off your fucking clothes!" he roared louder.

Now, there's a huge fucking difference between taking off your fucking clothes, and trying to outsmart him, and outright dying at the hands of a madman, so I just did what he said. Because seriously, if I refused him, was that the way I want the world to find me in the end? No, sorry, that's not the way I want my story to end. Let's go for what's behind curtain number two. I get it, I truly do, the thoughts that are running around in your head right now: Run! Fight! Kick him in the dick! Let me express again what the scenario was. There's a gun wedged hard against my temple. I feel the cool metal of it. I can blatantly see the safety is *NOT* on, and the magazine is clipped in and probably fully loaded. Like I've said before, it takes only SIX pounds of pressure against that little trigger, and then my brain will collide with the wall. I could shove him away hard, he could move that trigger softly, **BOOM**, my baby is going to die, and my brains would need to be scraped off the walls. I can't even think about the possibility of losing my unborn child. I happen to like my brains, as they've been with me for thirty-two years, and I have trained them and exercised them to almost genius fucking status, and I want to KEEP them inside my skull.

Still don't agree with me? Then, let's probe the crazy that is my husband. I had watched a video of him with another woman, and his reply to the whole thing was to laugh, tell me how he'd screwed someone else, and complimented me on my damn *toasted shrimp*. He told me he *would* kill me. Told me he owned me. Oh, and let's not forget the bigger picture here. Try to envision it with me, okay? HE'S GOT A GUN, FULLY LOADED, TO MY HEAD. Most twisted part: he's fucking smiling.

The butt of the gun moved in a quick violent motion, and my world went black. God only knows how long I was out for.

An indescribable scorching pain along my pelvis and across my lower back was what woke me. When I looked down at my body, my eyes blurred instantly, and I was gasping at air to stifle the shrieks of pain that were bubbling in my throat.

*What I saw almost killed me.*

Beads of cold sweat exploded across my cheeks and forehead.

I couldn't believe what I saw was real.

He branded me with his name. My skin, it *burned,* and I'm panicked and sick. Blisters have formed in the shape of the name David, and I feel the intense throbs of pain pulsing and screaming at me. The burn had extended through my epidermis and into the dermis, its second layer, and I moaned out in agony, because I knew I would have these scars for the rest of my life, however long that might be. My stomach was rolling...and then I felt them...

The *cramps...* My body felt beaten, but my stomach felt wrong. It felt so wrong.

Looking around, I found myself lying on my bed, still naked, cold and shivering, with a thick layer of sweat pouring out of my pores. The muscles of my lower back and stomach were convulsing, and there was an intense cramping and clenching of my uterus.

*Oh, God. No, please, please don't take my baby.*

In the blur of my eyes, I saw David as he sat at my desk with the papers from my bag strewn all over the floor...*he knows I know*... The way he looked at me was sickening. If I doubted before what I had found about SamMatt Pharmaceuticals, there was no doubt now. Those papers were *his*, and what was on those papers would put *me* in jail for the rest of my life, yet I was totally innocent. The huge offshore bank accounts with my name on them were all *his*. He framed me, set me up, all that time, so he could steal millions of dollars from my father's hospital. Aurora was telling me the truth. He never did love me.

I could feel it then, the life of my child seeping out of me. I felt her leaving me and I couldn't protect her. I couldn't keep her safe. I felt my heart just dry up and shrivel, harden, and die.

The monster turned his face in my direction, gun still pointing at my head, "What the fuck did you do? You went through my private belongings. This is the end of you. Do you understand that you just killed yourself, baby? I can't let you live after this."

"David. Take me to the hospital. The baby. The baby," I cried.

"Baby's gone. I took care of *that* while you were asleep. That should have been a blowjob, anyway."

*What?*

*No.*

*No.*

"No. No, David, no-no-no-no-no-no," I sobbed. "Oh, God. What did you do? What did you do to me? What did you do?"

His face was in mine instantly with the gun held to my chin, "What else did you see? What else did you take?"

Red blood spread across the sheets underneath me, my uterus convulsed in pain. "Everything," I hissed. "And I made five copies of each. You'll never find them, but if something happens to me, everyone will." I smiled. "Oh, and check your secret accounts, dear. All that money you stole from *my hospital*? It's gone, you fucking piece of shit."

# CHAPTER 3

## Kade

Rage.

Samantha was visibly shaking as she whispered her story.

I should have killed him.

The sick part was that I knew there was so much more to this story, and she was completely spent just telling me *this* much. I knew this was overload. I knew what she was feeling. I knew she could see the images thick and visceral - real and solid right in front of her, because as she spoke, her emerald eyes followed the ghosts of the things that haunted the room.

"Okay, Sam. Enough for tonight, love, I can't let you suffer through this again. I...we'll talk again, more, but you need a break." I held her in my arms and kissed her on the temple, the one that I knew still felt the lingering apparition of David's gun. "I promise you, I will never let him hurt you again." Lifting her gently, I carried her into the bathroom and placed her softly on the chaise lounge.

I ran a bath for her as she sat and stared blankly at the ceiling. The look in her eyes was so broken and full of agony, it made me want to rip someone apart. Taking out all her soaps and scrubby shit, I placed them in order along the edge of the steaming tub. I knew what she needed after letting that filth out, *I knew Sam*; she needed to clean herself, rub herself raw with apples and fucking cinnamon. "I'm sorry I pushed you to talk today, but the thought of you being sick killed me. I know talking about him makes you feel dirty, baby. Go ahead, wash him off your skin."

Her vacant eyes still stared up at the ceiling.

*Holy fuck, Sam lost a baby.* I had to stop her from telling me more. Fuck, I just want to watch him die. Really slow. *All I saw was red.*

Closing the door, I left her in the bathroom and stormed into my den. I tried every fucking anger management piece of shit step the doctors had shoved down my throat for the last four months, but NOTHING helped. Explosive rage tore through me and I completely snapped.

I could only vaguely remember any of it.

It started like a little knot of venom in the pit of my stomach and began eating its way through my body, taking control. A surge of heat traveled over my skin, making me sweat instantly, and my heart was slamming painfully against my chest, pounding too loud for my ears to take. "BLOODY FUCKING HELL!" I roared, screaming a string of harsh words in my rage until my throat burned and my words ran dry. Slamming my fists over and over again through the drywall, breaking holes and tearing the flesh of my knuckles until I saw my own blood. That's what I was going to do to the motherfucker's skull when I caught him. The fucking doctors were going to have to remove my fists surgically from his internal bloody organs, just to bury the cocksucker. My knuckles burned, stung, and split over and over again as I repeatedly slammed them into *everything*. Cartilage snapped and cracked, bones splintered and popped. Yet I felt only numb blinding rage. Somewhere in the back of my mind, I could hear pounding on the door, muffled voices yelling my name, but I was too far-gone. I wished David was standing in front of me. I wished that I could hurt him every day for the rest of his life. I wanted to see him bleed and I didn't care about consequences. I just needed to see the cuts, rake my fingers across his broken flesh, and indulge in the crimson spray of his suffering. I wanted to burn her name across his forehead and watch it bubble and hiss with the blistering flames. I wanted justice. Revenge.

When my eyes became focused, and my breathing slowed, there was broken glass and furniture littered all over the room. The curtains were torn off the windows and my extremely large couch had been thrown right through it. Giant shards of glass were sticking out of the leather, and a cold wind drifted in from the other side. My desk chair was dangling by a wire in my flat screen television that had a brilliant desk-chair-sized-hole in the middle of it. The chair twirled and swayed in the breeze. *I don't think I'll be stopping my therapy anytime soon.*

Opening the door, I stumbled out into the hallway, and fell into the kitchen. My hands were a bloody mess and my throat was scorched dry. It was three o'clock in the morning and Jen was in the kitchen, holding one of my steak knives, shaking and crying. The blade of the knife glimmered and trembled harshly with the vibrations of her fear. "If you *touched* her, hurt her in any way, I will *gut* you," she warned.

"With a fucking steak knife?" I laughed, dryly.

Violently trembling hands held the knife out threateningly. "Where is Samantha?"

Before I could answer, Dylan rushed through the door with a crowbar and a baseball bat. "I got the crowbar, come on!" When he saw me standing there, he froze, and held the bat out towards me, another person, threatening me, this time with a blunt object. *They're acting like this from what they heard, imagine what they'll do when they see the fucking den. I don't care; it's my damn house.*

"Sam is taking a bath. I got a bit self-destructive, but I'm sorted out now and did a bit of redecorating in the den, *and...*" I looked directly at Jen and tried to give her some sort of reassuring smile while climbing to my feet, "I would never lay a hand on her in violence, not in the way that David did. So put your weapons down, and really, Dylan? A baseball bat? I have five different licensed firearms in this house and you went for the bat? Seriously, if you thought I was hurting her, you bloody call 911!"

Jen dropped the steak knife into the sink and slumped down onto the floor, Dylan was next to her instantly, pulling her into his arms. *Oh, get a freaking room.*

"You were screaming and there was glass breaking and I thought..." Jen stammered, tears falling down her face.

I raked my hands through my hair. They came back drenched with my own sweat, and I shivered. "Look...Sam told me about...about...losing the baby, about David putting a gun to her head, knocking her out and the branding. I just ran her a bath, closed the door behind me, and lost it. That man does not deserve to breathe," I said, with an eerie calmness as I began pulling paper towels off the roll and patting at my mangled hands.

Dylan rubbed his hands over his face, "Wait, what? She had a miscarriage and her husband got angry with *her*?"

Wiping the tears away with the sleeves of her shirt, Jen stood up slowly and leaned against the counter for support, "No, Dylan. Samantha didn't have a miscarriage. That bastard gave her an injection of a combination of Digoxin and Potassium Chloride. When you inject it into the heart of a fetus, it assures no chance of a live birth, and the death of the fetus is immediate. It's how they administer late term abortions due to fetal anomaly." Streams of tears poured down her face, and she gave up on wiping them away. "Kade, that was just the beginning. He had her tied down to their bed. He gained control of everything after her mock *miscarriage*. She wasn't dealing with a normal man. He was a psychopath, precise, and vicious. He put on a brilliant show for everyone and she was the starring puppet."

"Bloody hell," Dylan whispered.

*Me. I said nothing.*

*Because there were no bloody fucking words.*

*My heart was just ripping right out of my chest.* My Sammy didn't just lose her child; it was taken from her, from her *body*. And I could *see* it. I could see her in my head, blood between her shaking thighs, and him viciously laughing, standing over her. I can't *not imagine* it. I can't stop the imagery. It clenches at my throat and doesn't let go.

Jen rubbed the back of her neck and took a shaky breath through the tears. "He told everyone she had suffered a miscarriage and set her up with sick leave from the hospital. Then he told everyone she was depressed and didn't want visitors. No one knew where she was, and no one saw her for *weeks*," Jen whimpered and hiccupped. "No one thought anything of it, because, my God, she was so happy to be pregnant, everyone assumed she was just in mourning. Even her father said she was just taking some time away from everyone because of what happened. But after two weeks, I tried to visit her and no one answered the door. Then it struck me as strange, because Sam was the type of person to throw herself into work when she was upset, not hide from the world. She worked constantly, always on call, pre-call, post call, being a trauma surgeon was her entire existence. She wasn't a regular person-her life-everything was just *trauma*. When reality was that he had held her captive the entire time, breaking her day by day. He was a genius really; his whole plan was just pure genius." A loud sob exploded through her lips and she hung her face into her hands, "She's going to kill me for telling you, Kade."

Dylan turned on the coffee pot and reached up to find some cups in the cabinets. Pushing myself off the counter, I moved towards the table and awkwardly collapsed onto one of the chairs and sat still, listening to the sound of the coffee maker hiss to life. I needed to focus on the sound, because I couldn't explode in front of

Sam any more than I had. I had to be better for her than what he was. The water heated and hissed. My knuckles flexed and clenched.

Jen whimpered again, inhaled a long deep breath, and sat across from me at the table. She hung her head in her hands for a moment and then fixed her eyes on mine. "You know what you did in your den, is the reason why you don't know shit about what happened to her, right? She's terrified of how you will react. She's terrified that everything you've been working through with your PTSD, will get all messed up and she'd make your recovery worse."

"I will never hurt her, Jen. Never."

"But you want to hurt David. You look ready to drive for seven hours, meet him in the hospital, and blow his brains out. I can see it in your eyes," she said.

"Yeah, and? You don't think he deserves to die? Because he's living the same life and she's hiding here. She was a surgeon. A bloody *surgeon*, and somehow, he took that away from her, which I still don't bloody understand. Because the both of you are keeping secrets, he should die, and *I SHOULD BE THE ONE TO DO IT*. Who bloody better equipped than me? I wouldn't take a car there; I'd take a plane. I'd get there faster and I wouldn't blow his brains out. I would torture him for a very, very long time. Now tell me what else happened, or else, I'll start bloody redecorating in here too!" I slammed my bloody fists on the table repeatedly until she started to talk again.

"Okay, okay...*damn it, Kade!* I'm doing this for HER, not you! Not you! Okay... so little by little, he gave her tea each morning, it was laced with something, something really bad. Like a *good* husband, David completely played the part of being married to someone who'd become mentally incompetent from a grief driven breakdown. After three weeks, he let people visit her. We all saw that she was depressed and sick, lethargic. She couldn't even stay awake long enough to speak. She just lost her baby. Kade, she was about five months pregnant, and she had to give birth to a baby that she knew had died inside her. We all thought she'd broken." Jen shifted in her seat as if she was uncomfortable with what she was about to say, and let out a low puff of breath. "Then I got a call from one of the nurses in emergency, saying that they just brought someone who looked a lot like Sam in. David said she tried to commit suicide by taking a handful of sleeping pills. When they got her to the hospital, they had to resuscitate her, twice. She left a note on the side of her bed. All it said was she couldn't live with the grief. David was adamant about the hospital doing an extensive autopsy if she died, but she didn't, so he ordered toxicity reports of everything in her blood."

Dylan handed us mugs of steaming black coffee and slid a half-gallon of milk across the tabletop. "I don't understand, wasn't he lacing her tea? Why would he want people to find anything? Oh, wait, was he lacing it with the sleeping pills?"

"No, he wanted the doctors and lab staff to find exactly what had gotten her sick. See...in the regular spectrum of toxicity tests, they don't usually screen for certain things any longer, like cyanide. Cyanide poisoning is uncommon because it's a regulated substance. You can't get it unless you work in chemicals or pharmaceuticals. The lab was content with the show of sleeping pills, even though there were too few in her system to do the damage she was showing, but David pressed for the cyanide screening as soon as her tests came back with an unusually high level of acid in her blood stream."

Dylan knocked on the table with his knuckles and shrugged, "I still don't get it. Am I just a bloody idiot? Why did the bloody wanker want everyone to know she had cyanide poisoning, if he was the one who was bloody giving her the poison?"

A small shuffling by the door stopped our conversation. Sam stood halfway in the doorway, while tiny drips of bathwater crawled down her face and neck, dropping onto the kitchen floor from her still wet hair. The strong aroma of her apple cinnamon soap stained the air, flooding my mouth with saliva.

"Because he wanted to pin me for the pharmaceutical fraud he was part of. He knew I was moral and righteous when it came to medicine, so he planned that if anyone were to look into anything that was going wrong with his little façade, all fingers would point to me. I had gone through his papers, and found that *my father* and my husband had created a fake company with me as the president. The company was a counterfeit pharmaceutical company, one that made shitty generic drugs in third world countries," she took a deep breath and looked up at the ceiling. *Bloody hell, she couldn't even look at me.* "The hospital and various other non-profit entities, were billed for billions of dollars in counterfeit medicine; all okayed with *my signature.* Charities and private philanthropists donated to *my foundation* for years, without me even knowing it existed." Her eyes reddened. Glazed over from the memories. "My father and David built themselves an empire while I was deployed. I was so used. *My own father,*" her voice cracked. "I would never knowingly agree to any of that stuff. Do you even know the risks that are associated by taking counterfeit medicines? What if you're a patient in my hospital and you're being treated for cancer? You trust me, your surgeon, to give you the correct and best medicine that I can to shrink your tumor. However, the medicine I really give you is not potent enough with the right drug, and contains too many other dangerous contaminants, like fucking arsenic or cyanide. Which were their go-to shitty fillers. Why? Because they can make a patient look like they died from natural causes, or some underlying shit, and not from the treatment the surgeon was providing. I think my father thought I would die overseas and I wouldn't ever find out, but when I came home, he needed to watch over me carefully, so he got me a husband, the only person he trusted, his partner in crime."

"And this is what he was giving you?" Dylan asked.

"In very small doses, both arsenic and cyanide, among other things, but they were the most lethal and did the most damage to me."

"What the fuck did it do?" Dylan asked.

I *couldn't* ask. I couldn't speak a damn word. Held it in. Held it in, grinding my teeth, nostrils flaring, eyes stinging so she wouldn't get hurt any more. No more. Never again.

"The lovely cyanide will starve the body of its oxygen. It destroys the enzyme that is crucial for cellular metabolism. The death of the cells will result in the death of the victim being poisoned. As you can see, I didn't die, but I came away from the situation with a nice bag full of neurological issues, and limbs that tremor. The majority of people who are poisoned this way die."

"Huh?" Dylan questioned.

"Didn't you ever go to high school chemistry? It messed with the things I needed to make my body function correctly, to keep the oxygen flowing in me, and to keep me breathing correctly. It's like messing with a car's fuel system. A car won't run on mud instead of gasoline; the mud only plugs up the car's fuel system."

"I was poisoned with mixture of a bunch of their filler medications, so with the suicide note I *supposedly* left, it just compounded the idea that I knew these medicines would kill people, since I used it to try to commit suicide, and *my company* was using them. David held it above my head. Leave him, and he tells authorities, and I'd be the one in trouble, not him," she whispered.

"There was only one thing wrong with his plan," Jen said, quietly.

"What was that?" Dylan asked.

"He underestimated me. As soon as I was strong enough and woke up, I slipped out of the hospital. I packed my bags and Jen was going to drive me to the airport. I was going to by a ticket to one place, and disappear to another. But he caught me leaving, just before Jen got there. This time, I wasn't pregnant, and I fought back. I should have checked his pulse. Jen was so scared when she found us, and he even got a punch right into her face. She dragged me off him, and I didn't think he was alive. Not until that night in the bar when he sent that guy to kill me."

I sat silently. What could I have said? This was the first time in weeks she opened up; I wanted to absorb everything. *And yes, I was happily planning his death. He bloody well deserved it, don't you agree?*

Sam walked over to me and slowly unwrapped the bloody paper towels I had wrapped my knuckles with. Her lips pressed tightly together and she swallowed hard when she saw the damage. My stomach knotted from her expression. I deserved pain like this, not Samantha. Yet, all I did was add to hers. I didn't even think I could hate myself any more if I tried. *Yes, may I have a little more self-loathing with my coffee?*

I stared up into her eyes as she washed out my cuts. I felt nothing but her soft warm hands, no pain, nothing but her calming touch. Her eyes were red-rimmed as if she was holding back tears, yet her features were smooth and expressionless. Her fingers moved slowly and meticulously over the broken flesh, pulling out small fragments of glass and plastic. At some point, Jen had brought down Sam's aid-pack, and ointment was slathered onto the mess of my hands, and gauze was covered over my skin.

The moment, Jen and Dylan left the room to get some sleep, Sam walked to the door to leave, and then glanced back towards me. Her eyes were bright red, then surrendered to their tears, unfocused, and deadpanned. "Don't ever do that to yourself again. You need to promise me that whatever happened to me, or whatever happens to us, you will never take it out on yourself again."

"I wish I could, *Doc*, but, I will never promise you anything that I can't make good on. You deserve better than that."

Her chin trembled and she pinched her lips to hold back a sob. One broke through anyway, and shaking her head, she walked away. That look and those tears tore at my heart, but I could never promise her that. And I knew. I knew it was only a matter of time before that woman walked the fuck out of my life, because I was fucked up beyond repair. How was I supposed to stop it? *How do I stop being how I am*?

*This is* who I am.

# CHAPTER 4

## Samantha

I heard them talking in the kitchen as I walked downstairs looking for Kade, wrapped in one of his dark terrycloth robes.   Hushed whispers, fists slamming, Jen sniffling, of course, they must have been speaking of me. Passing the den, I stopped in complete shock.   Unease rolled deep in my belly. *Oh my God, he had lost control. Please let it have been a bat he took to the room and not his hands.*

Jen's voice hissed out, taking my attention off the wreckage of the den.   Then like uncontrollable projectile word vomit, she was telling them about the torture David dragged me through. *What the hell was she thinking? This is going to kill Kade and push him into the monster that he fears lies dormant in his soul.* Anger bubbled up in my throat, choking me.   I knew she meant well. Jen was just trying to help him understand, but even she didn't know everything. *No one ever will.*   There are things, words that just won't pass my lips, emotions and fears I won't let myself remember. I can't.   I have to be stronger than them.   I have to be, or they will consume me.

*Do you understand that?*

I leaned against the outside of the door, listening. My terror warped into a few worthless insignificant bunch of spoken words.   They didn't hold the weight of my experience. No, the weight of it was safely tucked away in my heart, so as not to hurt the ones I loved.

*Oh, my God.* Your warped curiosity wants to know anyway, doesn't it? Fuck it. As long as it's not you, right? As long as the story is about someone else and you can get to feel bad, get to be part of the experience *a bit*, and then walk away without all the years of anger and fear that really comes with *it*. I get it; it's human nature. It's okay, I'll be your spokesperson for domestic abuse. I'll be the face of victimization, and you can live vicariously through me. Go ahead, I've signed the release forms, and made sure no one else but me will be hurt in the making of the dramatization.

There is a reason why I'm a strong person. There is a reason for my inability to filter the things I say when I see an underdog, or feel oppressed in any way, or when someone tells me *I* can't do something. I fucking *earned it*. *I earned respect* when I put myself through medical school, and chose to use my talents to help save people who were fighting for my freedoms, and *I can't even begin to tell you about the hell that was in Afghanistan or Kuwait*. *I earned my strength* when a sick psychotic man took the perfect world I built for myself, shook it like a snow globe, and smashed it up against a wall. I have earned every breath I've ever took, while being choked at the hands of that madman. Can you even begin to understand what it would feel like, if the person you chose to spend the rest of your life with was trying to kill you? Torture you? You probably couldn't even fathom what it would feel like, if you found out your husband had another secret life, well hidden from the one you knew. You probably think it's impossible.

Nothing in this life is impossible.

Peek through his cell phone.

Look through the history on his computer.

Watch his eyes wander at a restaurant.

Listen quietly in the shadows as he speaks to one of his friends.

Think about the dark thoughts in your own mind and about the monsters that hide under *your* bed. Think about the things you're ashamed of thinking, feeling, and doing. Anything is possible.

*Nobody in this world is completely innocent.*

For three weeks after losing my baby, David kept a steady line of drugs flowing through my veins, and he was so ingenious about it too. Every few days, he'd change the way he'd administer them to me. Some days, they were straight into my blood stream with syringes. Some days they were gassed into the air, saturated into a cotton cloth and held over my mouth and nose, or just ingested into my stomach with a small sip of water. Minutes where I was conscious, I could fight him; fight taking the drugs, but everything was so cloudy and chaotic, I never knew what was real and what were the hallucinations.

Every day, I was chained and shackled to our bed, and every day, he'd remind me of how *nobody* was coming to save me. How *I was crazy* and a *criminal* for what I'd done with the fake company that *he created*. After two weeks, my body was so weakened and frail from the constant line of drugs, it began purging itself and shutting down. To live, I pretended to believe him, pretended to understand that I was his, nothing more than a piece of property, one of his assets. Pretend it was okay that he could do what he wished to me without my consent.

It's not enough to gloss over it, is it? You want to know more, feel more, huh?

My so-called husband was an uncontrolled, undisciplined *sadist*. Forget everything you've learned about dominant men, and the kink of BDSM, because a sadist is something I'm not sure you truly understand. Dominants, men or women, get off by controlling the sexual experience they give to their submissive partners. They will inflict pain or pleasure. It could be physical or emotional to *intensify* the experience for the submissive person. Even if the pain is unpleasant, they're doing it, knowing that the submissive is finding some sort of pleasure in the act.

A sadist, not so much. A sadist is someone who hurts you for his or her own pleasure, *never* yours. They get off on the pain they inflict on you, or anyone, and they don't give a shit about your pleasure. Oh, I'm sure that there are some sadists out there that enjoy pleasuring their property, but not my husband, not the man I found out I was married to. I want you to see the whole, ugly reality of a true violent undisciplined sadist, not only to get you to understand what happened to me, but also to stop you from romanticizing any option that I should have fought for my marriage, because I had made a vow. I vowed to marry someone who *wasn't real*. The real David was a sick man. I sure as fuck didn't sign up for everything he did to me. If Aurora wanted him, she could have him. I would wrap him up, tie him with a bow, and leave him on her doorstep. May they find happiness together, because I would never be happy with a man who demanded me to do the things she did, never.

On an extremely cold morning, I was awakened with the icy blast from a bucket of water that was poured over my head. "Wake up, my little pet," David's voiced cooed in mock tenderness. There was nothing tender about David. His insides were as hard as rock, and black like coal.

It took me a few minutes to focus my eyes and climb out of the drug-induced slump my body had been forced to endure. Sitting up as straight as I could in the bed, I lifted my chin to him. A mumbled slur fumbled out of my lips and he laughed.

He laughed at my inability to speak.

He laughed at my weakness.

Thick rough hands clenched my throat, pulling me up off the bed, over the soft white cotton sheets I once adored. I couldn't take in any air. In fact, I couldn't breathe at all. Warmth flooded my body, sparks of adrenaline-fueled fire burned across my skin, and I struggled to draw air into my lungs. My eyes stung and burned with pressure. His were dead of any emotion or expression. "Kneel," he demanded, releasing my neck, watching my body crumple to the floor.

There was a small creak at the door, the tiniest of sounds, as if a mouse had just stumbled upon us and was scurrying to find food. My eyes instantly tracked the noise, and they locked on Aurora, who crawled in on all fours with a goddamn spiked collar around her neck, violently pulled with a leash that was in one of David's hands. Her naked body was covered in brightly colored contusions, broken capillaries and venules, damaged by whatever trauma he'd inflicted on her. Crimson abrasions covered her knees as she moved them over the coarse rug, and a small bloody laceration marred her pretty lips. It was angry and red. My hands itched to clean it, and my mind raced to find something sterile to stitch up her cuts. Oh, my God, she was acting as if she were his *sex slave*.

I've only read about this sick shit in books. Books I usually choose not to finish, because they never end well.

"The look of mortification on your face has my cock so fucking hard right now, pet." Slowly, as if putting on some twisted morbid show, he stripped out of his clothing, throwing each piece at me, as I sat on the floor clawing my fingers into the plush threads of the carpet. "I'm going to make you watch me fuck her like a dog."

Aurora's head lowered submissively, but her bloodied lips smiled, and my stomach rolled. *Sick. Sick. Sick.*

I gave him my tears then. The last of them. Because the minute he was inside her, I was planning to hurl myself at him, and kill him with the buckle of the belt he'd just thoughtlessly thrown at me.

He'd thought he had finally broken me, slamming his hips against Aurora like she was *nothing*. Fucking her so savagely that I thought he'd rip her insides.

The one heartbeat he blinked, I attacked him, clawing his eyes, punching him and raking the metal of the belt against his skin. No technique existed in my fight, none of the combat discipline I had learned in the military; it was raw, ruthless…, and so fucking desperate. But, after a few good attacks, my arms began moving in slow motion, because they were too heavy and thick with fluids. I knew I'd surprised him, knew I had hurt him in some way, yet the blackness claimed me quickly. I raged in my semi-unconscious mind, raged to fight him, to fight the drugs, but my body just *quit*. I couldn't tell you what happened after. And God forgive me, I don't want to know. I don't want any more of those visions. *I still can't ever feel clean enough, no matter how hard I scrub. I still feel David's filth…everywhere.*

I was very sick, and *that*, I was absolutely aware of. Violently vomiting, I knew what was happening. I knew he was killing me slowly. I could feel my body shutting down organ by organ, but there was nothing I could seem to do. Most nights, I would find my conscious swim to the surface, becoming vaguely aware of my surroundings. Most times, I would feel the headboard jostling violently against the wall, and could hear Aurora's moans and laughter as if she was enjoying my torture.

I was almost dead when he called for an ambulance, the ink still fresh on the fictitious suicide note he penned in my name. Those morbid, carnival clown giggles and moans from Aurora, the ones I had spent my last breaths listening too, became echoed shadows of sounds. Cold, strange, invisible hands pulled and pushed my body. It felt as if I was being strapped into one of those old rickety wooden rollercoasters, my body just slumping against the cool metal of the cart, not being able to do more than listen to the low murmurs of disembodied voices talking all around me. Eventually, the little cart lurched forward and up, ascending into the warm moist atmosphere and the grinding of the metal teeth of the rollercoaster bucked and clinked beneath me. Higher and higher I soared to a place where gravity had no say, and my body hurtled up into space, weightless.

For a few moments, I was numb. Gone.

Dead.

Then I was freefalling back down to earth, wind whipping past my face, tangling the long strands of hair in trails of fire behind me like a comet across the sky.

When the world around me slowed down, and my rollercoaster car glided into its port, my heart began beating again. My senses could pick up things again. Beeps. Hisses of a ventilator.

Hushed angry voices fighting in whispers.

Heartbreak.

I listened to the low murmurs. "She was barely breathing when I called the ambulance. I gave her enough *of that shit* to kill a fucking whale. How is it that she is still living?" David's voice growled low in his throat. There was a horrible screeching, as the familiar sound of a hospital cart next to my bed suddenly thrashed violently against the wall, and a clatter of items scattered across the floor. The real nightmare was the voice that he spoke to, the one that answered him back. It was my father's voice.

My *father*. "Well, everybody is observing her closely now, so no more fillers. We can't get caught here. If she lives through this, when she gets home, we'll give her a round of Potassium Chloride, and then we'll be done with this. My hands are clean of this, Stanton, clean, you hear me? But I hold you responsible for this. She was not supposed to find out. I never wanted to lose my family over this." My father chose money over me. It was one thing to learn your husband had a secret life and wanted you dead, but to find that your father *wanted* you *dead* sears your soul with scars and agony.

My father. My husband. Two self-proclaimed gods immersed in their own lethal capitalistic world, spoke over my body as I lay still and silent; too lost in their greed to look at me, care, or to shed a fucking tear.

My fists clenched tightly as I thought about what those fucks had done to me. What my *father* allowed to happen, and what *David* did. I knew them *now*, and what brand of monsters they were, and I knew it could have been, should have been, so much worse for me. Yes, that is what I thought, because, seriously, let's get this straight... I should have died. Reality folks; the shit he put inside me would have killed most people. I like to think I lived because I was meant to save people, and that I was meant to be greater and do more. Everybody has his or her own measure of worth, and that was mine. *God had my back, not David's.*

For hours, I pretended I was asleep on that hospital bed, lying as still as death. I waited for Jen to come, and when she did, I told her everything. My voice was barely audible, dry and cracking. "They are trying to kill me...you have to get me out of here."

Her eyes shined with tears, "But you...honey...you tried to..."

"Jen," I fumbled for her hand with my trembling one. "Go...to Mana Storage...Jersey...I can prove..."

"You're serious?" She leaned her head low. "Honey, you tried to commit..."

"Jen!" I hissed desperately.    My breathing faltered, eyes sprang with tears, "He did this to me. Please believe me." I looked in her eyes. *Please believe me.*

Weak and humiliated, I begged her to help me get discharged, or to escape. *And she did.* Jen ran down to the ER and found our homeless friend, Mr. Carson, one of the hospital's *repeat attenders*. You know the people, the ones who continuously try to come into the emergency room with an array of ailments for a safe place to sleep, and a meal.  She offered him all the money inside her pocketbook to lie in my bed with the sheets over his head, until someone realized he wasn't me.  With two hundred and fifty three dollars rolled into a dirty sock, he crawled under the white sheets, wearing a giant toothless smile. Then Jen helped me walk right out of that hospital, without anyone seeing.

But that's all over now.

Well, you got your little glimpse of David's brand of abuse. I could tell you so much more, little details that would make you cringe, but you know what. I don't want to *think about it anymore*.  You still want to know though, don't you? Think of the worst shit you've ever heard, and multiply that by three weeks, turn up the heat and let that simmer in your brain for a minute. Honestly, that's not the story I want to be a part of. It's not the story I want to be remembered by, and I don't want to be known as a victim, ever. I want to be remembered for my story with Kade, for my achievements in my life, not for some piece of shit that abused me. Besides, they are my scars, *mine*, and those horrible things I lived through still *hurt*. But, do you know what scar tissue does for your body? Makes you stronger and tougher. Makes you realize that every breath you take is a gift.

I know I should not have lived.

*I should not be alive right now.*

Yet I was. I was alive and safe with Kade.

The man who could turn darker than he already was, *because* of my scars. Because he wants to own them, take them on his flesh to erase them from mine, but he can't. They were too deep inside me.

I stared out Kade's bedroom window, watching the first rays of the sun lighten the wintery sky. "Hey," he said softly, "come to bed with me."

My eyes glanced over his bandaged knuckles, and a cold shiver ran down my spine. Closing my eyes, I tried blinking away my tears. Kade Grayson was the only man I'd willingly give my tears to, because I knew he'd never want them, or take any joy in them.

"Hey, hey. No, no, Sammy, baby," he pleaded, cupping his hands around my face and gently swiping the tears with his thumbs. "Don't cry for me, love, please. I fucked up. I went crazy. It's just a few scraped knuckles, Sam, you saw it."

"We are both so messed up, Kade. How are we supposed to deal with this? How am I going to help you deal with this?"

"Together," he said, touching his lips against mine.

His answer was so calm, so final, and so *wrong*. I knew there was something so very wrong, because I could taste the guilt on his lips. *I knew Kade*. He was going to kill David, and even though I wanted David dead, I didn't want to lose Kade. I didn't want him lost to more violence, shattered by his own actions and demons. Nor did I want him in jail for something that had nothing to do with him. It was all over, it was all in the past. David and my father thought I was dead. Why did Kade need to know my pain? He would just be hurt by it.

I couldn't hurt Kade anymore, I couldn't. I needed Kade Grayson away from this whole situation. He still needed time to heal from the tragedies in *his* life. I just didn't know exactly what to do.

David Stanton's venom was spreading into every fragmented part of my existence, like spilled ink on a clean page, staining everything with his filth. His delusions of ruling the hospital world went beyond being the best surgeon, and spilled into categories that are more lethal. He was sick and twisted, and I needed him to stay as far away from Kade Grayson as possible. I should have just vanished when I had the chance. Less people would have been ruined.

"No more thoughts of him, love. Not when you're in my bed," Kade whispered in his husky British accent, slipping warm hands between my thighs.

*Damn it, the accent was melting me.* The fingers were working their magic too. "Don't you talk all Englishly with me, Grayson."

"*Englishly?*" He asked, stilling his hands, mouth smiling against my skin.

I loved making that man smile. "Yes, all accented, hunkified, and kissable...*oh, screw it*...just don't stop."

His lips captured mine, and I could hear my own breathing, the small gasps and moans as my body awakened under his touch. Pulling back his head, raising his eyes to mine, he smirked, "Bring that delicious pussy to my mouth, love."

And there I went, slipping into our little bubble easily. Losing myself to a world full of *Kade*, where I was safe, innocent, and yet fucking filthy all at once. My heart hammered insanely as I straddled him, and a scorching flush spread across my chest and over my cheeks. I could feel his lips curl into a smile against my flesh, and my body shivered from the want.

Hot breath scorched my damp skin, "You know when I was younger, I used to lick anything I didn't want taken from me."

I smiled, forgetting about everything that wasn't Kade.

That man's tongue is a wicked, wicked thing.

Delicious wet heat spiraled through me. Kade's touch was the only thing that ever washed away the contamination that David filled inside me. Kade made me forget, with his intense eyes, dark obsession, and his touch. His touch always made me feel cherished, wanted... completely *fucking possessed.*

His tongue slid over me, in me; lips played and teeth nipped. Wet fingers slipped through, curling and stroking.

Arching my back, I let the sensations coil and build. "Kade, oh God," heat fanned out across my belly. Tangled whimpers and soft sighs filled my throat, until I could take no more. Before the sweet rumble of release burst inside me, I crawled down the hard tight muscles of his body. Hovering my warmth against him. His cock slipped and slid under my body, grinding and gliding along my wetness. Sitting upright, I slid myself over the long, thick length of him, teasing and taunting. Hot hands covered my breasts, fingers twisting and digging into my skin. Heart pounding. Flesh burning.

But then he stilled.

Dark gray eyes captured mine. Unyielding. Unrelenting.

Sweet, *sweet* anticipation.

I could hear him breathing.

Heavy thick breaths. My breaths, shallow, and shaking.

His hands skimmed down my skin, rough fingertips grazed over my trembling body and reached for mine. A trail of heat was left in their wake. He linked our hands, tangling his fingers with mine, squeezing tightly, and brought them in the space between us. Pulling his face leveled to mine, we sat still, eyes locked together, my body straddling his. The way his eyes pierced mine made my throat thicken, my eyes sting with emotion. An ache stirred in my chest and throbbed for him.

Sliding himself slowly inside me, he tightens the grip on my hands and brings his lips against mine. The sweet sensation that rocks through my core is so intense, tears well in my eyes.

He rocked into me once, his teeth captured my lips, and his hoarse whisper sends me rocketing through space, "I will erase them for you, I'm going to kill them both, nobody...nobody will *ever* fucking hurt you again."

The thought, the emotions send me over. Convulsing and shaking over him, and he didn't stop. He thrust into me harder and faster, until the stars imploded in my sky, and all I felt, was the inferno that burned from inside him, thick hot and real. Ruthless. Savage. Brutal.

I'm going to lose Kade.

I'm going to lose him to David.

*I have to do something.*

# CHAPTER 5

## Kade

My eyes were still blurry and heavy with sleep, as I watched Samantha climb into her car from the window in my den, dressed with a deep flush on her winter pale skin. My laptop hummed softly behind me, surging up to life as I touched the steaming cup of coffee she had left for me to my lips. She had a day shift at the hospital, which I wondered how she'd stay awake through, because we'd been up all night tangled around each other. She had stretched and grumbled, then yawned loudly as she left our bed. When she was out of sight, I shifted to her side of the bed, searching for her warmth. I missed her already.

That only lasted for five minutes, because she came running back into the bed and flung herself at me to wake up, demanding that she not be the only poor soul awake at that ungodly hour.

I got up, and of course, watched her dress. It was like watching porn, in reverse.

Black lace slowly covered her perfect rose-tipped breasts. It seductively slid up her silky legs, and hid her smooth delicious pussy from my view.

"Now, undress again for me, real slow," I whispered.

"Shut up, Grayson." She laughed. "You should be getting dressed too, instead of slumming it in your sexy-pjs all day, cuddling up under those covers. Sniffing my soap," she smirked.

*Fuuuuck.* She knew I sniffed her soap? Cinnamon-motherfucking-apples. I bet she doesn't know about her underwear...*Yeah, can you see my smirk?*

Anyway, that was the best part of what I did for a living. Being able to stay home, spin around on my chair in a pair of boxer shorts, and make up imaginary stories, sometimes, butt-ass fucking naked, just spinning on my chair. *You know you're picturing it.*

Sam tore out of the house like a tornado, and even though she wore a calm smile as she always did, I noticed a worry in her eyes. A crease to the forehead. A meeting of her brows. So, from the window, I watched her leave, wondering what her thoughts were troubled with.

"Hey, wanker," Dylan called after busting through the door *without* knocking. *I'm not sure if I'll ever get used to having so many people around. Always.* It was no joke. Everywhere I turned, someone was *there*. Four months ago, I would have wanted to blast a bullet between his eyes the moment I heard his foot creak against the wood of the floor. *I guess I was changing, huh? Okay, don't think about the whole den-boxing match from last night, and the man-tantrum I threw at the hospital...bloody hell; I have to call my therapist today, don't I? Sod off, I feel like I'm changing. Growing. Something.*

Dylan stood in my office with arms crossed, waiting for me to snap back to reality.

I squeezed my eyes tight until reality came back. It was so damn hard, but my thoughts were still on a naked Samantha, riding me hard and deep last night. "We're going to need some privacy settings programmed to this new living arrangement," I snapped, clinking my coffee cup down onto my desk. The bitter hot liquid sloshed over the sides of the mug, and splashed a still steaming splatter of hazelnut across my hand and desktop.

It made me bloody want to punch someone in the face. Sam made me that coffee.

Dylan waved my cell phone in the air, "Oh. Yeah, sorry, but your phone was going off and I thought it would be important. Caller ID came up as the Sherriff's office…and there are only so many times I can hear that girlie Pink song go off as your ringer. Why don't you change that to something more your speed, like Slayer?" He laughed.

Without thinking, my body was airborne, sliding itself over the top of my desk, almost knocking my laptop onto the floor, and my hands were fumbling into his face trying to reach for my phone. The wanker fought me back, slapping my hands away like we were twelve again. Making matters worse, my shorts were now full of the spilled hazelnut coffee. *At least my desk got cleaned.*

"Give it here, twizzletits," I said, snapping it out of his hands, "and I happen to love *Raise Your Glass* by Pink. It was a highly enlightening song for me," I explained, unlocking the code to my phone.

"Yeah, how's that?" he laughed, backing away.

Pressing the callback button on the phone, I held it to my ear and listened to the rings. "It was the song I got to watch Samantha do a striptease to with a mop. Fell in love with her instantly."

"Way too much information, mate. You could have left out the whole mop thing," he chuckled, walking out of the den. "But I always said she could have been a stripper," he yelled from somewhere down the hallway. What a *twonk*.

Before I could bloody curse at him, the phone clicked in my ear, "Good morning, Sheriff's Office. How may I direct your call?" A woman's voice crooned through the speaker.

"Kade Grayson for Deputy George Tatum, please."

"Sure thing, hold please," the voice drawled. *Bloody tart.*

After exactly two minutes and thirty-eight seconds of an instrumental hell that sounded a lot like *Call Me Maybe*, just as I was about to shove a pencil into one of my ears, George's voice, urgent and serious, silenced the horridness of what the public ignorantly believed was music.

"Grayson?"

"Yeah, George. I'm returning your call. What's going on?"

"Good news from the city. They just arrested Samantha's father, Doctor Michael Matthews. He is being charged with a twenty-one-count indictment that included pharmaceutical fraud, identity theft, and federal health care fraud charges."

Relief flooded through my body, as I collapsed onto the couch. "Federal charges? Wait, identity theft?"

"Apparently, Dr. Matthews, the president of the hospital, was still using Samantha's identity to move money around and sign a host of implicating papers," he laughed. "They executed the search warrants at the hospital last night, both penthouses, as well as warrants to seize up to $245 million in alleged fraud proceeds from various bank accounts."

"What about Stanton?" I hated saying his name.

"They took him in for questioning."

"What do you think is going to happen?" I asked.

"Don't know all the details yet. I just wanted to let you and the little lady know that they are both in custody."

"Best bloody news ever. Thank you for everything, George. I mean it." My heart pounded. I bloody felt like dancing.

"You bet. The jurisdiction is being all hush-hush about it, but I will definitely look more into it for you, and then call you back when I find out more information," he said.

Hanging up, I raked my hands over my face, and tossed my phone to the side. I wondered how the line of questioning was going to go in *that* interrogation. *I guarantee they were going to blame everything on Samantha.* It didn't matter though, because she was innocent, and both of those sick fucks would never know that she had a hand in taking them down.

They thought she had died in a car accident.

They even thought they buried her.

They had to assume that somehow, after her death, another whistle blower came in. Those two wankers held a lavish funeral for her, like she was some sort of celebrity in the city. Even their mayor showed up, police escort and everything.

But now, she was finally safe.

I felt like a kid. Balled up giddy happiness, last day of school excitement, hope, just the fucking unimaginable laid out future for us. She will finally feel free…no more chains. *Rewrites, happy endings. I rewrote her life. What happy ending could I give her? That perfect life she wanted?*

The one she didn't get with him?

Could I be a *husband?*

*A father?*

*A dad?*

I wanted to give her anything, everything.

"Dylan!" I screamed. "DYLAN!"

Fast heavy footsteps clumped down the hall, pants of an out-of-breath-I shouldn't't-be-running-I'm-still-fucking-healing-from-getting-shot filled the doorway. "What…" *pant…* "what…the…" *pant…* "bloody…hell?"

"Do you know anything about engagement rings? Or proposal things and such?" I barked. "How about diamonds? Like ENORMOUS bloody diamonds that sparkle from space."

"Do I look like someone who would know about that stuff, mate?"

"Okay… then what is the most romantic way you could think of to ask someone to marry you?"

"Why? Bugger! Jen isn't pregnant, is she? Bloody hell, what do I say to her?"

Jumping up, I started pacing the room, tapping my hands along the surfaces of all the tables and desks. I must have looked like a maniac. "And it can't be cheesy."

Dylan, confused as always, stood perplexed in my doorway. I seriously believed I got all the intelligent genes in our family; he was just given all the *pretty*.

With all the racket I was making, Jen came barreling into the office too. "What is all the commotion about?"

"Uh, um… do…do you have something to tell me," Dylan asked her as I paced, folding his arms across his chest, nervously.

"Um, like what?" she asked, visibly perplexed.

"Do I have to get diapers?" he asked.

"Why, did Kade shit himself?" she laughed.

Dylan huffed loudly. Eyebrows knitted together, "DO I NEED TO GET BOTTLES?"

Jen rolled her eyes and shook her head as if he were crazy, "Don't you think it's too early to start drinking? You just got up…"

"IS THERE ANYTHING IN YOUR OVEN?"

"I'M NOT BAKING ANYTHING, YOU MORON! WHY ARE YOU YELLING AT ME?"

*My God, you have surrounded me with idiots.*

It's wrong to want to take a bat to their heads, right? Maybe I could just hold the bat and sneer at them both threateningly, just to see what could come of it. It might get them both to piss off and shut the bloody HELL UP.

Stepping in between them, I practically had to shove my body between the both of theirs. *Did they even realize I was there?* "Mate. Come with me. I'm going to buy *my* woman a ring. Then I'm going to go right to that hospital and ask her to marry me. Or should I just say fuck the ring, and beat her to the hospital, ask her to marry me, and let her pick out her own ring?" Then I turned to face Jen, who I could hear getting ready to rev up for a shriek, "If you *squeee* right now, I *will* shoot you."

She bloody *squeeed* anyway.

# CHAPTER 6

## Samantha

The cold leather of the steering wheel felt like a hard band of steel beneath my fingertips. It ached a chill in my metacarpals, seeping glaciers into my marrow. It made me think of death.

Its *finality*.

Its *loneliness*.

I craved to crush the wheel with my fists. Feel it turn brittle and crumble through my fingertips. *I will erase them for you, I'm going to kill them both, nobody...nobody will ever fucking hurt you again*, he had told me. How long after the kill, would it take him to lose himself completely to the evil of it? Again. How long would it be until he thinks of himself completely as his old friend, Thomas, a vicious killer, without regret, and without a soul?

My head felt strange. Thoughts blurred together, an alien kaleidoscope of shapes and emotions, both dark and haunting. My hands tightened around the wheel, gray clouds passed over the sun, darkening the world and my mood.

A high definition slideshow of Kade's bleeding hands from the night before clouded my vision, making it hard to drive. Being with me healed him, but learning about my past was hurting him. There was no good in him knowing any of it. None.

In retrospect, I knew Kade would never be able to handle my past. I knew going into this with him would burn us both, but there was no way of stopping it. There were far too many beautiful moments we shared to look back and wonder when we should have stopped the unstoppable. Now, I just needed to figure out how to move ahead, keep our heads above water, and help him through this.

He *can't be my hero*. There is no hero to my story. There are just two people who need to live past it.

I could feel the interior of my car closing in on me. My vision danced, and my lungs started playing a serious game of hide and seek with oxygen. Before I blacked out from a panic attack, I pulled over onto the shoulder of the road and turned off the engine. *Damn*. I squeezed my eyes shut. *I needed to be at the hospital in less than twenty minutes and I'm having a major anxiety attack.* Blood pumped fiercely through my temples, pounding an arrhythmia of unsteady throbs in my chest. Lunging across the front seat, the seatbelt constricted against my throat and chest. I clawed my hands into the glove compartment for one of the brown paper bags I stored inside. It seemed like millions of items sprung out when I opened the latch, scattering an array of first aid crap all over the passenger side. The brown bags fumbled out last, and I clutched at them wildly, slamming one up against my lips, immediately inhaling and exhaling into it.

*I'll get through this. I always do. It feels like I can't, but I sure as fuck will. I just need to make sure Kade will be okay.*

My phone beeped a text message inside my purse, and I tore through it with one hand searching, blindly searching, while the other hand still held the bag to my lips. Inhale. Exhale. David that filthy-little-dicked-demented-son-of-a... Inhale. Exhale. *COCKSUCKING MOTHERFUCKING DRYHUMPING PREMATURE EJACULATING PIG!* Inhale. Exhale. *KADE SHOULDN'T have to DEAL with any more VIOLENCE! I should have twisted that knife in David when I had the chance.* Swiping open my phone, I read the message from Kade:

*We'll get through everything together, baby.*

*I love you.*

*XOXO*

Inhale. Exhale. Inhale. Exhale. I was practically sucking on the paper bag.

Staying with Kade was just going to make his obsession with David and me worse. He's unraveling from my history, burning to know me, yet engulfing himself in flames with each minute detail he learns. I didn't want to watch him suffer. What would Kade do if I left him right now? Just left, went after David and ended it all. Keeping Kade safe and sane, away from all this craziness? Would he be able to heal? Would he go on with his life, or would he crumple into his old, reclusive, self-destructive ways?

I found myself giggling into the bag, thinking he'd probably stalk me until I was old and gray, a strange menacing old geezer lurking in my bushes, always trying to protect me.

I reread his text message. *We'll get through everything together, baby.*

I inhaled deeply and exhaled slowly. Yeah, *we would be okay, wouldn't we? Just look at how far he's come in the last few months. We'll be fine. He is absolutely right. He's strong, he'll deal with my past, we've both walked through the fire, this was just remembering the flames.*

I looked through my windshield and down at my watch. Damn it. I was twenty minutes late! I could have driven back and forth from the house to the hospital twice in the time I tried to calm myself on the side of the road. I needed to focus, and keep my head on straight.

Starting my engine back up, I continued my drive to the hospital, feeling more calm and hopeful, yet, still with a twinge of anxiety as if Kade was up to something wrong. Just a small tickle in the back of my neck, an itch that was just out of reach, but something that needed my attention at some point. I needed to make sure he was going to let the police handle everything, I knew it was only a matter of time before they found enough evidence to put David and my father away for the rest of their lives.

Yet, the closer I got to the hospital, the louder the uneasy feeling nagged at me. I shoved it away though, tonight, Kade and I would talk. *With clothes on*, that was the key. Pulling into the parking garage, I swiped my hospital I.D. through the toll machine, and watched the lever rise over the windshield of my car. My eyes were so heavy with exhaustion that I wondered how many pots of coffee I could get my hands on before having to see my first appointment.

Parking in my regular spot, I walked as if I were in a dream through the lot. I knew I would be fine as soon as I started working. As soon as I could shake the feeling that Kade was going to be doing something insane, like drive seven hours all the way into New York City, slit David's throat, and somehow be back before dinner the next night. As soon as I get to my office, I'll call him, threaten him, and promise to tell him anything else he wanted to know tonight. Maybe we could speak with the therapist, too. That would guarantee we both kept our clothes on while we spoke.

Using my ID card again, I entered the building through the emergency exits, a small beep echoed in the hallway, which alerted security I was coming in, and the row of bulbs that lined the ceiling flickered on and off. Creepy.

Climbing the staircase to the second floor family clinic, I could hear far away laughter of a group of people, most likely orderlies, taking a cigarette break in one of the stairwells above me. The strong smell of tobacco flittered across my senses.

My office was at the end of the hallway on the second floor, with an entire wall of windows that faces the tree-lined campus of the hospital, sun filtering in warm rays, even when the weather outside was still icy cold. I loved to stand inside the beams and feel the warmth as it hit my skin, bask in being alive, being able to do what I was put here to do, if only a fraction of what I have done. I missed being in a trauma unit. The adrenaline rush, the puzzles to solve, and the lives I could save. Maybe one day, again…*maybe*…I'd been hearing really great things about a new drug for tremors.

My hand touched the knob of my office, such a peculiar thing to remember, the icy smooth coldness of the metal handle and the metallic, yet floral smell of it. That acidic, aromatic scent was what confused me, citrus and sandalwood. It muddled strange sensations in my brain. The odor was so strong that I could almost taste it, like bitter rust and roses along my tongue. A strange wave of flutters rolled through my belly, but I dismissed it instantly, and I pushed through the door, thoughtlessly slinging my coat on the back of my chair, and my bag on the desk. For some ungodly reason, the slats of my window were closed, and I moved to open them, craving the brightness.

The mirror that ran the length of my office wall echoed my reflection. For a moment, I paused, confused, and disoriented. The pale-faced woman in the mirror stared back at me, eyes wide, mouth slightly opened.

My chest tensed, muscles tightened and coiled, ready for something, anything to jump out at me. My belly fluttered again when I noticed an enormous beautiful bouquet of red roses surfacing from the veil of shadows of the corner.

I knew I smelt flowers.

*Oh, my God, did Kade get me flowers?*

My heart thudded faster.

*He texted me he loved me and got me flowers?*

A dark velvet jewelry box sat in the middle of the arrangement, exactly like one an engagement ring would come in.   That *instant* was like pure electric surging through my chest.

    *Oh, my God.*

    *Was Kade going to ask me to marry him?*   My pulse sped up, my breathing accelerated, and I wanted to scream, YES, YES, YES, at the top of my lungs before I took another breath.

    I stepped forward, eyes stinging with joyous tears, heart pounding with excitement.

    Then I saw the man behind the flowers, standing larger than life, in that darkness full of shadows and emptiness.

    David.

# CHAPTER 7

## *Kade*

Everything was set up perfectly.

Okay, well, I didn't know anything about proposal shit, but it was perfect to me. I ran through the halls of the hospital, nurses and visitors flying out of the way just to get to her. My fingers tingled to sweep the hair that always hung against her cheeks, to watch her smile when I asked her to become my wife. There was no doubt in my mind, not one ounce of apprehension as I flung the door open to her office and stepped inside. I *knew* her answer was going to be yes, because she knew me, she knew I would give her everything she ever wanted. I'd give her everything that was taken from her, everything.

The room was empty, save for the bright afternoon sunlight filtering in from the window. *Damn, she must be in with a patient.*

My eyes quickly scanned the room. Her coat is neatly hung on a hook and her bag lay on her desk.

One of the clinic nurses came in behind me and cleared her throat, "May I help you, sir?"

I spun around, smiling like a bloody kid at Christmas; a huge Mt. Everest sized diamond, hiding deep within my pocket. "Hey, Evelyn. Where's Sam?"

"Oh, Kade. I didn't recognize you. Um, Samantha hasn't come in yet. I tried calling her cell, but I can't reach her. She missed all of her appointments today. I've been rescheduling them all day."

*What the hell was she going on about?*

*How could that be? The stuff she left from home with this morning was laying on her desk, her coat hanging on the hook. She had to come here this morning. Fuck me sideways; this tart must be stupid. They must give nursing degrees to anybody.*

Yet, she stood there. Stern. Serious.

My jaw tightened. Fists clenched. Somebody was bloody lying to me. Something was wrong.

"Bollocks. She has to be here, Evelyn. All her bloody belongings are here. Her coat. Her pocketbook. Stop messing with me," I snapped.

"I'm not, Kade. I'm being serious. I haven't seen her all day," she said, raising her brows, and handed me her phone. "Look at all the texts and calls I've sent her. She's replied to none of them."

Assumptions can kill you. They are the devil in disguise of a normal everyday moment. Assumptions are never really considered; they are just the reality you believe as truth. I assumed that Samantha was at the family clinic. Safe. I never doubted her whereabouts. I never considered that anything could go wrong. Not until it was too late.

I called her cell, but there was no answer, so I left a message.

Then I left five more.

*Her coat was on her desk. Her pocketbook too, but I couldn't find her.*

She never showed up to the clinic that morning. No one had seen her. The words kept announcing themselves in my head. *She's gone*, they taunted.

I called Jen.

Jen hadn't seen her, and Dylan had been with me all day. They dropped everything and were on their way, just as worried as I was.

I left another message on her voice mail and looked at the time. It was three o'clock in the afternoon. That meant she had been missing for at least five hours.

Blood rushed past my ear, throbbed in my veins. Panic.

A few minutes before, I assumed Samantha was fine, didn't even consider anything could go wrong. Just as tomorrow, I assumed the sun would rise and another new day would begin, but not for me, not if Samantha was gone. If she were gone, my world would forever be plunged into darkness.

*Just bloody calm down. Think.*

The question to answer, was did she leave on her own, or was she in trouble? Was there an accident? Couldn't be, her stuff was there. Did she get locked in a closet somewhere? If she was in a bloody closet with someone else, I will rip every inch of his skin off, and make myself a suit.

Grabbing her purse, I looked through her stuff. Her wallet was still inside, so she couldn't have gone far. She had to be in the hospital somewhere. Maybe there was a trauma, and she was needed in emergency? *We're a bunch of bloody morons, that's got to be what happened!*

My eyes dropped to her desk.

A small pale pink *Post-It* note was stuck dead center on her desk.

A small note; addressed to *me.*

*Kade,*

*Sorry. This is too much for me. I'm suffocating here.*

*Everyone will be better off if I leave.*

*Samantha*

Holding the note up to my face, I crushed it silently into my fist. Complete self-destruction in 3, 2, 1.

The edge of my vision exploded in reds and oranges; licks of heat and flame. Quick and savage, my fist holding the note slammed into the mirror that ran along her office wall, shattering it into webbed strands that traveled to every edge. My reflection was broken, fractured into thousands of pieces, completely fucking destroyed. Just. Like. Me.

Crushing my hands against the sharp splintered mirror, I slid them down harshly, taking in the burn of pain as the uneven edges sliced through my palms. Dr. Jekyll, meet Mr. Hyde.

*I'm going to destroy this room.*

*Every bloody inch of it.*

And I did, until Dylan and Jen found me on the verge of smashing Samantha's desk through the window, crumpled up letter still balled up in my bloodied fist. Dylan tackled me. It wasn't hard, because I didn't fight him, just sort of sunk onto the ground and handed Jen the letter.

Her eyes scanned over it, hand to her mouth. She wiped my blood off her hands onto her pants, disgusted. *Fuck you, bitch, this is how I deal with shit.*

"I have to get out of here before I destroy this hospital. Need to be alone," I growled.

People gave me a wide-open path to leave the hospital. Nobody stopped me, detained me, or even called security. They just let me tear the place up behind her office door. Being thought of as dangerous and savage, does have its fucking advantages, doesn't it? Not one person thought twice about provoking me, stopping me, or calling for fucking help. Everyone there was a stupid, pathetic sheep, because all they did was make my brutal tendencies feel bloody liberating. As if I had every right to explode so violently, because of feeling wronged. The sheep just fed the wolf.

The drive home was almost lethal, as I never once touched my foot to the brake, not until I slammed on it in front of my house, and lunged out of the truck. There were no deputies to stop me, no soft smooth voices to lure me to calmness, there was nothing; nothing but blurs of movements and hazy moments. And rage.

Disconnecting from the world, I closed myself in my den, just watching the dark crimson blood seep out of the wounds on my hand, as I obsessively opened and closed them. Open and closed them.

When the outside skies grew dark, I heard Jen tiptoe into the room, "I am so sorry, Kade. I had no idea she was planning this." She held a bat in one hand, most likely for her own protection. *Smart.* I wanted to beg her to hit me with it.

"It is because of *that* woman I'm still fucking breathing.  There are too different Kades, there's the before Sam one, and since Sam one.  I'm going to die going back to the first one," I seethed.

She lowered herself to the floor next to me, leaning her back along side mine, against the stone of the fireplace, and laid the bat across her legs.  Looking down into my hands, she asked, "What is that?"

I held it up, a small lilac ribbon on a clip, twirling it between two fingers.  "Her ribbon."

"That's the one you found in the crash...*you kept that?*"

"Hold it in my pocket wherever I go."

"Why?"

"Smells like apples and cinnamon, smells like her. She wore it the first night I saw her, and I can't let her go just yet. You need to leave me alone, Jen.  Not at a good place right now.  I feel like I could climb a bloody bell tower and start shooting."

"When I found her and David that day, freaking bloodied and...God, it was horrible, Kade.  She didn't want me to help her.  She didn't want me to come with her. The only reason I knew what happened was because I was at the hospital.  Then we got her out of there, and she asked me to drive her home to get some stuff while David was working, and pick her up when she was done to take her to the airport – she was going to start over alone.  But when I got there, they were physically fighting, and he grabbed me and punched me...Anyway, she never wanted to drag anyone into this...Maybe she..."

"What happened that day? She's fucking gone, so just bloody fucking tell me. How the bloody hell did she end up in *my* hiding place?" I snapped viciously. "And don't waste my time by telling me about what *you felt and what you went through*. All I want to know about is *her*."

Puffy, tear filled eyes looked back to mine. Strands of hair were plastered to her face from the tears that streamed down her cheeks. Haunted eyes shifted down, not able to look into mine a minute more. "She wanted to take her aid packs and some clothes, so I dropped her off. She...uh...told me to give her an hour...so I did. I ran back to my little place and packed a bag. I wasn't going to let her leave alone. She was the only family I had, so I couldn't let her go alone." Her attention turned to her hands, picking and playing with her nails as she continued. "When I got there and she wasn't out front, I ran up. And he...he was dragging her by her hair across the rug. He was trying to get to the surgical knife that was full of blood on the floor. I threw a picture frame at him, and when let her go, he turned to punch me and she...well...she...ah..."

"Tell me, or use the bat," I hissed.

"STOP IT, Kade! She stabbed him in the back. Over and over, okay. She wouldn't stop. She just grabbed the knife, and instead of running, she went back after him until he was lying still on the floor, and she had blood all over her. I grabbed her off him. God, Kade, he looked dead. He looked so dead, I wanted her away from him. She tried to go back to the hospital and get her father, but I got her in the car and told her to drive. She just focused on the driving and that was it...we hardly spoke for like seven hours, and she was just bleeding and bleeding, but she wouldn't stop. She was screaming at me to leave her, and just let her hide, but I couldn't. She didn't want me to be involved. She doesn't want anyone else hurt by them, Kade. Don't you get that? She left because she fucking loves you," she cried. Wiping at her tears, she whispered, "She left because she didn't want you to be hurt."

"Whatever, Jen. Now, she's bloody running around, hiding, with the whole of her life probably packed in the trunk of her car. Fucking alone. Thank you for telling me she stabbed someone in the back. Completely makes me understand how she could just walk out and leave me, too. Please get the fuck out."

She broke down then, sobbing and whining. "It's just not fair to you. I just can't believe she'd do this." I could see myself wrapping my hands around her little pathetic neck, and shaking her fucking brain against her skull until it looked like dull, pink, gelatinous Jell-O.

"Life's not bloody fair, princess. She did what she wanted to do. The end," I whispered, harshly. Getting up, I walked out, slamming the door behind me and stormed into my room, locking the door. *Fuck everybody.*

I ripped through my closets for brandy. Found four motherfucking bottles and poured them straight down my throat. Double-stuff-fuck-everybody.

I *think* two days blurred by, where I was sick with gut wrenching pains and fucking agonizing aches in my chest. Gravely, I clung to my desolation, reveled in its bitter coldness. But those fucking two arses that lived with me, were relentless in trying to *'get me to talk through my feelings'* or *'put to practice my anger management strategies.'* Which led me to theatrically cursing out my therapist and threatening to *'chain him to the back of my bloody truck and drag him around town until his flesh scraped itself to the bone.'* I also somehow started a small fire in the master bedroom. Who knew apple and cinnamon soap was so bloody flammable. They should label that shit. I guessed Dylan and Jen were almost reaching their boiling point, when they invited their pussy of a friend, Francis, over to 'talk to me.'

As soon as I saw *Fran's* face at the door, I punched it. I was left alone after that.

Obsessions grew.

My mind filled with ghosts. The rooms in my house became haunted by her. Her phantom hand still held mine. All I saw was her apparition and nothing else. The stone walls, the bed where we fucked, the counter, the bath, everything, everywhere was closing in on me, not one surface was free of her spirit's possession. I fucking missed her. I turned off every light in the house and locked myself in my bedroom, and in the darkness, I stayed. It was comfortable and easy. Yet, her specter still visited, making me remember every single touch, and each beautiful whisper.

I thought about what would have fucking happened if I'd never met her, if I never walked into my brother's bar that night, if I never asked Dylan her name. *What would I have been?* Still alone, sitting in the den, fingers on the keyboard pretending I knew what the world was like on the outside. Drunk. Hiding. Angry. I'm better for knowing her.

Yet, this pain...this emptiness...this hole in my chest, not letting me gasp in enough air to breathe, was going to kill me. Her being gone was going to kill me. How do normal bloody people deal with heartache? Because the way I felt, so bloody gutted, I was shocked that more people didn't go on rampages daily. The bloody way I felt, the bloody things I thought of doing, bloody hell, I was definitely going to Hell in every religion.

Another day blurred past when Dylan stood in front of me and said, "I just got off the phone with Mrs. Heldist."

"Who's that?" I hadn't showered. Or changed my clothes. I stunk. I hoped it would offend him enough to leave ME ALONE.

"Your personal assistant," he said, jerking his head back and pinching his thumb and index finger over the bridge of his nose.

"Oh," I answered flatly.

"She's worked for you for ten bloody years, so how can you not know who I was talking about?" he stammered, shaking his head.

"Never met her. I just call her *Help Desk,* when we talk on the phone."

106

"Bloody hell, you must have been a pleasure to work for. She just booked you a flight to see Mum. You need to get away from things that remind you of *her*. You need to realize it's over. You need to accept this." His arms crossed over his chest, waiting for my retort.

"Sod off! Psych 101. There are five stages of grief and I'm owning that shit. They ARE *my* bitches."

"What are you…?"

"Sod off!" I roared baring my teeth at him. My face heated, fists pounded against the tabletop, and my chest tightened and panged sharply. "You don't get to tell me I have to accept shit! You and Jen, won't even fucking allow me to deal with stage one! Leave me the fuck alone. I don't want to believe she would gut me like this, because that shitty thought makes me go to the next fucking stage. And now I'm at stage fucking *two*. ANGER. I'm livid. I'm outraged! I'm so bloody fucking angry, I want to kill someone!" I screamed in his face. Visions of explosions and burning walls appeared in rapid moving slide shows through my mind. I gritted my teeth trying to make them disappear, heat flushed through my chest, I wanted to hurt something, someone. "I *can't* believe she would do this to me."

"I know, mate. I know," he murmured. His eyes were soft and gentle. I wished he wasn't my brother, so I could have punched him.

*God, this storyline of a life you wrote for me is a sick twisted fucking joke.*

Pulling out my phone, I checked for messages, *again*. My chest ached when I saw not even one. My once loud and obnoxious phone was heartbreakingly silent. No whispered messages with her perfect voice, no more funny texts, and no more silly selfies. I leaned my head against the wall and slid down the coolness of it, crumpling down until my arse hit the floor. *Somewhere out there in the world, was my Samantha, erasing me. Forgetting me. Writing me off. Deleting my chapter.*

I pressed my hand to my chest, trying to rub away the ache.

Without another word, Dylan pulled out one of my small suitcases and packed it with an armful of clothing.

I could hear my own breathing, heavy and harsh. The anger took a toll on my body. My mind. I squeezed my eyes tightly against the flashbacks and violent images that always took over. I didn't want to go back to the way I was, I didn't want to only feel how brutal and savage life was, so I fought to clear my head of the violence. It was much easier to face my demons with Samantha. She always had this calm tender way to redirect them. Maybe it was her voice, or the warm feel of her skin, I didn't know. Maybe if I didn't push her to talk to me, she would still be here.

Oh, look. Psych-central, I'm making my way to stage *three*, bargaining. Whoever it was that made this theory, got it down perfectly. If I could just get her to answer her phone, I could tell her how sorry I was.

If only I never told her about the shootings and about Thomas…

If I could have just kept my mouth shut about David and her father…

If I got the chance to tell her that they were both in custody...

Still bargaining and negotiating with my demons, I found myself packed, showered, and seated on a small jet bound for England that was taxiing down a private runway. I had been sent home like I was expelled from school.

*This sucks.*

*Twenty bucks says my plane will crash. Scratch that, wouldn't matter. I'd be the only poor sap to survive, and everybody would blame me for not having my phone set on airplane mode.*

Digging into my pockets, I switched my cell to airplane mode. There still were no messages from her, and I couldn't send her any more, since her voice-box was full.

I sat on the plane for precisely seven hours, twenty-nine minutes, and forty seconds, staring out the window, watching the earth spin far beneath me. How fucking insignificant does that make a person feel? A small crumb of stone sliding away from the base of an enormous mountain. Never having been part of the whole or its foundation. Just tumbling over the dirt and rubble, alone.

Every time the flight attendants tried to shove liquor down my throat, I growled at them. A weasel-eyed, greasy haired, oil faced man sat somewhere in front of me, and complained incessantly that the warming blankets weren't warm enough, and that his sherry wasn't dry enough. I screamed into that air that if he didn't shut up, I'd experiment with how far a human being could shove their foot up another human's arse. After that, nobody spoke to me. I didn't need to go visit my mother, I needed to find a damn cave far away from civilization and just be left ALONE.

I landed at Heathrow, and winced at its vast whiteness. There were too many stark lights. Too many bloody people milling around, getting in my way and stopping abruptly, just to have me slam into the back of them. I toyed with the idea of screaming the word BOMB, until my throat bled, but thought better of it, knowing it would then take me forever to get back to the states, or get my voice back. Grumbling to myself, I trudged all the way to the luggage pickup, and waited *years* for the piece of shit to start spinning and spitting out the bags.

*You know* mine came out last, right? With a loud sigh, I lifted up my bag and trudged alongside the crowds of people living their happy little existences.

In the middle of the bright lobby stood my mother, holding an enormous handwritten sign that read: WAYWARD SON!

Bloody hell.

My life was already a nightmare; *this was a horrible thing to do to me.* I hated my brother for it. Most of all, after that long plane ride and thinking; I was starting to hate Samantha for it, too.

Mum's hair was a lot grayer than I remembered, yet it suited her beautifully. She had lost some stones too, which made her look somehow older and grandmotherly. Tears filled her soft gray eyes, and her smile widened when she noticed me walking towards her.

"Oh, Kade, look at you," she whispered softly, dropping the sign and holding me at arms length. Then she dragged me into a hug, and smacked me on the back of the head, "You need to visit me more. Dylan told me you needed an intervention, how are you really, love?"

"I'm fine, Mum, just bitter and angry, as always. Come on, I need to get away from all these people."

Mum hooked her arm in mine and nodded quietly, wiping away her tears with her free hand. "Sure, love. My car is in the *Meet and Greet*."

In the car, *it began*.

The queries. She all but held an interrogation light up to my face, trying to get me to tell her everything. I ran my hands down my face, doing my best to ignore the dramatic meddling. *This was supposed to help me? I tried to stay calm, I tried to focus on things that Sam would say or do when my thoughts got too violent. I tried. So fucking hard.*

"Did you love this woman?" She asked as she pulled into her driveway.

Joy. A question that was easy to answer, but would open up a universe of hell for me. "Yes," I muttered.

She froze, like I knew she would, and held her fingers up to her lips as if someone had told her the Queen was coming to tea.

"Don't bloody act like that," I snapped, climbing out of her car. Grabbing my bag from the back seat, I fixed my gaze on her, "I do get it, you know. I get how every-bloody-one sees me. I just wish that everyone would leave me alone. I'm a grown man, and yes, I bloody well loved her, and I still do. Let me deal with it on my own." God, with everything that I had ever put my mum through, I didn't want to fight with her about this. I didn't want to hurt her any more than I already had, but she needed to let me be.

"You keep up with your ways, Kade Charles, and very soon, doctors are going to be able to place the bloody word *syndrome*, after our family name!" She yelled, storming into the house. I followed after her, a heavy yeasty scent of fresh baked bread filling my senses. Slamming her keys down on the hallway table, she spun around and jammed her hands on her hips. Her eyes narrowed at me and *I knew* the mother of all *shame-on-you*-tornadoes was about to sweep through the house. "Those doctors did not encourage me, Kade. They had me planning your funeral. They had me burying my son at sixteen. Look at you, now. Dylan says you're finally getting help and healing…what this has done to our family…"

She was revving the engine for the guilt trip, her one-way ride into my already stress-filled-damaged-guilty-as-hell-self-condemned-soul, when a strange man walked up next to her. He was wearing what looked like a pair of silk pajamas.

*Okay.*

*Does she see the strange man?*

*The one standing next to her in his **pajamas**?*

Strange man put his arm around my mother's shoulders. *Hmm. She didn't scream bloody murder. What the bloody hell was I missing?*

Was he the dog walker? Gardener? Mail carrier?

He bloody well better be something of the like, because he was way too young to be anything else I was thinking about, standing in my childhood home in his bloody silk I-just-shagged-your-mum-pajamas.

"Kade, love," she said when she finished her guilt flavored monologue, "this is Henry Moors, my significant other."

"Your *significant other what*?" I demanded. I pointed a finger at him, "He bloody better well be the dog walker!"

"Kade!" She huffed. "I haven't had a dog in five years." She turned to Henry, and patted him on the cheek lovingly. "Ignore him, dear, my eldest son has less personality than our bath towels."

*Our* bath towels? *What the fuck were these people trying to do to me?* "That's it, I need air. Nice to meet you, Henry. Have fun with shagging my mum. Mum, later." I walked out her front door, slamming it so hard that the windows rattled back an angry response.

Without a clear thought in my head, I just walked.

Of course, once I stepped foot outside, it began raining a thick mist of icy cold daggers, it *was* England after all. With tightly clenched fists shoved deeply in my pockets, I stormed blindly through the streets, acknowledging nothing and no one. I only glimpsed shadows of copper-haired figures taunting me in my peripheral vision. My clothes and hair becoming heavier and heavier the more the sky's tears soaked through them.

I only stopped walking when a tall gate stood in my way, and a dark looming mountain of a building stood like a god behind it.

Realizing where I stood set my heart thundering against my chest, trying desperately to climb up my throat and eject itself from my flesh. The moment my eyes locked onto the abandoned edifice was voltaic. Blood rushed through my heart and surged through the vein in my neck, causing my cheeks and forehead to blaze with heat.

Demanding and harsh, the building stood menacingly over me. Saint Benedict's. The place I lost my innocence. The place where Thomas took my life. Where all my demons were born sixteen years ago.

Fingers clasped into the chain links, muscles pulled my body up and over the fence; I walked across the overgrown campus and up the crumbled and cracked stone steps. *Time to face these demons head-on*.

Fuck you, Thomas.

Fuck you.

And fuck you Sam, for leaving me.

# CHAPTER 8

## Samantha

David stood in the corner, smiling with eyes like one of those sinister, scary as hell circus clowns. Expensive over the top slacks and a crisp blue Armani shirt. He regarded me with a silent condescending stare. Looking at me as if I were already an obituary in his morning paper, over the loss and utterly bored. Everything in me froze. Time stilled and moved along in exaggerated sluggish motions. Long elegant fingers lifted the velvet box that sat in the bouquet and opened it, revealing my once beloved diamond studded eternity wedding band. "Time to come home, *wife*," he whispered darkly, plucking the ring from the box.

Tilting his head, he looked straight into my eyes. His normal golden brown iris's were void of all color, just deep black pools of dilated darkness, and his smile...his smile was *chilling*, making an icy tremble crawl down the back of my neck. Those were the eyes, and that was the smile of a killer. My killer. The man who desired to cause my very last breath.

The instant, I stepped back towards the door, David was closing the distance between us. With one hand, he was raising a gun to my face. The other clutched a dirty brown sack. A glint of light reflected off the diamond band that dangled mockingly from his pinky, as his index finger teased the trigger.

My legs immediately weakened and turned cold, as I clawed at the door. My hands numbed as I desperately turned the knob and fumbled with the lock. Adrenaline kicked in, hormones raced and released into my bloodstream. I could hear my heartbeat, pounding in my ears, and I willed it to slow down. *I needed to neutralize the threat. Gun in hand, get it out. Take control of the weapon. Achieve a position of advantage.*

First thing I did was try to scream my damn head off.

David closed in fast; gun rose higher and slammed his full weight on me, crushing me against the door knocking the wind out of me so my screams could not be heard. I slammed my fists into his face, raked nails along his skin, "Shoot me then, shoot me! I'd rather die than go with you!" My fists and nails met with hard solid flesh, unmovable, and impenetrable.

His laughter rang harsh and savagely in my ears. The hand holding his gun wrenches a handful of hair at the nape of my neck, violently yanking my face closer to his. Hot wet lips smash savagely over mine with such brutality that my bottom lip tears open on one of his teeth. There's not an ounce of tactical training that I can remember. It's just pure instinctual fear and a screaming rush of adrenaline that had me punching and biting back. The hard metal of the gun pressed against my skull, as his free hand grabs wildly at my wrists, trying to stop the onslaught of my defense.

Pulling away, his face is covered with blood. Whose blood exactly, I couldn't tell you. I tried for another blow to his face, but it was stopped by a vicious elbow that he slammed my face against the wall with. The hit to my head rang loud in my ears, and made my vision double. A thick warm cloth closed over my head and plunged my eyes into darkness; the theft of fresh air stifled my breathing. I screamed out, but a heavy pressure slammed against the coarse, salty tasting bag gagging me, as a mouthful of the coarse fabric was shoved into the back of my throat. Sharped edged plastic wire ties closed around my wrists with a loud *zip*, while I retched and coughed until the material was gone from my airways. My throat scorched and ached, tears flooded my eyes, stinging and biting my lids. Anger and panic ripped through me when I tried to move my hands to lift the hood off, only to feel the sharp pain of the tight plastic ties that bound me.

"Shhh…" A low voiced hissed, seeping warm breath through the material and into my ear. Hot sweaty hands forced my shoulders down until my body was lying facedown on the cold tiled floor. The slow, strong roll of his hips over my ass again and again had me choking, and I struggled frantically to break free. "I love watching you fight, pet. If I only knew months ago how much of a challenge you'd be, I would have tried to break you sooner. This is quite fun, wife, I might even keep you alive as my pet," he hissed. His hips continued their relentless obscene taunting thrusts, and even through our layers of clothes, I could feel the bruises form and my skin scrape with the friction.

Sick fuck.

*Sick. Sick. Sick fuck.* I struggled to scream, to push the heavy material out of my mouth with my tongue, but the end result was me just gagging on the cloth as it filled my mouth more.

A heavy pressure on my head crushed my face against the ground, as I struggled and kicked out my legs, then the sharp precise burn of a needle into the flesh of my arm brought me to the precipice of oblivion. My thoughts shrieked in utter horror, as the surge of whatever poison flushed like pure acid through my veins. The heat coming off his skin seeped into mine, as he gathered my torso roughly in his arms and dragged my body along the ground. My legs and arms weakened until I could no longer move them on my own volition. The floor tiles scratched and scraped beneath me, as he towed my body to whatever destination he wished.

I had no say.

He was supposed to think I was dead.

David's going to kill me, and Kade is going to break completely.

"Kade," I garbled weakly into the darkness of the cloth, as I plunged into a black hole of nothingness.

*Please, God, just don't let Kade find my body. Please, please, please don't hurt him again like that. Please don't hurt him again.*

*Please.*

*Just let him think I left.*

*It'll be easier...*

*To forget me...*

*If he...*

*Hates…*
*Me…*

# CHAPTER 9

## Kade

While Samantha Matthews-Tucseedo, who-bloody-ever she was, continued her bloody fucking life without me, I stood somewhere across the Atlantic Ocean from her, under Europe's cloudy skies, on the cracked foundation of my past.

Saint fucking Benedict's, *where high school students come to die. England's best educator for the criminally insane and mass murderers.* My beloved bloody high school. *Bitter, much, you ask.* Fuck yes, I'm bitter. Tragedy makes people bitter; it makes you petty, hateful, and vicious. My doctors had told me eighty-five percent of all gunshot wounds are fucking survivable. Only a half an inch difference would have made all the bloody difference between life and death for me. If only Thomas had raised his hands a bit more that day, aimed that gun a tad bit higher, I would have never had to deal with any of this suffocating grief.

With muscles coiled, I pulled myself though a glassless window, falling into an empty abandoned corridor. My shoes echoed a loud slap against the cracked floor. Sharp concrete scraped against the flesh of my hands. I smelled blood instantly, yet all I felt, was numbness.

I walked with a purpose, a destination. Decay peeled at the walls, rot and mildew crawled along the ground. It was the place that nightmares lived, a backdrop for horror movies. Thick vines of ivy crawled through the windows and scaled the walls long ago. Desks and chairs were everywhere, toppled over, encased in strands of ivy.

For sixteen years, I've lived with emptiness and darkness in my heart. Since Thomas shot a hole through my chest with a 9mm, complete with a motherfucking exit wound, *and* the bullet blasting into the wall behind me. It was a black hole too, one of those massive objects in space caused by the gravitational collapse of my world. A star exploding as a supernova so intensely, it sucked everyone into my darkness. I let the violence of that day define who I was as a man. I spent my adulthood hidden inside the walls of my house, writing about the horror of violence. Yet, there were never adequate words to reveal the hell and destruction of what it really was. There would never be any way to explain the absolute primal agony, mental, emotional, and pure fucking physical agony that comes with such torture and grief. Every goddamn night after the massacre, I prayed for my ending. I hated every breath I took, each and every single healthy one. I should have died that day. I was the first one hit, he blamed everything on me, *fuck,* Thomas said it was *all my fault.* Said it was everybody's bloody fault.

The abandoned school walls spun around me, blurred and pulsed. An icy breath of life flickered through the corridor, and a lone loose door swung slowly in its upward draft. The cold vacant hallway welcomed me like an old friend. I could hear the echoes of the other students, voices loud and laughing, unknowingly walking towards the last chapter in the book of their lives.

Suddenly, I was sixteen again, awkward in my body, carefree and innocent, unaware of the horrors that my life had in store for me.

I could taste the last smooth drag of my Marlboro, before I held it between my thumb and middle finger and flicked it into the street. Thomas and I, always sneaking drags before each class. He was laughing about something that morning, chuckling about some project he was going to be a part of, and how excited he was finally to show me what the bloody hell he was talking about.

"This is a killer project, mate," he laughed. "Best thing I ever bloody thought up, and it's all for you."

Distinct, astonishingly precise details were coming to life around me. Inconsequential bits and pieces of the minutes *before*, the last few beautiful moments of my youth. Standing there in that abandoned school, I remembered them all. In. Exact. Horrifying. Flashbacks.

Running up the stairs, the soles of my Converse hit the ground, echoing, echoing their tap-tap-taps.

Thomas' boots *slap-slap-clump* against the tiles. His deep laughter as he climbed higher up the steps, racing me to class.

The rustling of the leather jacket I wore and the smell of cigarette smoke lingering on my clothes.

The creak of the classroom door. The look-through glass smudged with grit and dirt.

Mrs. Turner's smile. Her big blue eyes. Long lashes, blinked, and smiled.

Ticking of the classroom clock above her desk. Tick. Tock. Tick. Tock.

Blink and smile.

Dusty white chalk tickling the back of my throat.

My girlfriend, Lizbeth, flipping the pages of a book. Paper against paper. Pencil twirled around a brown lock of hair.

Then, Thomas was holding a gun, standing in front of the door, blocking the exit. Smiling.

Shooting.

And *smiling*.

I could still feel the fire in my legs where the bullets ripped through my flesh. "So you don't run, mate. I need you to watch the show."

The flashback so real, my scars actually ached. Squeezing my eyes closed, I could feel the icy breeze drifting in through the abandoned buildings broken windows, yet I felt so much more. The memories so vivid, the years between then and now blurred, and disappeared completely.

Thomas was standing in front of Lizbeth, taunting her... "Do you believe in God...Lizbeth?"

All she could do was cry and nod her head.

"Lizbeth. Lizzy, Lizzy, Lizzy. You can't bloody be surprised by this little turn of events, could you? I believe I told you just this morning that I could kill you."

Her tears poured down faster. She reached out to grab my hand and squeezed it tightly. I froze, God forgive me, I froze. I could do nothing to save her, say nothing to save her. I. Just. Froze.

We both flinched as Thomas threw something behind us, and the hot fiery blast of a pipe bomb exploded under the computer desks. The bloody thing was made out of sparklers and PVC fencing tubes. Tall flames devoured the books on the shelves, and floated pages of burning papers across the classroom. The sound of my heart beating, so loud and fast, so very loud and fast.

As I lay there, legs bleeding, not having the courage even to stand, I watched him shoot every bloody one of those kids. Mrs. Turner even dove in front of us, and I will never forget what the face of a hero looks like. Real heroes don't wear capes. They are just normal everyday people, like teachers, who step into the path of danger without a second thought to help someone else. She died for Lizbeth and me that day. Died trying to save us.

She didn't save Lizbeth though. Lizbeth lay dead on the ground, before Mrs. Turner's crumpled body landed on her.

Then the searing explosion of fire tore through my chest. Deep red blood spread across my shirt, and I touched my hand to it. I never knew why I did. I think it was a natural reflex, feeling the warmth of my own life on my fingertips.

His face slammed into mine as he jammed the barrel of one of his guns under his chin. The guilt and hate. "You should have stopped me, mate. This is all your fault." The warmth of the wet mess after he pulled the trigger.

All my friends. Dead.

He killed them all, as I lay there bleeding out on the classroom floor.

Now they're all just headstones.

I never got over what happened that day. Nightmares, flashbacks, feelings of numbness and anxiety. I lived through something that other people only read about, watch movies about. They could only imagine it. *I lived it*. The only person who ever understood me since that day was Samantha.

I sat down heavily on the cold ground where the bodies of my dead friends once fell. My heart ached for the woman who had helped me begin to heal. Sam was the only person that understood the chaos of my mind, one I hardly understood myself. She challenged me on everything and helped me see other ways of thinking and feeling things. She made me human again.

I sat and listened as the corroding walls spoke to me in soft chalky whispers, and singsong cadence of dripping water. Reminiscing with me about our youth. *We're the same inside*, it said, towering over me. *It would be so easy to stay here with me*, it cooed.

*No. Fuck you, Thomas.*

And I know where your mind is going right now.

*You want a reason why he did what he did, don't you?*

*Well, SO DO FUCKING I!*

*So do all the parents of all the innocent children who have ever been gunned down in schools where they were supposed to be safe.* **There is no answer good**

**enough.** *There will never be one good enough, or one to help you understand.*

So much bloody time gets wasted trying to find exact tangible reasons for such violent behavior, desperate to find *something* to blame. Yes, all the blame and reasons in a pretty little wrapped up box, complete with a yellow crime scene ribbon that warns: DO NOT OPEN. If it were only so easy, yeah?

Was it because of bullying?

Did he play violent video games?

Could it have been that horrible music he listened to?

You want to know the bloody reason? It was because of all of us. Of me, of his parents, our friends, and teachers. Every-bloody-one of us. Thomas couldn't cope with everyday shit. He was always frustrated and always pissed. He would walk to school in the morning and laugh, "Let's see who gets to live or die today." Of course, he'd go off on the girls who would ignore him. He was popular with some girls, but others, the ones who rejected him, he'd throw a tantrum like a bloody toddler, taunt them – humiliate them. He was quiet and sad, and so mis-fucking-understood.

Before school that morning, in the front seat of his car, Thomas recorded a video message, leaving the tape and YEARS worth of journals in an open box. The video began with: "I can't bloody wait until I blow a hole in each and every last one of you bloody selfish motherfuckers." His journals showed how the entire thing was premeditated and choreographed. Precise hand written details of each weapon he used, and how he came to own it, down to the bloody fucking outfit he wore. He truly believed that gunning down everyone was the only way he could be *heard*.

Understand me yet? *HE JUST WANTED TO BE HEARD.*

And, bloody hell yes, I blamed myself for the massacre, I still do. He was my best mate, and if I only could have LISTENED, if I only could have helped him through his shit, got him the help he needed for his violent tendencies, he and everyone that died that day, would still be here.

So no, it wasn't that he was bullied. It had nothing to do with any violent video games or violent movies. And it sure as shit was not because of any loud disturbing music he listened to. It was that nobody bloody listened to *him*. Not even me. Because if we *listened* to whatever the fuck he was going on about, we would have *known*, we would have got him *help*, and *we would have stopped it before it ever happened*.

Fucking hell. I looked up through the cracked ceiling and into the sky. I wish I just could have helped him. I would have saved them all.

My mother found me in the cemetery that was ironically across the way from the school. Back leaning against Thomas' headstone, looking up into the clouds just as evening was settling in. A sheer curtain of rain around me, everything muted in soft shades of gray.

"This is the first time I've ever seen you come here," she whispered, lowering onto the wet grass next to me. "Dear Lord, Kade, the grass is all wet." She placed a gloved hand on my leg and gave me a little nudge, "I miss him too, Kade. He was like a son to me. Yet, I hate him all the same for what he did to you and the rest of those poor children. I always blamed myself for the way you handled the tragedy. I didn't know how to help you. I didn't know what to say or do. I still don't, love."

"Ironic how everyone lives with the guilt of what happened, except for the person whose fault it truly was," I whispered back. Sometimes, the need to claw my way out of my skin, to let go of the crushing grief, was overwhelming. Then there were times like this, sitting on Thomas's grave on a cold wet night, when the grief was so suffocating and breathtaking, all I could think of, was to bury myself next to my friend, and let the world continue on its own without me.

"I was in such bloody shock, love. It was all a bit too much for my nerves. I was so happy you lived through, but you hardly did, did you? That first year, I don't think you slept at all." The cold leather of her gloves touched my hands and chills raced up my spine.

"When I got home from the hospital was the hardest, mum. Trying to sleep was the bloody worst. *Still is*, actually. All I saw were their faces. Cold dead expressions. Staring up to the ceiling. As soon as I'd fall asleep, I'd wake the next minute screaming, tangled in the cold grasp of Thomas's claws, but were only my blankets when I'd open my eyes.

"We've never really spoke about any of it, love. I could never find you in a state where you were approachable. Now, you've changed, haven't you?" She twisted her fingers together, a nervous habit I loved. "I tried, love. I did. I brought you both all the way to the States, to try to get you from the media and the God awful doctors with all their rubbish."

"Mum, you did fine. It was hard to listen to the news reports tell everyone that I was in on the whole bloody mess. I'm glad you took me away. It let me find myself. It helped me to find the only way I knew how to cope, when honestly, I just wanted to die."

"This woman, Samantha, she was helping you through all this?" she asked, hesitantly.

My mother's eyes glistened in the lamplights from the streets as they came to life. Climbing to my feet, I held out a hand to her and helped her stand. "She brought me back from the dead. I never realized how ugly my insides were until she showed me what beauty really was." Gently pulling her elbow, I led her across the grass, away from the rotting remains of nightmares and unending vengeful memories. "Let's get you home, Mum. It's fucking freezing out here, and it's getting dark."

Nodding her head thoughtfully, she placed her arm in mine and walked me to her car.

She had parked near the entrance. I never asked how she knew where I would be. *I'm your mother*, she'd say, *that's how*. We drove in silence and walked into a dark and empty house. I glanced at her questioningly in the entryway, and she just shrugged, "Henry is staying at his friends flat for a few nights. Go change into some dry clothes. I'll put on a pot of tea. Or would you rather have coffee?"

Sam would have always chosen coffee. *Tea was for you uppity Brits,* she'd tease.

"Tea is fine, Mum. Thanks."

Peeling out of my wet clothes, a wave of wet chills ran over my skin. A foreign feeling of acceptance followed slowly after it. Sam and I were over. Period. *Get over it. And get over what Thomas did, straighten out your head, be* **fucking normal**.

For once, be normal.

"Come sit beside me, Kade," she said, patting the couch cushion next to her. Two steaming cups of Earl Grey were set on the coffee table. "Tell me about her," she urged, "Tell me everything, son."

Staring at the twirling mist of steam floating off my cup of tea, I ran my hands over my face, letting out a heavy sigh. "She was bloody brilliant, Mum. Samantha was the kind of woman who every single day, would buy a half a dozen cups of coffee after her shift at the hospital, so she could drink one herself, and then hand the rest out to people she thought needed a warm drink. She'd hand deliver a buttered sandwich to the vagrant that practically lived in the emergency room each day. She was different, so different than anyone I'd ever met before." My eyes reached my mother's smiling ones, "She was one of those women who always blended in with the background, never brought attention to herself, but when your eyes adjusted to everything around her, then her presence was so bloody overpowering, it hurt. I didn't love her because she was beautiful or sexy. I loved her because she made everything around us beautiful, because she made me look at the fucking bloody world differently. She made me a better man, and I swore I'd try my best to encourage her to reach *over* her limits. I thought I was enough for her. Bloody hell, she never mentioned she was unhappy enough to leave. And the way she left, mum, fuck, she left me a note on the desk in her office."

Getting agitated, I stood up and started wearing a trail into my mum's carpet. "What the fuck was she thinking? What the hell did she think this would bloody do to me? I fucked up. I should have hid myself from her. Not told her anything, I thought she understood me, I felt like I belonged with her...She unraveled me all at once, and I threw myself at her. Told her everything...let her see me raw. Why the fuck would she want a broken man? I get why she left, I just didn't think that she was like that, I thought she was different." *She left because she knew I would take her father and ex-husband's life to make her safe. She couldn't love a cold-blooded killer. What kind of a person am I? Could I do that, exactly what Thomas did?* "Now, I just want to fast forward, and get the hell over her."

She sipped quietly at her tea, and then placed it back down on its dish with a soft clink of the china. "When I was a schoolgirl, my first boyfriend and I thought we'd marry and have children. Oh, dear. It was all we could talk about. We planed the date and named our future babies." Her lips curved up with the memory. "When we broke up, I was sixteen, and at the time, I truly thought my whole world was at an end. It hurt like nothing I had ever felt before. Yet after, both of us lived through it. I met your father a year or so later, and we married and had you and your brother. He married eventually too, and had five of his own children. I see him every once in a while at the market. All those feelings of not being able to live without each other, now just add up to a smile or a polite wave in the grocery store all these years later. That's the way of the world, Kade. Life goes on."

"Yeah, Mum. Nobody knows that better than me," I muttered, bitterly.

She tapped my leg and smiled, "Why don't you go off to the pub for a while. It's still early and Barney's, that new place on the first floor of the new hotel, always has loud music going on and a room full of pretty birds, Kade. Go take your mind off of everything. Get pissed and live a little. Live *simply*, love."

I thought that was the best advice anyone had offered me in a while, so I bloody took it. With a heavy heart, I found myself walking down to the pub, hearing the low thump of a rock ballad a block away, and I inhaled a deep breath of crisp cold air. England always smelled different to me than the states did. Older. Mustier.

The pub was crowded, more like a club attached to the lobby of a hotel. The infectious sounds of *Radioactive*, by Imagine Dragons, hit my ears as soon as I stepped in. The gasp after the first verse took me away, and after my first pull of a brandy, I was far beyond the pub, in my own fucking universe.

And that was where I stayed, with an entire bottle of brandy.

Until I got knocked back down into the atmosphere, spiraling and plunging in a bloody free fall back to earth. A head of ginger colored hair, the same ivory coloring of the skin, cheeks flushed a deep rose from dancing… I bet if you could've seen my face right then, my eyes were glazed over in sheer animalistic lust. Someone needed to pinch my mother-bloody-freaking arm or something, because I was seriously having the dirtiest of fantasies staring at that woman *who could* be Samantha. Then I tripped and fell, quite drunkenly I might add, landing right at her feet. *Yeah, that happened. But, that was just a random gravity test. It's all good. Bloody gravity is still strong.*

Stumbling up to stand, I almost lost my nerve. Her eyes were a golden brown; they weren't green, making me almost turn away.

Then the first cords of a piano whispered through the speakers. *Just Give Me a Reason*, by Pink. All I saw, was Samantha standing in front of me, not the stranger who was smiling and sliding her body against mine to the heart wrenching rhythm of the song.

She spoke. I heard no words, just listened to the song, watching her lips move in the strange shadows of the dance floor. Her head tilted, locks of Samantha-like-hair tumbled into my hands, Samantha-like-smiles danced on her lips, all invitations to take what I needed.

"I can't believe this. You're *Cory Thomas* the writer. You're *like famous*…" Her voice whined high and irritating. It would *not* be good to rip her throat out. *No, it wouldn't.* I'll just jot that little drunken note down for later, insert that shit in a book. Love to kill people in books. Priceless.

"Don't talk," I whispered. Don't do anything but look like Samantha, just one night. *Just one more night.*

Her teeth bit down on her bottom lip and I cringed. *Samantha would never pull a fake porn-star pose like that.* Pulling the woman closer, I swayed her to the music, laying a hand across her bare neck, and another skimming under the waist of her shirt.

"I'm game if you don't fancy sleeping alone tonight," she whispered, standing on tiptoes to reach her hot breath into my ear. Warm hands gently tugged at my pants, sliding a palm over my cock. "Doesn't that sound good?"

"One condition."

"What's that?" she purred.

"You don't speak anymore, and I'm going to pretend you're someone else. Someone named Samantha," I said, sliding my hand down her neck, spreading my fingers across her collarbone and feeling her heart pound against my palms.

"That's some kink you're into," she giggled, drunkenly.

"Shut up," I snapped, pulling her off the dance floor and into the lobby of the hotel.

She waved a keycard in front of my face and giggled, pulling me towards the elevator, and shoving me into an open one. Immediately, her eyes were closed, lips slack and she began unbuttoning her shirt. She offered a pair of small high breasts with tiny dark brown nipples. I leaned heavily against the wall of the elevator, the handle that protruded around the inside dug into my lower back.

Slipping her hands into the waist of her pants, she dug into her crotch and started going to town on herself, moaning, and rotating her hips.

I thudded my head against the wall. Everything was spinning.

*Ding.* Sixth floor.

The elevator doors slid open and she was shoving me out, yanking me into a room numbered 601, and slamming the door behind me.

Drunken hands grabbed at my buckle, fumbled with my belt, and unzipped my pants. Lowering herself to her knees, she smiled up at me.

*Shit.*

Every part of my body screamed.

*Shit.*

She had shitty brown eyes.

All I wanted was green.

She lowered her mouth to me and before she could lay one disgusting finger on me, I shoved her face away with an open palm, fingers splayed tightly and harsh. "I can't bloody do this."

"What? Why? Call me Samantha. I'll be whoever you want me to be," she slurred. "It's all good."

"No. Fuuuuck, I really *can't* do this. I don't bloody want anyone but her."

I left her there, half-naked, eyes wide. Lipstick smeared down her chin. Was it smeared when I met her? How could I think she looked anything like my Sam? My perfect Sam.

I walked around aimlessly, drunk as all hell, and ended up back at my mum's where I threw up my entire night into the wastebasket of the guest bedroom. My body crumpled to the floor and I lay there cold and alone, hugging a garage pail full of vomit. Closing my eyes, the room spun quickly around me, and I gradually fell asleep.

The tranquil whispers of Sam's voice rippled through my mind, "It feels like you can't breathe, *but you can*. It feels like you'll never get through this, *but you will*."

What if I just didn't want too? Huh? Bloody hell, Samantha, what then?

# CHAPTER 10

## Samantha

I wish I knew how much time had passed when I finally awoke. It would have been a bit easier to gauge how much danger I was in, but with the heavy burlap bag over my head, and the stench of vomit that lined the inside of it, I could not think one straight thought. My body felt as if it were sitting on some sort of hard surface, my hands were still tied around my back, and my legs felt bound together at the ankles and knees with something that made me itch with madness. Secured so tightly that I could not move, and when I tried, the pain and ache of my muscles and bones screamed out of me in tears, letting me know they must have been stuck in this position for a while. It felt as if someone had taken liberties with my body in a boxing ring. My head hung heavily to one side.

Something a small distance away made a soft thump. I rolled my head in the direction I thought it came from. "Hello," my voiced slurred slowly into the darkness.

A loud grumbly laugh burst out from somewhere right over my head, so close and abrupt that my head flinched back from the sound.

Bright light blinded me, as the hood was yanked up violently from my head, and I gasped for the fresh air that assaulted my nose and mouth.

There, standing in front of me, wearing a smug smile was David. Shoulders back, proud strong chin jutting out and perfect posture, arrogant and cocky, radiating an air of superiority around him. The glint of a filthy serrated knife peeked out from behind his back, intimidating, and mocking me. He smirked at me when my eyes fixed on the blade of the knife.

Rusty. Filthy. Staph infections. Tetanus. *He knew exactly how to torture me.*

Slowly, he moved over me, dragging the tip of the knife across my throat, burning a small lick of flame in its wake. Tilting my head as far away as I could, I cringed, biting down on my tongue from the sheer disgust and hysteria that was taking over my body. I knew it was nothing more than a scratch, but the way his eyes were basking in my horror, my mind started to race into panic mode. *I can't let him do this. I can't let him control me with fear.*

Calming my face muscles, I locked eyes with him and cleared my thoughts. *I can't let my emotions take over and chaos win.* Focus. Stay calm.

Slowly, he brought the blade away from my neck, dragging it gradually down the front of my shirt, over my breasts and stomach with just enough pressure to bite through the material. I wanted to run and scream, fight back, *anything*. All I could do was tighten my muscles, and clench my fists closed against the back of the chair. I knew he was seeing signs of my panic; my skin was probably pale as hell, my nostrils flaring, and beads of sweat breaking out across my skin, and the quickening of my breathing, as my chest fell and rose in terror. I tried to count, I tried to calm myself, so help me God I tried, but I knew David was going to kill me. I knew my hours on this earth were numbered, and I was not in any control. All I could do was fight back the tears. *I wasn't going to give him any.*

With the knife, he slowly sawed through the ropes between my knees and ankles, deliberately taking his time, smiling, knowing he had all the control. Then he stood and pressed his body against mine to reach to saw the ropes binding my hands behind me. One slip of that knife and the pain would be unreal.

"Stand up," he whispered into my ear before he stepped back.

I grabbed hold of the back of the chair to help me stand, and sat down again quickly before he could see me fall. I couldn't breathe. This man was an entire army in himself, and I felt like I had no armor against him.

Then I thought of Kade.

*Oh, my God, Kade must be going insane right now.*

"Get down on your hands and knees, pet and crawl to the door."

*This man was going to kill me. I wasn't going to crawl for him anywhere.* I had just enough energy for one laugh, before his fist met my temple and my world blurred with rainbows and jaw numbing pain.

"You're just as stupid as your brother was," his hazy face whispered into my ear. Thick strong hands grabbed onto my hair and savagely yanked my head to face his. Strands of my hair snapped and pulled from my scalp, sending sharp needle-like stings over my skin. Low guttural sounds escaped through my clenched lips, causing him to smile heartlessly. "He tried to fight me, too," he chuckled, darkly. "He thought he could outsmart me, just like you. It's such a shame that *suicide* runs so rampant in your family, isn't it? Especially when he was helped by me." The wet slide of his tongue up my cheek made my stomach roll in disgust, but the acknowledgement of him playing a part in my brother's death, made me scream and slam my head against his. Primal screams of anguish tore from my throat, senseless words and guttural shrieks, as if I could kill him with the sounds of my shattered heart.

"You fucking piece of shit, David. You're a fucking coward, you son of a..."

His crushing fingers around my throat silenced my words. "Will *these* be your last few breaths, pet?" Pressing his fingers tighter around my throat, he laughed, "Your brother went quickly, a lethal mixture of a little Oxycontin to make him feel good, and a bit of Potassium Chloride to stop his heart."

Lowering my jaw down against his crushing hands, I squeezed my shoulders tight and pivoted on the balls of my feet. Slamming my hands into the crooks of his arm, I gasped for breath as his hands lost their hold on me. The weight of his body blasted into me, forcing me up against the wall, knocking the air from my lungs. The pain in my chest was like fire. The filthy blade of his knife was once again pressed hard against my flesh.

"Tell me why you killed Michael! Tell me why you killed my brother!"

"Don't act stupid, pet. You and your brother were so righteous. Just like you, he wanted no part of our little extra curricular money earning. Your father and I have been building the SamMatt Pharmaceutical Empire for years. It's a billion dollar industry, baby. I have everything. I *am* everything. He was trying to stop me, and he was collateral damage. You, though, I was surprised when you just left and didn't try to stop me. Even shocked me a bit when you emptied all the accounts and hid my money. I always thought you were too strong willed, but I never knew how unintelligent you really were."

The burn of the point of the knife sliding along my jaw, separating my skin, made me squeeze my eyes shut and puff out a strangled gasp of breath. "What the fuck do you want, David?" I stammered, through my pain.

"Oh, I want my money, pet. And I will get it eventually. I have every intention of getting every single penny. However, right now, I'm enjoying this. This beautiful torture we have between us. I love playing God to you, pet. Will you beg for your life, little one? *Beg me.* You'll either bend to me, or die. I *will* control you. Getting away from me will be fucking useless to you, because I'll haunt your nightmares, pet. I'm going to make sure you never forget *you are mine.*" Placing his hot open mouth over my cheek, he bit into my skin, making me cry out. "You'll never be rid of me, pet. I'll always be right up here," he whispered darkly, tapping me twice on my skull before slamming his fist into my head, blackening my world.

A thick heavy blanket of warmth settled over my body, dragging me deeper and deeper into my darkness. No matter what I had ever been trained to do in my past, facing real danger-*real fear, and knowledge that you are about to die*, was sickeningly terrifying. You could sit back when it's over and think, *I should have done this*, or *only if I did that*, but to no avail. Brutality is not prejudiced. Violence is never kind. When it strikes, it doesn't give you a chance to understand it or change it. Tragedies overwhelm, overtake, and conquer. You have no control over it. You can just respond to it. Sometimes, your body is just too beaten to respond hard enough. I knew enough of seeing the effects of combat and violence firsthand, as a military doctor, but I was away from the violence. I was the one that dealt with the after effects of it, I was the surgeon, not on the field, I saw no action up close. The dying was brought to me in choppers, Hummers, and stretchers. Sure, they trained you for things. I knew at every moment I could die, you make sure you wear your boots with your correct blood type on them, and hope that no one needs to know the info, but this…this was a madman with a personal vendetta, with my named tattooed to it. I was no longer in the military. It had been years since I held a soldiers hand. I could barely remember the chaos of it, much for of the loneliness. That empty blackness that engulfed me was an easy out. Just floating in a sea of shadows and anesthetized emotions, waiting to feel again-and sunlight to warm my cold, cold skin.

My eyes eventually fluttered open to the frightening thought of having the flu. My body ached everywhere, inside and out, as if I'd been wrung out. My eyeballs and the muscles that held them in their sockets pulsed to the throbbing pain that slammed inside my forehead. I didn't remember how I got there, wherever there was, and my thoughts were too distracted by my aching pains to think it through clearly.

*Wasn't I just at work?*

*Didn't Kade give me flowers?*

A sharp boom of panic thudded hard in my chest, as I tried to move my arms and legs, which I found to be too heavy. Panic surged through my chest, exploding in bright burst of light behind my eyelids, as I screamed into the empty room.

Nothing.

No one.

*Kade wasn't at the hospital with flowers, David was.* David killed my brother and made it look like a suicide. My father helped him with *everything*. They are going to poison me again. *They are going to inject me with filth, and I have no way of fighting this.* Panic surged up my chest and into my throat. My limbs shook violently, my own heartbeats drowned out the sounds of my screams.

Still no one came.

*Stay calm and focus. Where the hell am I?*

Scanning the small room, deep red paint peeled from the walls in long curls. It lay in crimson colored piles along the filthy tiled floor, looking quite similar to splatters of fresh blood. In a few places along the damp walls, rusty water dripped down like a small rushing river, pooling into a puddle of corrosion and decay. The floor tiles held thick spider veins of mildew and mold, growing black and chalky white. A hideous mattress, ripped to shreds, coils popping through, was slung haphazardly in the corner of the room, next to a cracked porcelain bowl that seemed to smell as if it held fifty years of feces. Panic set in. Gagging back vomit. The smell hit me so hard that I lost the entirety of my stomach, gagging until the burn of bile scorched my throat, but my stomach still convulsed.

I crawled up to my feet, pulling myself up by latching on to the sill of the boarded up window, and weakly made my way to the only door. The knob was locked still. Taking another survey around the dust covered room, I nodded to myself, and a cacophony of loud high pitched hysterical giggles poured from my lips. The noise that sputtered from my lips fed my panic. It flared itself into gulps of air I couldn't get, and black spots formed in front of my eyes.

There was an open shower stall in one corner of the room, with a ripped curtain that dangled from one hook. Dark mold grew from it creases and it smelled like rotted earthy remains. With shaky hands, I pulled on the curtain, and with no more than an ounce of pull, it tumbled down, collapsing in a puff of white ash. I gagged and covered my face, wondering what toxins I was inhaling. *Mold spores?*

Turning the spigot on, a downpour of red rusty rain drizzled weakly from the showerhead. I let it run until the water was clear, and stepped into the icy water to wash off the blood. I stared down between my bare feet at the filthy broken tiles, and watched the water spiraling around the drain. Circling and circling; pouring itself in. The chill of the water felt good against my skin, it numbed the bruises and aches to a dull roar. Yet, I could still feel the ghost of David's hands and heavy fists on my skin. That would never wash off, would it?

Panic again. Leaning back against the cold tiles, gasping for breath, my knees gave out. My body slid down the wall, broken chipped tiles slicing bites into my skin, and I landed painfully hard against the floor. I lowered my head between my knees, and let my sobs break free. It was okay to break down, because there was no one here to see me cry.

When night fell, the only light in the room was that which filtered dimly through the boarded slats of the windows, from the one lone light source outside. It made striped shadows across the walls and gave the room a morbid flavor.

Sharp spiked cramps racked through my stomach as I crawled towards the toilet bowl, where I wretched and heaved until I thought I would split in half. My head swam and throbbed in sharp pains so that I could barely see. All I could do was feel, feel the scorching burn of my insides in my throat, and the tight convulsions of my body trying to expel its filth.

Somewhere behind me, a soft click and rustle. Light flooded the room.

With his deep laughter, David was instantly behind me, grabbing me by my hips, and pulling me flush against his body. Even without the recognition of his laugh, I would have known it was him the second his precious Clive Christian cologne hit my senses. *Citrus and sandalwood.* It was suffocating.

His arms slithered up across my chest, pulling me tight, and burying his face in the crook of my neck, "My little wifey. It's been too long since I sunk my meat inside you," he chuckled, darkly. "You know, for a brief second, I'd thought you actually died. But, I knew, baby. Tiny little bothersome cockroaches are hard to kill, aren't they?"

"How...how did you find..."

His laughter tore at my insides, stabbing sharp razor-like cuts through my ear canals. "A little mishap with unsealed documents. You greedy little bitch, still wanted to be a doctor, in this little tiny redneck town, they sent your new name and social security paperwork to our home, pet. Seems like they didn't believe you when you tried to prove you were in danger." Laughing against my skin, his tongue ran the length of my face. "And really, pet, when one is trying to change an identity, you shouldn't let people twitter thousands of pictures of you in his little economically awesome car."

The harsh burn of a needle pierced through my flesh, and quickly spread a strange heat through my veins.

*NO! FUCK NO!*

I could feel the tense sinewy muscles of his arms locking me in, and my stomach convulsed again, heaving nothing but air. "What did you give me," I choked, gasping for air.

"No...no...shhh...shhh...my little cockroach. No questions, all I want is too hear you struggle, Sam. All I want to do is watch you suffer, now."

His hands moved quickly, in a blur, fisting and tangling into my hair and dragging me onto the filthy mattress. The brutal pull of the strands burn and tear my eyes, as I fall hard against the coiled spring and metal that poke out from the top of the bed. They scrapped and scratched into my skin, biting burns and stinging flesh.

He turned his back and began to unbuckle his belt.

And for a minute, I seriously surrendered.

*Fuck this shit, you win. I'm done.*

But then, my mind fills with Kade.

My gorgeous, dangerous, Kade, who had survived a massacre by the hands of his best friend when he was just sixteen. David had taken everything away from me. The perfect marriage I thought I'd had. My Dignity. My career. My identity. My freedom. My family. But I can't let him take me from Kade. I can't let him hurt Kade.

Cautiously, I slid my body against the wall, slowly, inch by inch. Instantly, he's in front of me, his hands closed, clenched into a tight fist, slamming into the wet drywall, so close to the side of my face I could smell his skin. "You can't leave, pet. I haven't run out of uses for you yet," he whispered.

I didn't flinch. I would not let ANYONE try to terrorize me with their fists. I will not let him hurt me without a hell of a fight. *Underestimate me, go ahead.* I needed an opening; I needed a clean, clear strike. I needed patience, but the edge of my vision was darkening, and my limbs weren't responding to my brain. I moved sluggish and awkwardly. Whatever he'd given me, was some sort of paralyzing agent.

"You're not going to get out of this alive, Sam, unless you tell me where the money is. When you tell me, then we can negotiate your life." He stepped back. "You don't have to bruise the skin or break the marrow to hurt someone. Oh, but I so want to. To bruise your skin. Your perfect skin, with your perfect mind, with your wild and carefree ways, you're like a wild rare little flower, and I want to rip off your pretty little petals."

I wipe the tears and mucus from my face with a slow heavy hand. I'm standing in a pool of my own vomit, as I slowly slid down, not able to hold my own weight. My body felt broken and covered with a thick blanket of weight. I find myself wishing this were just a movie. The end of a scene, where the audience thinks the heroine is just about to succumb to her terrorist. However, movies and books don't usually end that way. The gorgeous hulking alpha male comes charging in just in time, and she doesn't end up taking her last wet gurgled breath, bleeding out into her own bile. But, this isn't some dramatic scene in a movie, is it? It's real, and it won't end pretty.

There's nothing that's going to stop David from killing me.

He's an out of control monster. Real. Breathing. Not a movie bad guy that will receive an Emmy for portraying such truths. There is no fair play here, there is no long monologue where I get to reach for his gun and exact my revenge. This is it. My real end. This sucks, and it isn't the way I wanted my life to end, but you don't get to pick this kind of shit in your life.

*I will promise you this, the man better kill me quickly, because the minute that man comes close enough, and I can get my arms to move, I'm fighting with everything I have left in me.*

"And what's fun, is that this time, I don't have to bother making this look like a suicide. I can just torture and kill you slowly, because everyone but that fucking nutcase writer thinks you're dead."

Blacking out. Hard to breathe.

"Do you think your little writer will come and save you?"

Yes, I wanted to say. Yes, if he knew where I was, yes he would, but my mouth wouldn't move.

"Just because you believe in something, it doesn't make it true. Just like you believe I've done some very illegal things, but, it's not true. It was you, all along, it was you. Your name is all over those papers, but rest assured, he will find you, *eventually*. But believe me, he's not going to want your rotting corpse when he gets here. Besides, wife, I left him a little note. He thinks you left him to start your life over without him. You think he's too possessive and jealous and suffocating."

Drool dripped out of my mouth. I felt it stream down my chin and land across my chest. *As soon as Kade finds out what you did*, I garbled incoherently, *you'll be dead*. He'll blow your brains out in broad daylight. In cold blood, he won't care. *I know I'll be avenged.*

"Having this power over you is intoxicating. Dance little puppet, hang yourself with my puppets strings. To you, Samantha, I'm God, because I have the power to let you live, or let you die. Every minute, *I* choose your outcome. Just like at the hospital. I will break you, my pet."

His hands tore at my shirt, fists pulled at my hair, bruised, and pounded on my skin. I could do nothing. Nothing to lift my arms to defend myself. Nothing to make him stop. My body was useless, frozen. All I could do was take the pain. Over and over, live through it, without giving him what he wanted.

"Come now, pet...I want to watch the suffering. I want to see your tears. Give them to me," he whispered fiercely, as he ripped my pants open with the knife. His clammy hands slid over my flesh, following the contours of my body, making my skin crawl and rage on the inside.

*Oh, God, no. Please, don't let him do this to me.*

Trailing the knife up my stomach, he slipped it under the front straps of my bra, slithered the cold metal under one of the cups, and savagely sawed through it with the blade of the knife.

He stroked my bare skin, and then brought his lips to my neck, raking his teeth sharply against the cuts and bruises that lay there. "Oh, Sam baby, your nipples are so hard. You like it rough, you little whore?"

*No! Not with you. Please don't*, my mind screamed.

The cool steel of the blade skittered over my nipple, and drew circles around it over and over again. I waited for the pain, but there was nothing but the terror and anticipation of it, making me want to claw out of my skin.

Scraping his unshaven cheeks over my breast, he flicked his tongue against my nipple. "I bet you're soaking wet."

Lowering his ear over my heart, he smirked and wrapped the hand that held the knife around my throat. "I can feel your pulse beating so quickly, pet," he whispered, darkly. "I can snap you little neck right now, can't I, Sam?" Yet his hands slid down my sides.

*Oh fuck no. Please don't let this happen, please. Please let this drug wear off. Please let me be able to fight back.*

Thoughts raced though my head as he moved his body lower on mine. "Your heart beats like a little hummingbird's. I love your fear, Samantha."

Jesus Christ, how could I ever have loved this man? How did I not see the emptiness in his eyes? Black holes of emotionless shit. *Please stop, David, please stop, don't do this to me.* However, no words could come out. I cried in silence, inside my mind.

The tip of the knife skimmed down the swell of my belly, taunting me. Then he was tearing my panties with the serrated edge of the blade, as he laughed and licked the skin of my inner thigh. His tongue branded me with unimaginable terror. My mind screamed with panic and wailed for rescue. For something, anything, for the ceiling to cave in over us, killing us both, or my heart to seize up and die. But there was nothing. All there was were parted lips, heavy grunts of breathing, the smell of sweat from his efforts, and the pool of saliva dripping from the corner of my mouth. Dormant muscles, heavy and unmovable, lay paralyzed under the tip of his knife and under the brunt force of his body. I couldn't even move the muscles of my eyes to look away. I wanted to leave myself, jump out of that skin and abandon its terror, but the terror rode me hard and held me steady. My extremities turned to ice, making me shiver from the inside, and slowly my blood flowed to an alarming sluggish speed. "Yes, pet. Yes," he grunted. "Give. Me. Your. Tears." And he gruesomely lapped up each one.

I prayed he'd kill me after, because I'd never be able to look at Kade in his beautiful gray eyes again.

# CHAPTER 11
## *Kade*

My phone was ringing. I could hear it, muffled deep inside the blankets of the bed I was sleeping on. *Yes, I was alone, thank you for thinking so highly of me. No, I have NOT touched another woman since I had my hands on Samantha. My dick was completely useless to me.* The stupid thing was still waiting for Sam, protesting against any use of pleasure for me. Stupid, selfish-Sam-obsessed dick. I was lucky it still pissed right.

I let the phone continue to ring that stupid bloody song that reminded of Sam.

Five damn times.

Someone called me five damn times. If I heard that song go off once more, I was going to crush the phone into little bits of crumbs, mash it in a blender, and shove it up the caller's arse.

Peeling my eyes open, I searched through the covers to see what bloody moron would be calling me at two o'clock in the morning. Stumbling around on the bed, I found the phone and read the moron's name.

*Of course*, it was Jennifer. I believed she was crowned Queen of the morons, and hundreds of idiots sacrificed their intelligence for her daily, because of the cleavage she always showed. Stupid tart.

"Yeah?" I snapped harshly into the phone.

"Do you *ever* answer your phone?" she asked, annoyingly.

I sighed heavily into the phone. "What do you want, Jen?"

"I want to know if you are okay!"

"You do bloody realize that there is a five hour difference between where I am and where you are, right?"

"What?"

"Jen, it is two o'clock in the bloody morning! What do you want?"

"Oh, shit. I thought you guys were five hours behind us, not ahead of us."

"Trust me, love, we are *far ahead of you.*"

"Kade, stop making fun of me. You're such a crude jerk. I'm just calling to see if you're okay."

"Well, love, I'm not. See, I'm trying to sleep and my bloody phone keeps ringing and waking me up."

"Seriously. Your brother is worried about you and he doesn't want to call and push, so I did."

"Thanks, *Nurse Ratched.* I believe he didn't want to call because it's two in the bloody morning. He never cares about pushing me; he's like a thong, always trying to creep up someone's ass."

"Are you...are you fucking drunk, *again*?"

*Yep, I might still be.*

*Wait let me think...*

*A bottle of brandy for breakfast this morning. One for lunch. Oh yes, and another for dinner. I believe I think she might be right, give the lady a prize. Crude, yep, that's me. I have a perfectly good explanation for being so crude.*

*I'm drunk as hell, and I have an even more perfectly better explanation for being drunk as hell, but right now, I'm too drunk to remember. Which is perfectly fine.*

*I haven't been sober at all here, probably due to all the awesome pubs. Oh wait, now I remember...it was the bloody fucking fact that I had my heart ripped out of my bloody chest and thrown clear across the world. Double-stuff-fuck-everybody.* I laughed loudly into the phone, "Bloody hell, you're just a happy little bundle of bitch to wake up to. My brother is so bloody lucky."

"Fuck you, Kade!"

"Mmm, sounds mildly interesting. Maybe when I'm deeper in my pit of despair, I'll want to dive even lower and stick my dick into you. Yes. Have your bloody people call mine, and we'll pencil you in. I'll schedule some vaccinations first. You're a nurse, you should bloody know... Do they have any that protect against stupid useless soul-destroying cunts?"

She spent a few joyous seconds in what sounded like the slamming of her phone against a table, until I could hear my brother yelling and wrestling her for it. Being piss-ass mean made me feel so much better.

"Who is this?" My brother's voice sliced through her unladylike cursing on the other end.

"Your brother," I barked out a laugh.

"What? *Kade?* Why the hell is my girl trying to beat you through the bloody phone?"

"She sounds wrong in the head, mate. You should get that checked out."

"Oh, bloody hell, Kade, you're drunk again? Fuck you."

"Mmmm. Incest. Yum. However, your clever little woman there has already propositioned me. Are you both so bored already? Have you thought about therapy? Ah, bloody hell, Dylan, I wouldn't trust the whore though, since she was friends with that bitch."

"You are a miserable broken sod, and it's no bloody surprise why she up and left you."

Click.

*Hmmm. Maybe now I could bloody sleep.*

And I did. Until I was sober again, the next day, and I found myself feeling half dead looking out the window, not wanting to do anything but write the world's worst apocalyptic horror story, where no one survives. *Maybe I'll start with a beautiful ginger haired heroine, who contracts a raging infectious disease from wherever the hell she'd been hiding, and her stupidity and selfishness wipes out the whole of humanity.* Maybe I should even name the character, Samantha Matthews. What could possibly happen, she sues me? Then she'd have to face me.

I was starting to hate that woman.

It had been one week. Seven days. A grand total of one hundred sixty-eight hours since Sam left, and things didn't feel like they were going to get any better, they felt worse. I was deteriorating back to being my charming reclusive self. *Fuck this world.*

Look, truth be told, I knew I'd get over Sam. I knew life went on, and all that crap my therapist would say. But Sam was my obsession, my addiction. She bloody made me quit her cold turkey, and I was going through withdrawals. I let her bloody destroy me. I wanted her to. I knew she wasn't coming back, I knew it was over, I had faced it, yet, all I wanted was to be bloody well left alone, and nobody would listen. *I stared at myself in the mirror for hours, wondering who the fuck it was staring back. Was that me? Surrounded by the cold lonely shadows, blood-red eyes, rambling hopelessly about a woman who I should be grateful for, showing me there was hope? The muscles at the back of my jaw twitched just beneath my skin. She might have abandoned everything we had, but she fucking loved me, and for that, I should be grateful, for that. I should sober up and move on. Let her go. Just bloody let her go. I had erected a fortress of isolation around myself; she was the only one to get in. She showed me how to live better, and I should. I bloody fucking should.*

My fist slammed into the reflection, shattered the mirror into shards of a broken me. Falling, scattering, fists against the cracks, until my reflection was gone. My head softly thuds against the place where the mirror once hung. Forehead to the cool metal, knuckles seeping blood, I say her words as her voice echoes in my mind. *I'll get through this. I always do. It feels like I can't, but I sure as fuck will.*

Then my cell phone rang, *yet again.* It was one of those rings, too. You know exactly the one I'm talking about, *that ring*, the one that after you answer it. *You knew* it sounded different because it brought the message of bad news.

157

The ominous ring screamed from my phone and vibrated little electrical shock waves through my hand. The number was unknown.

"Grayson," I snapped into the speaker.

"Grayson, it's George. Huge clusterfuck here. I just got word NYPD never brought in David Stanton. They had another doctor from the hospital they were questioning, some guy named David Resner. No one has seen Stanton since the day before the warrant was executed. He's MIA."

"Yeah, well, I couldn't care less. Sam skipped out on me seven days ago. I don't have a clue where the fuck..." I trailed off. My heart seized in my chest and convulsed. *Fuck, no.*

*Oh, fuck no.*

*They were both gone for seven days?* "What the fuck do you mean no one has seen Stanton? No one has seen him for the last seven days? Are you telling me he disappeared the exact same time as Sam?"

"They have a warrant out for him, but he skipped town. No one knows where he is. Fuck, Grayson...I didn't know she left...I thought we made her feel safe here...it's a shame really, she would have made a great witness against them in court."

"George, shut up and think for a bloody second! Is there any way that, I mean could David have had a clue that he was going to be brought in? Do you think he knew she was still alive? Do you think he knew what was happening on our end? How did he know to leave?" My

158

stomach wrenched with pain. "George. George, Sam…she wouldn't just leave a note, would she? She…wouldn't…"

"What's going on in your head, Kade?"

"Last week, Sam left me a note in her office saying she was leaving me. She's been missing for a week. She's not answering her phone. She just left all her stuff in her office in the hospital and disappeared. She only took her phone and her car."

"Just left like that, huh? Same time that Stanton went missing? I'll be right over, Kade," he growled into the phone.

"Fuck, mate! I'm in ENGLAND! Go to my house and talk to Dylan and Jennifer. I'm catching the first flight I can. FUCK! George…" I ran to the closet and started throwing my shit in my bag. My mother stood at the door to the guest room worrying her lip.

"Fuck, George. Please…*fucking find her*. Just…I don't even care if she fucking left me…just find her, okay? You just find her. Find her and if she left me, fine. FUCK, George, it's Sam, *my Sam*…she wouldn't just leave me like that…she bloody fucking wouldn't."

"Yeah, Grayson. We'll find her," he said, disconnecting. The harshness of the dial tone throbbed in my ear.

Anger ripped through my insides. "BLOODY FUCK!" I screamed, slamming my clothes together. Fucking hell, I bit hard at my bottom lip to stop my throat from knotting and my eyes from tearing. *Fucking hell, she could be fucking dead.*

Dead.

Dead.

Dead.

*Glazed green eyes staring blankly into the sky. A pale bluish hue to her cold skin. Sticky congealed blood caked and drying beneath her once soft warm body. Purplish chapped lips open, empty of breath. Pulse still. Blood stagnant, thickening, drying, tissues rotting, seeping into the earth. My beautiful Sam, decaying, melting and crumbling into dust that flits away from my fingertips. I breathe in her ashes. Absorb them into the tissues of my lungs. She helps me breathe. Her and her cinnamon apples.*

"Kade?" my mother's voice whispered from the doorway, shaking me from my imagery.

I wiped at my face, zippered up my bag, and leveled a glare at her. Hands twisting hard around the luggage handle, squeezing it as if it were Stanton's neck, snapping it completely off. I should have killed him long ago.

"Kade, love? Talk to me. What's happened?" Mum asked.

Sucking my lips in, I couldn't form the words in my head. Couldn't process the truth, the heavy fear that was eating me inside out. I crushed my hand over my mouth, squeezing my eyes tightly shut. *Samantha Matthews would never have just left me with a bloody note. He fucking took her, he fucking killed her, and now I'm going to end him in the most brutal way I could possibly think of.*

Her soft hand touched my shoulder and I tensed.

"They never had David Stanton in custody. He…uh…he has been missing as long as Samantha has been," I mumbled, barely audible.

"What does that mean?" she asked, giving my shoulder a bit of a squeeze.

"It means that…fuck, Mum. It means she might not have left me and he just took her. Bloody hell," my tears were falling. A grown man crying like a baby. "She could be dead. He wanted her dead. Oh, God. I didn't believe she loved me enough to bloody stay, and she's probably dead."

Opening my phone, I called my PA. Without even saying hello to her, through tears, I demanded she get me on an airplane instantly. Yelling and cursing, barking and ranting, I made not one shred of sense. Softly my mother took the phone from my hands and explained to *Help Desk* what was happening, while I slid down to my knees and finally broke down. I could hear none of her conversation over the thundering pound of the blood that rushed into my ears. All I heard, all I saw, and all I felt, were the sight, sounds, and feel of my hands around Stanton's throat when I finally killed him.

"Get in the car, love. Henry will drive us to the airport. Mrs. Heldist just booked us on a private, long-range jet to Adirondack Regional Airport. We'll have a car waiting for us there. It's about an hours drive from there, right love? We'll be there in a few hours." I looked up from the floor. My mother stood over me with a bright red backpack slung over her right shoulder, and stern determination across her brow. "Let's go, love."

I grabbed the broken handle of my luggage and swore when the sharp edges of the handgrip bit into my palm. Climbing up to my feet, I steadied myself and wiped away my sweat and tears. *"We'll* be there?" I asked.

"Well, I certainly can't let you go all the way there on your own, love. You can't even speak with your assistant without bloody flipping out, so how are you going to handle being on a jet for a few hours. I'll be there to box your ears, love."

"You'll just get in the way, Mum, and when I find him, I'll most likely be going straight to jail after."

"Well, dear, if you find him, I'll help you bury whatever's left of him," she said, smiling tightly, as she walked out the door.

# CHAPTER 12

## Samantha

*Am I still alive?*

Shifting slowly, my muscles fought against any movement. They roared in pain and ached with helplessness. My eyes snapped opened to a blur of light when I felt the tiniest movement of my fingers, the twinge of motion and lust for freedom. Hesitantly, I stretched each finger, one by one, until I knew how much mobility I had, and realized I was no longer tied down.

"Sir says you will be able to move around again by tonight," a soft feminine voice drifted past. Keeping my head still, I moved only my eyes in the direction of the voice. I *knew* it was Aurora. You hear some people in your nightmares on a daily basis. Her and David's voice, I would be able to pick out of a crowd of screaming monkeys in Grand Central Station.

A flawlessly groomed Aurora sat on a rusty folding chair in a finely ironed shirt and long flowing red skirt. Perfectly manicured fingers folded, locked together in a perfect lady-like gesture. She crossed one long leg over the other and offered me a tight smile.

My throat was parched. Sharp needles of pure misery slid down my esophagus as I tried to swallow. "Where...is...he?" I croaked hoarsely.

Her smile widened at my pain. Deep chocolate brown eyes danced in joy with my struggle to speak. She shrugged her shoulders coolly, and shook her head, "I'm not quite sure, but I'm positive, Sir, is doing something important."

I tried licking my lips to coat them, help them to move, but all I tasted was the salty tang of blood. "Did you...did you just call him, *Sir?*"

"Would you like some water?" She asked in a creepy gesture to comfort me.

*Thanks, bitch, but I rather skin myself alive then drink whatever you're offering.* "Are you fucking stupid?" I seethed. "Aurora. I need more than a damn glass of water. You need to help me get away from him."

Her eyes narrowed. "I can't do that. I would never go against David. I belong to him," she whispered. "When you tell him where you hid the money, he will let you go, so just do what he says. Everything will be fine then. You can go back to doing your things with that writer, and David and I can finally be together like we always should have been."

A sudden wave of nausea slammed against my body, filling my mouth with vomit, and left me retching straight down my chest. Holding my head as still as I could, I cringed at the feel of the liquid dripping down my bare skin, but there was no way I wanted her to know that I was getting my ability to move back. I gasped and spit, then locked my eyes with hers. "You should go and find the truth first, before you go and produce a Disney princess movie out of this situation. That man is going to kill me no matter what. He has already tried."

"Nonsense. When you were sick after losing your baby, he was there for you. You're the one who tried to hurt yourself, not him. When you overdosed on those drugs, he almost snapped," she said, wide-eyed.

"You really believe that? Violent people like David Stanton don't just snap, sweetheart. They make precise-well-thought out choices for their victims, and act on them. David injected me with a drug that caused my unborn child's heart to stop beating, and then the sick fuck gave me a mixture of poisons to stop mine."

"NO!" She shrieked. "Stop making up stories! You *are* the sick fuck. I know what you did to him when you ran away. You almost killed him that night. I found him and called 911. He was in the hospital for weeks, because of you. Do you want to be arrested? Just tell him where you hid his money and he will let you leave," she hissed.

"Take a good look at me, Aurora. Do I look like someone who is just going to get to leave? Does he do this shit to you?"

Her gaze shifted down towards the floor, indifferent to my appearance, shook her head and sighed. "You don't understand our lifestyle or our nature, and that's why he should have never married someone like you. He married you for appearances only. Your father forced him. You were supposed to die overseas. You were never supposed to make it back here, you know." Talking about my death so nonchalantly, as if I were just some unloved pet goldfish ready to be flushed down the toilet. This fails to surprise me on every conceivable level.

Twinges of muscle spasms traveled just under my skin. Deliberately without Aurora knowing, I tried out soft miniscule motions across my body, feeling out the range of movement I was getting back. I needed to keep her talking, pass the time until I got complete control over all my muscles again, without her knowing I was mobile. I couldn't let her be aware that I could fight back. The element of surprise was the only weapon I had right now. The anger settled inside of me, pooling in the pit of my stomach. All the panic and terror from what had been done had to be set aside, called back later, at another time. I needed to be in control of my emotions to get myself out of this situation. Just like in a war. I was facing my enemy, standing on the front line, two against one, and I did not want to lose. "What lifestyle? Are you talking about the way he treats you like his slave? That's okay with you?"

Lips pursing, then puffing out a small laugh, "I'm a natural submissive. And believe me, whatever you think that is, it has a different meaning to me. David Stanton is a sheer unadulterated dominant, and you would never be able to let him control you like I let him control me."

Leveling my voice to a calm croak was maddening. I wanted to scream and claw my way out of the room. My toes were wiggling now, and the muscles of my calves tightened when I flexed them. "So, this is all just role playing for the both of you, and apparently me. Innocent loving sex play, right?" I licked at my lips again, which caused her eyes to zone in on them, "So, tell me then, if it's all just playful, why have I been drugged, beaten and..."

*Fuck* the word stuck to the back of my throat, heavy and filthy, coating my inside with cancerous cells that threatened to overtake my mind. "Raped."

"Raped? Really? You are so delusional. Do even understand what kink is?  What David's sexual desires are?" She scooted forward in her seat, smiling. "Would you like me to tell you? Sir says I have to stay in here until you are able to move around. I could teach you all about what we like, and I can show you how good it feels," she said.

Yeah, right there, my mind...*officially blown*. I was dealing with someone who demonstrated the mental capacity of a fourteen-year-old horny boy.

What the *freak*?  "What, are we bonding now? This conversation is insane. This has nothing to do with sexual fucking preferences and levels of kinkiness. I was married to him, sweetheart. I knew he liked it rough. Couples play games, experimenting. It's fucking healthy- but *this*...this, what he's doing to me is not healthy, Aurora, it's a fucking crime!" I started feeling the tingling sensation of pins and needles along my skin, as I flexed whatever muscles able to move, as slow as possible. "We're not talking about two people enjoying a bit of slap and tickle and bright red handprints on ass cheeks, with a side of rope burns for bracelets, Aurora.  I didn't want what he did to my body. I don't want to be here. That man hurts me because he is pure fucking evil."

"He's not as horrible as you are making him out to be..."

"My, God, Aurora, if you really believe that, you're dumber than I originally thought you were." I was getting full feeling in my legs now. *Maybe if I get her pissed off at me, she'll slip up and make a mistake, look in another direction. I needed her off guard, because I was pretty weak to be fighting, so I needed all the advantage I could get.*

"No, David is brilliant and wonderful. He's perfect, and you're just jealous."

"Yes, he's so perfect, ask him to walk on water. If he can, then by all means, I give him the right to do this to me, but if he can't..."

"He loves me, he's never loved you," she stated. "You're just jealous."

"And you are *romanticizing rape and violence.* How do you think this is going to end? This isn't a fucking lifetime movie that you can pause, or a book you can snap shut. I get playing roles and dom/subs and sex play, but this is *beyond.* Can you leave here? Can you honestly look at me and think what he is doing is fucking normal? Maybe for you, but not for me, lady. *I don't like this.* This is someone holding me hostage. *It is a criminal act.* I would never let another human being hold me hostage or hit me...I'm not playing a part in a sex game."

Aurora leaned forward in her chair and a streak of crimson anger flushed her cheeks. "You don't understand the power I feel when I'm in my submissive mind. I am *Perfect* to him there."

*Yep, just a PERFECT PIECE OF PUSSY. Nothing more.*

Taking a slow deep breath in, I felt the shift of control in the muscles of my shoulders and back. Clenching my inner thighs, and slightly tightening my stomach abductors, I knew I finally had full control of my body again. A swell of relief drifted over my shoulders, and I scanned Aurora's eyed for any acknowledgment from her that she knew I could now move. Nothing. She had to think I was still under the influence of whatever paralyzing agent he'd injected into me, probably *Suxamethonium Chloride.* There was one thing that could not be denied, as I laid in front of her, naked and still. Aurora had a lot of problems with fucking reality. That woman sitting before me, blinded, and in love with a sadistic misogynistic man, and he was the King of her *Auroraland.* Nothing I could say would be able to touch that. Nothing I could do to save her, I just needed to save myself from this crazy train wreck. "Look, Aurora. I think you and…Sir…make a beautiful couple. You both obviously fit together perfectly, and I don't belong here." I gave her the smallest smile I could muster, which tore a spike of pain across my bruised face. "Why don't I tell *you* where I hid the money, and then I just leave you both to a happy long life together. Sir would be very proud of you if you were the one who found out where I hid it. Can you imagine his surprise?"

Her eyes turned into tiny slits as she slowly stood up and walked towards the disgusting mattress I had been thrown on. "I said I was submissive, not stupid," she hissed, leveling her face with mine.

*Shoot, that didn't work. Well, time to go.*

Adios, bitch.

Instantly, my fingers clamped tightly into fists and my body sprung up. With the momentum of all my weight, I slammed my fist into the side of her head, hoping the force would rattle her brain against her skull and knock her out quick.

Of course, I barely had enough strength, but I felt the surge of adrenaline burn across my skin as she scrambled to get away from me. I lunged after her with a fury. Hurting people went against everything I was ever trained to do as a surgeon, but there was truly only one thought in my head at that moment. *Escape.* And the bitch was blocking my exit.

Hitting her with my hands made her move, but slamming her in the head with the metal chair got her to fall.

*GOD, that felt fucking GOOD.* And for a split second, I had the urge to go all bloodthirsty Kade-like on her stupid ass, and then thought better of it. She'd probably like it too much.

Running my hands over her pulse and head quickly, I knew she was fine. She would have a splitting headache when she woke up, but I wasn't planning on sticking around to find out and help ease her pain. I needed to get out of there as fast as I could. Ripping through her pockets, I found the key to the lock on the door, and then looked down at myself, realizing how bloody and bruised my naked body was. And sick to my stomach, *holy shit, was I sick to my stomach.* I gagged and dry heaved, as I quickly stripped off the clothes from her limp body. I had to stop three different times, because the convulsions in my stomach where so powerful that my temples and chest burned from effort and restraint.

Thank God, she wore a pair of flat boots. They were probably three sizes too big for me, but at least she wasn't wearing those lethal stilettos today. Wiping the filth off my chest and stomach, I quickly dressed in her clothes and boots and quietly opened the door. Then, with my trembling battered body, I walked right the fuck out.

Mission set. Goals defined. My thoughts focused, cleared. Escape. Kill David. Get back to Kade.

Nothing was going to stop me from getting back to Kade.

Nothing.

If something did, I was going to kill it.

# CHAPTER 13

## Kade

After five straight hours on an airplane with my mother, and a handful of flight attendants who listened in earnest as my mum regaled the story of our tragic relationship, I seriously had to encourage myself not to open the emergency latch and jump to my highly desired death. Every single tendon in my entire being felt as if it was getting coiled tightly into an anxious stress filled band of steel. Images raced through my head as I was up in the air. Not in control, helpless. Thousands of feet in the sky, thousands of miles away, fucking bloody helpless.

Somewhere, hundreds of miles away, miles below the metal box I flew in, my Samantha was in trouble. There was nothing I could do, and nothing that anyone could say that would make a damn ounce of difference in anything. The blood pounded in my head the whole flight. Torture was in not knowing what was happening below.

"Mr. Grayson, would you care for a drink? Is there anything that I could…"

"For all that is good and holy, just go the bloody hell AWAY," I snapped.

My mother's hand reached out from her lap faster than my eyes could see, and she slapped me upside the head like I was a disagreeable teen. "Kade Charles Grayson! I did not bring you up to be a dick to women."

"I'm good like that, king of dicks, and that bloody hurt," I snapped.

"You are acting like an arse!"

"Bloody awesome, thank you. I might add that to my business card. May I quote you? For one bloody moment, could you, and everyone around me think about what I might be going through sitting here helpless? All I could see in my head are images of her somewhere hurt, so forgive me if I snap at the twits who are trying to shove a bit of liquor down my throat!"

I was allotted two hours of silence after that, which I spent hyperventilating into a bloody brown paper bag in the back cabin, and going over the last conversation I had with Deputy George before I boarded the plane. I gave him permission to access my computer where the GPS to Samantha's phone was. You're wondering why I hadn't done that myself to begin with, yeah? Well, I bloody tried, but I never got a signal. I figured it was just a cheap piece of shit, or she'd taken the tracking application out to make sure I wasn't going to follow her. I should have tried harder. I should have believed in her more. Fuck, I should have believed in us and never doubted her.

The only hope I held onto was that of Stanton's greed. If David Stanton did have Samantha, he wasn't going to kill her until he had his money back. George explained that Stanton had complete control over all the computer modules and bank accounts at the hospital, their insurance claims… They signed checks…forging signatures continuously for millions of dollars to a fraudulent pharmaceutical company they owned; he wasn't going to walk away from all that work easily. No bloody way. Knowing everything that Samantha had told me about him, he would terrorize her until she gave him the money, and I knew she never would. I knew that for a fact, because Samantha didn't have the money. When we went to the Sheriff, she gave him a key to a safe deposit box with all the evidence she had stolen from David when she ran away. I still don't know the details, but did it matter? Sam was being held somewhere probably getting hurt, alone, while bratty flight attendants tried to get me on the piss.

As soon as I felt the landing gear lower, I was out of my seat with my bag around my shoulders, daring the flight attendants to ask me to sit back down.

No one said a word to me, which was excellent, because I was nearing my breaking point. I'm talking Christian Bale in American Psycho, here, but with a British accent and the chainsaw.

When I stepped my feet on the blacktop of the runway, my knees weakened with the realization of just how much time had passed since she was last seen alive. I awkwardly stumbled into the waiting car that was to take us to wherever the sheriff's were gathered, dealing with the mess. I could visibly see the warm mist of my breath as I climbed in, but I felt not one degree of the coldness. I was completely numb, and strangely, for the first time since the age of sixteen, my brain was completely calm and focused, because I knew it had to be, because I had to fucking save her. Taking a slow deep breath, I sat in the back seat, pulled my phone from the pocket of my jacket, and turned it on. As the driver spoke in whispers with my mother, the light from my phone illuminated the car, and I vividly remembered Samantha and me locked in a closet in my brother's bar and my stomach dropped. I wanted a chance to feel those lips against mine again. I wanted the chance to give her the ring I'd been holding in my pocket since the day I was going to ask her to marry me, the day she went missing. I needed to see her again. I needed to hear her voice. I just plain fucking needed her. With trembling fingers, I hit the contact button for Deputy George and waited for my world to end.

"Grayson, did you land yet?" he barked. Not even a proper greeting. Curt and serious. *Oh, bloody fucking hell.*

"We're driving to town now. What's happened?" I replied, my voice cracked and shook, immediately giving away my emotional mindset.

"We tracked the GPS to her phone," he began, and my heart thudded painfully hard against my chest. I swallowed back the urge to scream and stayed fixated on his voice. "We found her car off the side of the road on Forest Home Road."

"Was there an accident?" I asked, clenching my jaw.

"Negative. The car is in perfect condition, half a tank of gas, keys on the front seat and her cell phone in the trunk. We did however find bloodstains in the trunk, Kade. It's been a few hours, but we're waiting on lab results. I'm at the hospital right now with your brother, waiting on the video surveillance recordings from last week. Seems like this hospital doesn't have the proper upkeep of their security equipment, so we called in the head of the their security firm to help find the time stamp and evidence from last week."

"That's all there is?" I whispered into the phone.

"So far, yes. I'm sorry I don't have more information for you, but I'm certain to get this sorted out as fast as we can. How far are you away from the hospital? Why don't you come here and we'll go to the car site together."

"Yeah, I'll see you in a few," I mumbled hanging up. "Please head to the Adirondack Medical Center," I said to the driver.

My mum's soft-gloved hand touched my forearm, "What information did you get, love?" Her voice was cautious and caring, making me want to sob out in agony.

"Sheriff's office found her car with her cell phone in the trunk, abandoned on the side of a desolate road. There, um was blood inside the, ah..." I couldn't finish.

"Oh, dear," she whispered, covering a hand over her lips.

I could do nothing more than turn my head out the window of the car and watch the evergreens as they blurred by. The *dark and dismal mass that was otherwise known as the Adirondack Mountains.* Somewhere, in that surrounding black of the forest, was my Samantha. Did she know how to navigate in the thick nature of the Adirondacks? Did she know how to survive in this brutal weather? Or was she somewhere inside with that monster, being held prisoner? The thoughts gutted me, but I held onto my sanity with a tight grip. The only way I was going to save her was if I kept my head about me.

When we finally pulled up to the hospital, Jen was outside leaning against the brick columns under the canopy of the large building. She was uncharacteristically smoking a cigarette, a cherry tip, blazing brighter as she inhaled a pull. She pulled herself off the wall as I climbed out of the car, and began wiping at the tears that emerged from her eyes, and walked toward me. "Oh, Kade," she sobbed, "this isn't happening, it can't be. How could he have known she was still alive?"

I took the cigarette from between her fingers, and instead of flinging it into the parking area, I took a long pull, and exhaled. There was no way to answer her question, so I ignored it. What difference would the answer make anyway, it was already done. "Where is everyone?" I asked.

"There in the security unit on the ground floor," she whispered.

Taking my last pull of the cigarette, smoke burning and scratching its way down my throat, I flicked it onto the walkway and strode to the sliding doors. I didn't check to see if she or my mother followed. Though, I did hear my mum's voice say, "Well, Jen, dear, I'm sorry we have to meet under such horrid circumstances..."

I shut the rest out. The niceties made me want to gouge my own eyes out of my skull. It was simply astonishing to me, how everyone in the world could be calm and act so bloody normal, while Sam was missing. Fuck, I was trying my damnedest to hold myself the hell together and not fall apart, but my body was knotted up into clumps of pure hate and bottomless despair.

"Security unit?" I snapped at the security officer behind the front desk. Placing his hand on his little toddler like walkie-talkie, he eyed me as if I wore a strap-on bomb. "I'm Kade Grayson, the Sheriff's department called me. I'm here to meet Deputy George down in security," I said, pronouncing each word slowly, so I would calmly get my point across without having to use the knuckles of my hands that tingled to introduce themselves to his eye sockets.

"Oh, yes," he said pointing to the right, "it's just down the hallway to your right. Just follow the signs." *Bloody moron. Bloody splatters of crimson spray splashed against the wall as a bullet tore through his head; gray matter clung to the desk and dripped thickly down his idiotic security uniform.* Imagining his death made me feel better.

I could hear Jen's voice somewhere behind me as I stormed through the corridors to the security unit. Florescent lights beat down on my face, surreal and alien. Samantha once told me she found a strange kind of peace inside the cold whiteness of a hospital; a comfort in its chaos and trauma. I think maybe because she brought in the calmness, because she could heal everyone's pain. Now, someone needed to do that for her.

Through the maze of hallways, I could hear the sounds of male voices, harsh and loud, until I rounded the corner and found the open door to the office. Before I even stepped foot inside, my gag reflex attacked, and I had to pull myself up short of the doorway. Dylan was just inside, both his hands grasping the front of his hair.

"Bloody, fucking hell," he was saying, over and over. "Bloody, fucking hell."

My hands grabbed onto the doorframe as I tried to focus my breathing. "What? *What? What!*" I heard myself screaming.

Sheriff Lane's wrinkled face was in front of mine, hollow cheeks and oil filled pores, fumbling out words that I couldn't hear over the white noise that filled my head. Just past his face, blaring in grainy black and white images, six enormous security screens played the video of David Stanton pushing a full laundry bin into the garage area, and dumping a body sized load of laundry violently into the trunk of Samantha's car. A bouquet of dark flowers was tossed in on top of the heap and it didn't move at all.

*Sam's body was in that bag and it didn't move at all.*

"NO!" I screamed. "No. No!" My fists slammed against the walls, splintering holes across the paint. Pain rocked up my arms when I didn't stop, "Take me to the car. We have to find her. We have to find her!"

*This isn't David trying to get the evidence she took. This is David getting his revenge. This is David not caring about getting caught and he was desperate now, desperate for her to give him all the money, desperate for her to die.*

Dylan and George wrestled me to the ground. Their voices urged and pleaded me to stay calm, and I tried, I swear I tried, but I just watched my world get hauled savagely into the trunk of a car, and I could do nothing                to                help                her.

179

"Over a week," I roared, stilling my efforts to fight. Dylan's hands grabbed my arms tighter, his forehead pressed against my shoulder blades. "It's been more than a fucking bloody week since this happened. I have to fucking find her."

With Dylan still holding me steady, the fucking sheriff slapped a pair of handcuffs on me and shoved me into a rolling chair, which slid across the office and slammed me up against the far wall. My head bashed against the wall, and all I could hear was the harsh gasps of my Mum and Jen as they entered the office and realized what had happened.

"Okay, everybody, just calm down!" Sheriff Lane bellowed. "Kade, you are not helping this investigation at all by throwing a tantrum. It wastes our time, babysitting you here. Time that we need to go looking for the victim."

*Fuck me, he didn't say her name. He just dehumanized her to me like he knew she was already fucking dead.* The guttural sob that tore through my chest was *in-fucking-human.*

"We have to do something," Jen cried softly when her eyes locked onto the video loop playing Samantha's abduction. "He's really going to kill her. He's going to torture her until he finds the money! My God, we need to do something. She might be...*oh, God*," she sobbed.

"You all need to realize that there is a great possibility that she is already dead. The blood in the trunk was a match with blood Samantha donated to the hospital for the last blood drive. So put your adult pants back on and let us do our job without getting in the way.

180

Understood?" His pale brown eyes softened as he looked straight at me, "You also need to realize that the woman who is missing was trained for traumatic situations and spent six years in the fucking military, and the blood that was found on the *outside* of the trunk was someone else's match, but we have no DNA evidence as to who. What we do know is that we have her hospital ID card code with her coming in and leaving twenty minutes later, and we've all just seen on the surveillance tapes who really left. Now, Deputy Tatum here is going to stay with you, and escort you all home. I have a department full of deputies and rangers combing through the woods in the fucking dark for anything that will lead us to find her."

Calmness overcame me. If it fell between the two, Samantha had more experience with violence. She knew the monster well. She had seen more violence and lived through more pain than I ever did. She'd survived worse than David.

*Right?*

*She was a fucking surgeon. She could shank a bitch, gut her, feed her own intestines to her for dinner, and fucking keep her alive while doing it. It's David's arsenal of weaponry I'm fucking worried about. If he starts pulling out his handy dandy bag of pharmaceutical toys and shit, she can't fight against him.*

They had to find her.

"There is nothing more that you all could do for her tonight, so go home and get some rest. I know you think that's an impossible feat, but you have to try. Tomorrow, when daylight breaks, if you want to volunteer in the search parties we are setting up, you can, but you need to leave your emotions home, Kade. It will not help her for you to lose control."

*Too fucking late, control has already been lost.*

# CHAPTER 14

## Samantha

Slowly, I cracked open the door and swept the room for David with my eyes, I would have given a limb for a gun right about then. My hands tightened and braced themselves against the wall as I slipped out silently. It didn't feel right, being so *vertical*. That wasn't the best of signs, but I wasn't giving up, and I wasn't stopping for anything. My skin was too raw and too hot. It burned from the inside out. It prickled and stung like thousands of little needles were piercing my skin, making me shiver with chills that crept into the nape of my neck, but I couldn't stop and self diagnose. I had to concentrate, keep my eye on the target, and get out alive.

Aurora's clothes were huge on me, and I practically had to tie them around *things* to keep them from dropping around my ankles. With slow calming breaths, I silently closed the door of my prison.

The room on the other side was crammed and cluttered with battered mismatched furniture, and hundreds of piles of tied up newspapers. Cartons of what smelled like rotting food littered every surface with swarms of bugs hovering over like little black clouds. One circular tube of fluorescent lighting flickered and buzzed in the middle of the ceiling, and tiny silhouettes of bug carcasses filled the bulb. From the rush of icy air that surged in through each broken window, torn cream curtains ruffled and fluttered like long menacing spirits. The sight of the room crippled me with a mixture fear and disgust.

*How long have I been here?*

Keeping myself as close as I could with my back to the wall, the room spread out in front of me. I made my way towards the closest window.  The frigid draft sent chills across my skin, making me wrap my arms around my chest for warmth.  *How long would I be able to stay outside in this cold? How long until the sunrise?*

My eyes quickly scanned the room for anything I would be able to use.  A few dishes.  Mounds of papers.  No utensils or weapons.

There was one long candle cradled awkwardly into a metal holder. *That's going to have to do for now.*  Look. Keep fucking looking.  Grabbing it quickly, I shoved the metal candleholder in the waistband of the skirt, scraping my hip as I did so.  *Keep looking.*  My eyes scanned through everything. My hands held tightly to my chest, not wanting to touch one single piece of filth.  Climbing over the piles of papers and *fuck I don't even know what,* I tried my hand at wrestling with a rusty old latch of a piece of furniture.  After a few strong tugs, the drawer came open and a puff of dust and debris exited. I wanted to scream. I wanted to scream and mother fucking OCD clean.  I felt like...I felt like things were crawling across my skin.  I moved my eyes faster around the room. There had to be something there to use as a weapon, anything. *Come on.*

My eyes dropped to the ground, where a small box of matches lay open, matchsticks scattered across the rotting floorboards.

*Matches.*

Matches?

I'm going to burn this motherfucker down.

Someone will come to put it out. *That's my way home.*

Crawling across the floor, I began picking up every matchstick I found, praying the box they had come in was bone-dry. My knees sank into the soft decaying wooden planks of the floor. They crumbled and snapped under the pressure. Yeah, this place was going to light up real quick. Maybe I could find some gasoline or other flammable substances to help it along. My gaze fluttered around the room, quickly taking an inventory of everything as fast as I could. Then my eyes froze on the closed door to the room I was held prisoner in.

*Son-of-a-SUBMISSIVE-BITCH!* Aurora was still out cold in there, wasn't she?

There was a tiny, miniscule part of me that wanted not to care. Leave her there. After all, she helped David with whatever he had planned.

Clenching my eyes shut tight, which hurt like hell, I inhaled deeply and sighed. That wasn't the person I was, though. I wasn't the type of person to leave someone to die in a burning building, no matter what she ever did. Maybe you could. Maybe the majority of the people in the world could, but I would never be able to look at my reflection in a mirror again and live with myself, knowing that I could have saved her and didn't even try. I mean, come on, even with the limited knowledge that you hold about the way my brain works, you know I could never leave her. I was a trauma surgeon. I couldn't leave her and start a fire where I knew she would die. I just couldn't. That's not what I'm made of. That's not how I was created. I was put here to fucking heal people, to save them, and I refuse to give up who I am for anything. And...I'm not going to lie. It's the thought of seeing her in a bright orange jumpsuit, behind bars, being someone's little bitch that made me want to save her even more. Yeah, major critical visual stimulation for me. I wanted to be visiting her in prison, smiling in front of the thick bulletproof glass, and eating Twinkies in front of her.

Still on my hands and knees, I shoved all the matches into the little front pocket of my new shirt, and crept across the floor back to the room. All I could think about were the plethora of fungal infections that lived on everything I touched. I needed to do this quickly.

Silently opening the door, I slithered in and crouched down next to her almost bare body. *Damnit!* I forgot I stole her clothes. Screw it. The gigantic campfire I was about to unleash, would have to keep her warm.

Hooking my elbows under her arms, I dragged her unconscious body slowly across the floor and out the door. I was so weak from whatever drug David had given me, by the time I hauled her to the window, I had the cold sweats and labored breathing. I might have vomited once on Aurora's leg, but let's be blatantly honest here, *she deserved it.*

Hefting her body up and out of the window just about killed me, yet I did it, and she flopped out and onto a decomposing porch with a loud thwack. Again, *she deserved it.*

With trembling limbs, I lunged back to the piles of newspapers and set to work on lighting them up. Quickly starting in one corner, I moved around the room, striking a match to light and holding it against the stacks of paper, until I watched them curl up in flames. Damn, adrenaline rushed through me. I felt the heated burst of it across my chest and scalp, and immediately, I was high. Great, somewhere hidden in the depths of me is a closet pyromaniac. *I couldn't wait to tell Kade.* Over a dozen little fires raged, rapidly growing into tall scorching flames that licked black rings of smoke along the ceiling. Within a few moments, the place was an inferno.

Climbing out of the window, with the heat of the flames biting at my back, I threw my weight up and over. My body landed on Aurora's. Once again, *she deserved it.*

Grabbing her by the ankles, I yanked her body as far as I could from the burning cabin and carefully scanned my surroundings. I had no idea where I was, or even *when* it was. The night was dark, moonless, and tall evergreen trees blocked out most of the view. One narrow pathway, just barely visible and wide enough for a car, stretched out just in front of the cabin. The ground was covered with a light dusting of snow and ice. That wasn't helpful at all to me, because I didn't want to leave any tracks behind for David to follow.

*Okay, maybe I did.* Leaving Aurora's body up against the nearest tree, I ran towards the pathway, making sure to leave a clear set of footprints behind me. I did this for a few minutes, then jumped into the surrounding forest and doubled back the way I came. Halfway back, I climbed up the thickest covered tree I could find and watched the cabin blaze with fire from above.

I stayed there. I didn't run. I waited. I hid and I watched, because now, *I was motherfucking* hunting. Someone had to see that fire, right? Someone had to be alerted and people had to come, right? I knew David would, but I was counting on others. If I ran out into the dense woods, I would freeze, and I'd most likely be lost for days. I had to trust my gut instinct. Stay close to the enemy and watch him.

My body started to numb with the cold. I tried swaying back and forth on the branch of the tree to get my blood flowing, but that just made my ears ache with my accelerated movements. I climbed to a higher branch with better pine needle covering from the wind, when I heard the low motor of an engine. Just through the darkness of the dirt road, bright headlights crawled toward the cabin. *David.* He completely runs over my tracks and doesn't notice his lump of submissive mistress leaning limply against the tree.

The car slowly pulled up next to the front door of the cabin and its door swings open with a metallic hollow creak. David climbed out. Long elegant trench coat, slicked back hair. I wanted to throw a rock at his head.

Slamming the door closed, he walked around the old boat of a car and unlocked the truck with a key. *Who does that anymore?* Bending over the rim of the trunk, he seemed to be looking for something. When he stands up, he's got a huge bag in one hand and a huge roll of rope in the other.

*WHAT the hell was that rope for?*

My head spun, and the icy air started biting into my skin savagely. The bark of the tree was so cold that I felt aching in my bones. My fingers and toes turned numb, and my ears pang with sharp stabbing pains that shot across my jaw.

The rope dropped out of his hands the instant he saw the bright flames escaping, reaching, and clawing their way out of the windows. His voice screamed out in anger with some unintelligible words and I watched as he opened the front door to a roaring inferno.

"Samantha!" he screamed, as he backed away and ran around the cabin.

Nothing but the swoosh and crackle of the fire answered him back, as the roof of the cabin burst into brilliant sparks of fire. Dark leaves of the smallest tree closest to the cabin started bursting into flames, creating a domino effect. It spread quickly across the top of the tree, which caused a larger tree to catch fire. Along the far side of the cabin, a half dozen old cars lined the perimeter, all instantly lighting up and three large dark red barrels that were positioned next to the cars, exploded in succession, rocking the ground. The tree vibrated and trembled and I wrapped my arms around it, so I wouldn't fall. My luck, I'd fall right at his damn feet.

*Shit. Shit. Shit.*

"Samantha!" David taunted from below, laughing. "What do you think will come out of this, pet? Do you think you'll get to walk away from me?" With the bright blaze of the burning fire, the forest was eerily lit up, and the shadows of flames danced before him. He held his arms outstretched and slowly twirled in a circle. He looked bronzed and utterly evil in the harsh glow of the fire. "Do you think I'd let you get away, my love? Buy yourself a new life with all the money you stole from me? Give it to your new little boy toy? Think he's with you because he loves you? No one can love you, pet. You're just a slut. A dirty whole to warm a dick for a few moments, not a particularly pleasurable one, either. A useless little fuckhole."

Another tree started burning, and another, until the woods that surrounded the cabin were engulfed in flames. The heat of the fire warmed my skin, almost to the point of singeing the fine hairs on my arm. The snapping and crackling of the trees being devoured by flames became deafening. *Shit. I was going to have to climb down and get the hell out of this forest.*

Snapping off a decent sized stick, I hurled it into a pile of fallen branches just behind David. He spun quickly, his back towards me and lunged into the area like a crazed animal. I climbed down the branches, sweat bursting from my pores and my heart slamming against my chest. Losing my footing on the last fucking branch, my body collapsed against the ground, burning tree limbs fell beside me, and a monsoon of fiery debris came raining down. A hot spike of adrenaline thundered across my chest and I was up and running through the trees, not looking back at all.

"*Sa...maaaannnnnn...thaaaaa!*" David's voice sang over the crunch and swooshes of the flames. Then, just to my right, about a hundred yards away, I don't know, *fuck* I have no clue about distance and measurements, just not so close and not so far away, a huge mass of branches moved, snapped, hissed, and sizzled.

"Hello, Samantha," his voice said, tainted with rage and anger.

Then I heard them. The pops and sharp savage cracks of explosions. *P-taff! P-taff! P-taff-taff-taff-taff-taff!* Sadistic eruptions of gunpowder sounded as they ignited the inside of a round of bullets.

*He's got a gun*, I think to myself.

As the ground...

...slammed into my face.

# CHAPTER 15

## *Kade*

Back and forth.

Back and forth.

SLAM.

Back and forth.

That was me, pacing. Wearing a hole through the carpet. Storm raging, stewing, bubbling, boiling, breathing in savage, vicious breaths.

SLAM. SLAM. SLAM.

That was my fist punching walls as if they were Stanton's face.

I could do nothing. I was being *detained*. *Confined* to my own home under the watchful eyes of Deputy George Tatum. Dylan, Jen, Mum and I, all *babysat* under hawk-like eyes. He stepped aside to let me expand my pace, watching me sharply. He must have recognized the sparks of my barbarity igniting just from the haunted look in my eyes. My family knew better and stayed well out of punching range.

Like a bear out of hibernation, I was raw and famished, ravenous for answers, for action. All my senses exploded. My thoughts twisted into my own personal volcano, surging, bubbling, and detonating into white-hot noise. So palpable I could taste the molten rock inside my mouth, and the stench of putrid gases that boiled inside my mind. My muscles coiled tighter and tighter until the ache under my skin was so agonizing, I wanted to scream. Just before the pressure blew my heart right from my chest, George's police radio crackled and buzzed to life. "Check and advise on a 10-59 working fire. Got a Fire Tower saying trees are burning and there's been an explosion."

I watched his expression closely, the pulled brow and pursed lips. "Deputy Tatum, Copy." Loud static ripped through the line. "Fire en route, we're going to need all units. Over."

George immediately jumped to his feet, mouth against his radio, fingers pressing down the buttons. "Copy, this is unit 4052. Exact location?" As he asked the question, his eyes fixed on mine. Beads of sweat formed above his brow. His jaw ticked at its hinge. A small tight squeeze of his loose hand against his gun belt. *He knows this has something to do with Sam.*

The radio chirped to life again, "Behind Forest Home Road, above Lily Pad Pond. We have a fully involved fire. Need all units…"

George blinked once and answered, "Unit 4052 en route."

I grabbed my jacket and shoved my arms through the sleeves. He'd have to handcuff me to something to keep me here, and then I'd just saw my arms off, no bloody problem. Grasping the keys in my coat pocket, I dragged out my hand and ran to my safe. Dylan was behind me instantly. So was George. When I pulled out my firearms, George's eyes went wide. "What are you doing, Grayson?"

"Can't just stay here and go to sleep. I have be prepared in case Stanton comes here," I snapped, handing Dylan a gun.

"Grayson, I can't let you just pull out guns in front of me," he hissed.

I sprang up at his face like a cobra. He was a good four inches shorter than I was, so I menacingly looked down on him. I had nothing more to lose. "Piss off, George, I have a bloody license for every one of them. Last, I checked, I lived in America, and that gives me the Second Amendment, the motherfucking right to bear arms. I'm just going to sit here with my guns, *just in case* I need to protect myself."

"I'm not stupid, Kade, you're going to look for her. Now we have a fire to deal with. You can't come with me and you can't go out on your own," he stated, eyes locked on mine.

I offered him a wink, shifted my gaze to my gun, checked the fully loaded magazine, and slammed it in. "Try to stop me."

"You're crazy. You're going to get yourself killed, Grayson."

The most primitive part of my brain was telling me to shoot him, dead center in the chest, pull a Thomas on him, but experience has taught me that I have to think this through *clearly*, not give in to my urges, so I could keep my goal of getting Sam.

His brows pulled down, lips tightened and pinched to an almost white. "You are fucking insane. I can't let you do anything stupid, Kade."

"Right now," I growled, "the only stupid thing I find myself contemplating is not shooting a friend. I'm not insane, George, but I *have* to find her."

I know. I know...at this point, I wouldn't trust my sanity either, but what would you do? What would you *really* do? Observing it all together, my ideas point to only her defense, the logic being that I needed to keep her safe from *then on*. I had fucked up royally with her; because of my idiosyncrasies and my issues. I was easily swayed to believe that she would just walk the bloody hell out of my life. I lacked faith in us, and I guarantee for those last seven days, she paid for it. I was getting my woman back.

"Grayson, I repeat, you're going to get yourself fucking killed," George said under his breath as he walked toward my front entrance.

"George, I don't have much to live for if she's not here anyway. Just go, let's pretend you have no idea what I have planned after you leave. I'm no longer your responsibility," I smiled, as I nicely shoved him out of the door.

I watched the weight of my words against his radio cackling emergency, sway his emotions. "Kade, this isn't a good idea..."

Then I slammed the door in his face.

Turning on my heels, I snapped, "Mum, you and Jen stay here. Dylan let's go."

Immediately, Jen's red blotchy face was in mine, spitting and snarling like a rabid animal, "Fuck you, Kade. I'm not staying. It's all of us here that doubted her, not just you. You don't get to be selfish now, I'm fucking coming too. What if you need a fucking nurse, huh? I'm getting her aid-pack and then we go!"

*What do you mean if we need her aid-pack?*

WHY the FUCK did Jen have to enlighten my already stressed brain with overload? It was a given she'd be hurt, but the heaviness of having to use her aid-pack on her left me breathless. My mind whirled with images so real and disturbing that I had to clutch onto the closest piece of furniture to stay standing. The images weren't flashbacks of my friends in a high school; they were of my Samantha, beaten and bloody, her beautiful body riddled with bullet holes. Her blood in my imagery stunned me. Made me feel the weight of her absence. How it stretched down my limbs, melting them heavily to the floor. Feet encased in concrete, I thought I was immovable, untouchable. I was so bloody wrong. Toxic. Vengeful. Rage. Pure and hot. Destruction decay. Rip my twisted thoughts from my brain, physically claw and scrape them out until my head was fucking hollow, and I couldn't remember these thoughts.

Squeezing my eyes shut, I tried rubbing away the visuals. I couldn't catch my breath, and my muscles knotted and ached to bathe in David Stanton's blood. *I needed to find her voice. I needed to remember the way it sounded and calm the bloody fuck down.*

My thoughts shift and move, blur and hum. And I'm standing in her trailer again; she's leaning against her counter with barely anything on, mop in her hand. I smile at the memory, but it burns my eyes, and makes the bridge of my nose sting and tingle. *God, she was so beautiful. The mop slipped from her grasp, and clinked against the counter. Her eyes looked away, as if it hurt to look at me. "Beautiful," her soft voice whispered.*

*My body was against hers instantly, soft skin, hot flesh, and those fucking delicious cinnamon apples. "Yes. Beautiful. Stunning. Bewitching. Ravishing. Fucking angelic." Then her lips, moist wet, open against mine. Hands tangled, fists in hair, skin on skin.*

And then she's gone. Faded away as her soft voice echoed, "Beautiful" in my head.

I needed to find her. I shook my head of images, and blinked out the thoughts. "Let's fucking go, I need to find her. It's cold out there and she's mine. I have to go get her back," I snapped.

Reaching back into the safe, I grabbed two more magazines full of bullets, and stuffed them in the pockets of my jacket. Every one of them planned for a piece of real estate on Stanton's flesh.

"Got it," Jen's voice panted. "I got her aid-pack," she repeated as she slung it over her shoulder, wildly.

"Jen, have you ever shot a gun?" I asked.

"Kade, really? I've never even *held* a gun."

Handing her the firearm, I rolled my eyes. She held it between her thumb and index finger as if it were a dirty diaper. I raked my hand impatiently through my hair, "Look, if you see David, just point it in his general direction and keep pulling back the trigger. The safety is on. That little button right there."

Dylan turned to Mum and jerked his chin in her direction. "Kade, do you think we should arm Mum, in case Stanton makes an appearance?"

"Did your brain seep out your ass? Why would he come here? Why would I give Mum a gun?" I looked at our mother and shrugged, "Just stay here near the phone. We're just going to drive around and look, okay? I'll put the bloody alarm on."

The three of us storm through the door and run to my truck. "Let's go. Let's go," I yelled, climbing into the driver's seat. Turning the key, the engine roared to life and the heavy cords of a *Mad World* song blasted through my speakers. *Bloody hell, Samantha's favorite band.* I slammed the off button immediately. Silence exploded and stung at my ears.

Dylan jumped into the passenger seat and looked at me through narrowed eyes. A white mist of breath puffed out of his lips as he spoke, "What are you thinking?"

I looked at him deadpan, "Mate, I've lived here for sixteen fucking years. Forest fires don't start by themselves in the dead icy frost of winter, not unless someone fucking started it."

"Wait, you think David started a fire?"

"No, mate, I think Sam did."

"Kade, are you okay for this? What if you can't…"

I slammed my hands against the steering wheel, blaring the horn loudly. "When it comes to Sam, I could do anything," I said through clenched teeth.

"What if you can't?"

"I got this."

"You're going to kill someone for her?  Is she worth it?  Maybe we should let the authorities handle it, because I mean, bloody hell, Kade, *all this violence*?  Losing yourself to it, going to jail for a woman you met six months ago?"

"You know what, *you little fuck?*  In *one* day, back in 1998, something happened to me that changed my life forever.  It took literary forty-seven minutes in that classroom.  Forty-seven minutes shattered everything and changed me completely.  So don't tell me six months isn't long enough to be changed or affected by someone.  She makes me sane.  She makes me calm.  She makes me not want to fight or slink away.  She makes me want to live.  So yes, I am damn fucking ready to do whatever I bloody can to get her out of there, and to be back with me.  Because without her by my side, I'm half a fucking man, and it's the half I can't live with."

Dylan smiled at me and slammed his hand on the dashboard, "Bloody hell, you got this.  Let's go hunting then, mate."

# CHAPTER 16

## Samantha

The sound of the gunfire cracked like thunder over the blazing fire that was closing in around us. Sliding my hands down my body, I wait for any pain, but there was none. I snapped my head in David's direction. His gun was still pointed out, but it was Aurora's body flat on the ground, half a dozen bullet holes seeping blood across her chest and over the white snow. *Hell, he thought that was me.* He thought it was me moving through the brush and he killed her instead. From where I lay, I searched her form for any signs of breathing, any movement at all. There's no use trying to save her, she was dead the minute she met David.

*But, fuck, that, she didn't deserve.*

My body was on the ground; face down in the cold earth, a muscle memory reflex from the military. You hear gunfire in the open, you fucking duck, and find your enemy. My eyes shot up to David, and his emotionless eyes fixed on mine. "My bad. Thought she was someone else. Want to check her pulse, don't you, pet? Still have that drive to save people?" Snowflakes of fiery ash fell around us, gently floating, floating to the ground.

"David, what if she's still breathing?" Until the day I die, I will always, always be a trauma surgeon. I will always crave to heal people. That's who I am. *Just look at* me right now. *This is probably the day I do die, and I want to save her someway.*

*CRACK!* I violently flinched back as he brutally blew a hole in the middle of her forehead, in the soft creamy patch of skin that separated her flawlessly groomed eyebrows. A deep chuckle rasps up from his throat, "Well, now we know she's definitely not breathing. Does that stop your itch to save her?" *Fuck, how many rounds did he let go. Fuck. Think. Was it nine or ten. Fuck, I need to find out if that gun is empty.*

*Oh. My. Shit.* I couldn't think straight, and all I wanted to do was run. If I did, he would shoot me in the back, *if* he had bullets left. Would he get a perfect shot? *Goddamnit*, so far, gaging from the perfect hole on Aurora's face, I'd say he was a damn good shot, and he'd know exactly where to shoot me for maximum damage.

"Ah. Ah. Ah. Samantha," he wagged the gun at me, "I see you planning some stupidity in that empty little head of yours. Do you think you could outrun my bullets?" A fiery branch crashed down behind him, causing sparks to explode into the air around him. I heard my gasp, the intake of breath, the undeniable evidence of my raw fear for him to witness. He stood there, a small distance away, with the raging flames of an inferno behind him, and I truly believed I knew then what the face of pure evil looked like.

*This was what Kade's nightmare's were made of.*

He stalked towards me, shoulders tight, drenched in sweat from the heat, and gun pointed right to my head.

"Point blank range, little one. Tell me where my money is," he hissed.

"Nope...I have to show you. I can't tell you. You'd never be able to get it."

"You're wasting your time trying to be smarter than me, pet. You're not. Now, tell..."

"It's housed in a safety deposit unit in a private storage facility in Jersey. It needs my fingerprints, my retina scan, a code, plus another person with some kind of identification." No it didn't, I was lying. The money and all the evidence were handed over to authorities months ago, so they could build a case on him and monitor his movements, but I needed him to think that he couldn't get just a code, put a bullet in my head then walk away. "Why do you think I didn't go to the authorities, David? Why wouldn't I tell them everything you and *my father* did? Why would I hide in this remote place and pretend I was dead? Think about it, *sweetheart*."

Lunging for me, he pressed the barrel of the gun to my temple. "You tell me, pet."

"Two hundred sixty-five million dollars, David. My father gave up everything to get that money. Do you think he'd share it with you, instead of his own blood?" *God. Please let this work.* Holy crap, I was making this shit up as I went along. But it was just like dissecting the trauma. Think fast, go through all the scenarios and take the best actions for the wounds.

"Who else's fingerprints and retina scans do you need?" The hand that held the gun lowered to his waist, no longer aimed at me.

Hell *yes*, it *was working*. I smiled at him tightly, "My father's of course." I slowly slid my hands along the snowy ground, searching for something, anything I could grab to smash him in the face, and then go for his gun.

"It's so unlike you to lie, Samantha. Might it be that you like this game we're playing? I've seem to have lost one toy," he ticked the barrel of the gun in the direction of Aurora's body. "Maybe I'll keep you around until I find another one." He closed the distance between us, hovering over me, taunting, and hunting.

Psycho son of a bitch. How could we all have been blind to his madness? My hands searched frantically along the cold ground for anything I could use to defend myself.

*Well, hello sharp rock. Meet David's eye socket.*

Squeezing the rock around my fingers, I kicked out my leg at the hand that held the gun and swung my arm around, slamming the jagged rock into his temple. I saw one second of blood spurt from his head, before I slammed my other foot into his chin. I had no idea where the damn gun was, but both his hands were empty, clawing at his eyes, so I ran. I kept the rock in my hand. The crunch of the snow was beneath my feet, and then the wet dark spongy earth as the snow melted immediately under the heat of the flames surrounding us.

Under the rush of the fire, I could hear sirens. Under the snapping and hissing of the searing fire raging closer and closer towards us, I could hear...people. *That means we're close to a road.*

*We're close to a road.*

The skies above us clouded with thick choking smoke, and the smell of burning timber singed the inside of my nose. I covered my mouth with the crook of my arm and started fumbling through the brush, praying to get lost in the billowing veil of thickening smoke. Wildfires can move a hell of a lot quicker than me running. And the flames are bearing down on me. Soon, if the flames didn't burn me, I'd be suffocating from the raging fire that was quickly devouring up all the oxygen. Crackling and popping. Smoke drifting through. A large wall of flames rushed towards us with the deafening sound of a freight train, and I ran. I knew nothing about forest fires. I knew nothing about how to survive in one, so I fucking ran. I ran toward the blackness, where the air smelled cleaner, choking and gasping for breath. My feet hit the blacktop of a road. A road?

*Oh God, I'm on a road.*

David's loud panting and footfalls right behind me.

I stumbled, coughing out into the open. I needed to get to someone before David got to me. Through the thick smoke I could make the blue and red flashing lights of an emergency vehicle, but it was too far away.

Instantly, there was a heavy arm around my waist and I was tumbling into a shallow ditch, my face scraping against the sharp rocks and pebbles that filled it. David's weight crushed me.

Then white hot fiery pain.

I roared some kind of inhuman scream. The pain was agonizing, unbearable. David crawled off me laughing and shoving my body hard against the trunk of a tree.

Looking down, my brain screamed, when I saw the hilt of that huge rusty knife David had in the cabin. Right into my femoral artery. A kiss of white-hot agony, my entire body felt it, as the pain screamed across every inch of my flesh. As if I was being wrapped in barbed wire and squeezed. Sweat burst out of every pore of my face, and my stomach clenched and heaved violently. Blood poured out of the wound, around the knife, and I knew I had about twenty minutes to live. Fuck. If I pulled out the knife, I'd have less. Fuck. Fuck. I didn't want to fucking die. I wanted to see Kade. I needed to see him.

I can't take out the knife, but I have too. I have to put pressure on the wound. I have to save the leg. I had to stop the blood flood. I have to save the life.

But, David's there. *Remember?* Tears blurred my eyes.

He slammed his body over mine, causing the knife to angle itself up, opening me more, then laughing loudly, he pulled it out and fucking *showed it to me*. "Just think about the infection that will set in if you don't die quickly. Rusty, filthy dull blade. I might have even used it on raw chicken before I used it on you." *God, he was still playing on my fears.*

"And...you still won't have your money...you weak pathetic...little boy..."

Through my blurry vision, I could see a pair of headlights in the distance, and way down the road, I could just make out the flashing lights of the volunteer firefighters, trying to fight the monstrous blaze that was torching the trees. But everyone was too far away to hear my screams. To far away to watch as David slammed my bleeding body against a tree and break with his bare hands. I tried to fight him, clawing at his face, with the jagged sharp rock still in my grasp.

Yet, his hands overcame me. Doctor David Stanton, trained surgeon, with his long elegant hands. Hands with long, graceful, talented fingers, which once saved the lives of so many, were balled up fists of hate and malicious corrupted evil. Not caressing or saving, but, striking, bruising, breaking, and shattering *me*.

My brain was at war with my limbs, thinking faster and moving faster than I could physically do; all I wanted to do was find an opening. One where I could get to skin and slice, gut him while he's still alive. Except I couldn't, because I could hear my small, shallow breaths, as I tried to fight and felt the bitter agony of every savage strike against my skin. He hovered over me, straddling my body, his weight unintentionally pressed down against my thigh, numbing the burn. I knew he wasn't thinking straight, because putting pressure against my thigh, even though he was punching me in the face and chest, was actually saving my life by stopping the blood flow. Or maybe he did know, maybe he just wanted me to last a little bit longer for torture.

The shrill roar of a car sliding and brakes skidding tires along the snow exploded in my ears. I wanted so badly to have hope, so badly, but I knew I was running out of time.

"Freeze and put your hands where I can see them..." Through the smoke and haze, over the crackling and spitting of the flames, I heard Deputy George's deep voice.

Then I heard one last gunshot ring out. It bounced and echoed along the burning trees, drifted like a ghost amongst the smoke. After a raspy breath, a dark chuckle whispered into my ear, "See, my pet, I did have more bullets," the evil taunted. "But it's more fun to kill *you* with my bare hands..." Panting, and coughing from the thickening smoke, his body shifted off mine.

I wanted to look at my wound. I needed to clean it. Wrap my skirt around it. My vision doubled, my head throbbed and the trees spun around me. Trying to lift my head, his hands were instantly at my throat. I tore, and clawed at them, the warmth of my blood poured down my leg. *Shit. The blood ran thick and fast. Need a tourniquet. Need pressure.*

With a singing pain that made me shriek out in agony, I jammed my fingers through my wound, applying all the pressure I could muster.

Cringing, I looked toward the body of the deputy. *God, is he still breathing? Where was he shot?*

"Oh, pet. What is going on in that stupid little head of yours? Are you still trying to save the piggy? I just ripped a hole in your leg, and you still want to save his life?" Pain blasted and crashed up my spine as he shoved my body against the rough hard bark of a tree. Hands released my throat, but panic filled it.

I look around desperately for anything. Anyone. George couldn't have come here alone. Fuck, Kade has to be here somewhere.

"Kade!" I screamed.

"Oh. Ah...I see. You're looking for your lover? *Lover*. That reminds me, pet. What did he think of my name *branded* on your skin? Did he need to fuck you with his eyes closed so he wouldn't see me?"

The night was black and wet. Smoke and flames stung my eyes. David's voice was buzzing and humming, but all I heard, all I looked for were exit strategies.

"Ah, are we playing the quiet game, my pet? Should I make you scream then? I like when you scream, pet."

*Yes. Screaming. Then they'll hear me.*

I didn't have to force myself to scream either, David did that with the next sharp blow. I shrieked as I felt my skin tear, not that it mattered.

I saw my own blood. It dripped between my fingers fast and thick. My head swam and floated up. And I knew. I knew.

I couldn't save *me*.

My knees buckled. I didn't even know I had been standing until they collapsed on the wet snow. Down.

Down.

Down I fell.

But I never knew if I hit the ground. Before I landed, I was gone.

*Please don't let Kade ever find me. Please don't let him see me like this. It will destroy him.* It's going to destroy everything.

Then I waited for death to come.

But David's fists came for me first.

# CHAPTER 17

## Kade

Lost in a world of irrepressible dread, I prayed to whatever higher power that would listen as my fingers tightly gripped the steering wheel. The speedometer sat at a steady one hundred miles per hour, yet it still wasn't fast enough. Grinding my teeth with tension, I muttered, "The snow and frost should slow down the fire. The trees are too wet to stay ablaze. Something else must be burning."

With his hands braced against the dashboard and a harried expression, Dylan turned to look at me, "Kade, keep your eyes on the road. Don't look at me when you're driving this fast."

"This isn't bloody fast ENOUGH!" I roared, pressing my foot further down against the gas pedal. My truck crept up to one hundred and five and something started clanking under the hood. I ignored the noise. "It's not bloody fast enough," I repeated in a strained voice.

A small hand touched my shoulder and squeezed with what felt like mirrored sorrow. Jen sat behind me, leaning forward, her hand stayed fixed there. A somber and weighty touch. She cleared her throat before speaking. Then she whispered in a gruff tone, "The dispatchers said there was an explosion. Maybe there was an accident somewhere and this has nothing to do with Samantha."

"*Or*," I snapped, locking my eyes on hers through the rearview mirror, "Or, you could shut the bloody hell up!"

"Kade, you have to…"

"Shut. Up."

"Kade, mate, Jen is just…"

"SHUT. UP!" I hollered. My head pounded with tension and a heavy knot twisted in my stomach. It was working its way up my chest, ready to wrap its talons around my throat and squeeze the life out of me.

Mumbles and muttered curses flittered through the truck, until quite suddenly, a heavy silence fell, one filled with intense fear. Through the next break of the trees, we saw *it*. The horizon. It was on *fire*. Bright orange flames licked up into the dark sky, reaching wildly towards the stars with jagged spikes. Dark gray columns of thick smoke twisted and spiraled up, staining the sky. White wisps poured over the road. I couldn't see the road ahead of us, only the faint blue and red flashes of an emergency vehicle's lights that bled through the clouds.

I slowed the truck and drove towards the blaze in the sky. Puffs of thick white clouds rolled across the windshield, obstructing our view, and the strong smell of burning pine drifted in.

The sight of a police cruiser, cherry top lights flashing with its door slung open in the middle of the road, had me slamming on the brakes and skidding across the blacktop. My truck lurched to a stop, nearly crashing into the police car.

"What the bloody hell is that?" Dylan asked, in harsh whispers. "Is this an accident?"

No, there wasn't any accident.

Accidents *aren't* done on purpose.

In the surging smoke and wind, a large shadow moved, hovering just off the side of the road. A gust of wind noisily blew against the windshield, and in the shadows, David Stanton's face appeared.

Smiling.

Smiling.

*Smiling.* A dark motionless shadow of something lay at his feet. Time stilled and the world muted, hushed completely, except for the sound of my erratic beating heart. The smoke shifted, flowed left, and on the ground near the police cruiser's back tire, lay Deputy George Tatum, sluggishly moving as if he were hurt.

Automatically, my fingers wrapped themselves over the coolness of my gun. Unconsciously, my empty hand pushed open my door and my body ejected itself from the driver's seat. Kicking the door shut with my foot, I slid across the hood. The tightness in my chest was overwhelming, and I staggered forward without a care for my safety. *I needed to see who was lying at David's feet.*

The acidic smoke stung my eyes, yet I didn't stop. The dark unmoving form on the ground was my target. *I needed to see who was lying there, on the ground, at David's feet.*

*That couldn't be Samantha.* No. No. Samantha was full of life and smiles. She was not lying still on the cold filthy ground.

211

I didn't want that to be her.

I didn't want...

The pounding in my ears became louder and louder, until it was deafening. My throat burned hotter, the closer I walked. Wisps of smoke swirled around the small figure that was lying in a fetal position. Her beautiful ginger hair splayed out over the black tar of the road, coated with blood. A torn, muddy red skirt clung to her legs, her shirt shredded into thin curled ribbons exposing her bloody beaten torso. Her face was barely recognizable, yet her eyes...her eyes were open, staring past me.

"Oh, Mr. Grayson, *the famous Cory Thomas*, it's nice we finally meet, I was wondering when..." There were no weapons is his hands, and there was no emotion to his voice...

There was no thought at all.

This wasn't self-defense.

This was cold-blooded, and so well deserved, because he took away my beautiful Sam.

The gun was weightless in my hand. Flying to a perfect position on its own accord, aimed straight towards David Stanton's smiling face. Deputy George, crawled toward my feet, face full of blood and mud, but I *didn't care*.

I pulled the fucking trigger.

Dead center.

Right between Stanton's eyes. Dark liquid splashed out of the back of his head, spilling from his mouth, as he collapsed with a thick wet thwack onto the bloodied ice and snow.

*Then I emptied my gun on him*, hitting him with EVERY... SINGLE... BULLET. *This isn't a movie. He doesn't get to have a monologue where he could explain all of his bullshit excuses...this was life and his is over.*

*This doesn't make me Thomas.*

*This does NOT make me Thomas.* My knees buckled and crashed against the dirt in front of my Samantha.

My trembling fingers opened. My gun thudded against the muddy ground.

Jen was on top of Samantha, instantly. "Oh, my God. Oh, my God. Oh, my God. No. No. No."

*That's not going to help her.* Empty words. Empty prayers. Empty pleas. I have to help her. *Only actions will save her.* I have to help her. *The flames flickering in the sky above her body made me seriously wonder if God ever cared at all.*

Through dirt, mud, and filth, cold, ice and rock, I crawled to her. It was not over. I would NOT doubt her again. I would not give up on her again.

*Never* again.

*Never.*

"DYLAN!" I roared. "Get George! Get George!" I shoved Jen off her body and as gently as I could, I gathered her limp broken body to my chest. "Jen, get in the police cruiser and start it. Don't forget her aid-pack! Dylan, put George in the front seat and get us to the hospital, *yesterday*."

I carried her to the cruiser and delicately shifted my body into the backseat, keeping her on my lap. Jen slid in the backseat, while Dylan dragged George into the front seat and quickly ran around to the driver's side.

Jen's hands were on Samantha's neck, "Pulse! There's a pulse. Dylan Drive!"

She didn't look like my Samantha. She looked like...I can't even...her leg, her thigh was spurting blood until Jen yanked out the same kind of tourniquet Sam had saved Dylan's life with months ago. But this time, Jen was using it, and her fingers trembled and her tears poured down her face in rivets, blinding her. I needed to save her. I grabbed the bandage out of Jen's hands and wrapped it around the flesh I loved, and pressed the gauze into the fucking hole in her leg. I squeezed and squeezed as tightly as I could, and used the Velcro to strap it down. She was pale, *so pale*, and her entire body trembled and quaked in my arms.

George was grunting instructions to Dylan and the lights and sirens came on. Sam's eyes fluttered, her hands grabbed for me, but they slipped and slid with her blood. "Don't move, baby. It's me, Sam, I found you. Don't move at all. Just feel me. Just feel me around you, love. You're safe now."

One small squeeze of her fingers was all that she could reply with.

Jen sat on top of her leg, talking in small whispers, listing everything she saw, just as Sam would do in her head at a trauma. I lowered my head softly against her chest and listened for her heartbeat. There, in the silence of my mind, was the weakest of pulses. The most beautiful sound I had ever heard. The slow but steady beat of her heart as if under water, and I jumped in, drowning myself in it.

# CHAPTER 18

## Samantha

You want to know, don't you?

What it was like, during those last moments?

I know that ache you're feeling. It's what I would feel for my patients as they were thrust through the emergency doors. I wanted each and every one of them to live, no matter who they were...no matter what they'd done. I just wanted to take away people's pain. I wanted to heal.

Nobody on this earth deserves to endure moments like these, *no one*. No one deserves to look into the face of a monster and feel pain so intense that they pray for death.

I held my forearms tightly over my face, trying desperately to shield the blows, but David was vicious and unrelenting. Frantic panic bubbled up through my chest as I tried to kick out my feet and crawl away from the torment. My boots slipped and slid against the ice and frost, and its brittle crunching sounds cracked under our weight. It drenched my clothes and skin, until the stinging bitter cold bit into my shoulders and spine with sharp needle-like pinches.

*He didn't stop.* He just struck and struck, over and over; until I watched the whiffs of twisting smoke around him churn and spin like the waves on the ocean. Through my blurred vision, David's eyes looked empty, his face focused and sweaty with effort. Eyes the color of oily black pools.

"You. Pathetic. Brainless. Bitch," his words burst through the sounds of fists hitting flesh. Each word bit off, chewed up, and spat in my face. Jerking back, he grabbed for something I couldn't see, and swung it towards me, slamming it hard against my face. A white-hot explosion of gripping pain ripped across my skull and down my spine, as his fist, holding my goddamn rock shattered my right eye socket. I just prayed for unconsciousness.

It didn't come.

*I felt it all.*

I shoved at his hands, pushed against his face, and raked my broken ragged nails across his eyes. The rock flew out of his hands, but it didn't even cause a moment of pause. He counterattacked like a statue, hard and cold, and then hit me with muscles, fists, elbows, and palms, with such puissance it felt like he really *was* made of stone. A colossal mountain towering above me, too steep and impossible to conquer. An avalanche of crumbling rock pounding and crushing my bones and flesh.

Breaking his bloodthirsty frenzy, a high-pitched squeal reverberated off the trees, and the pounding of his fists suddenly ceased. His body moved and shifted into the heavy smoke, and relief crashed against my chest in a wave of hope. Yet, it was short lived, because I tried to move and claw myself through the wet mud and snow, but my body wasn't receiving the right signals. I frantically tried to tear up the earth beneath me, and crawl away, but the moment I reached up to drag myself away, unconsciousness took hold. Bittersweet numbness.

*Darkness.*

*A loud thunder of short explosions ignited in my head, one after another, after another. CRACK...pop-pop-pop-pop-pop-pop-pop-pop-pop!*

*Someone was crying.*

I hoped it was David. I hoped someone, some day, would make him cry, *but right now, I just want to float in this painless existence.*

A scorching heat enveloped my body, yet I still trembled with a deep bone-chilling coldness. I felt the sensations of my body moving, being carried somewhere.

Warm breath fell against my neck. A soft tender weight lay delicately against my chest. Something intense and burning was happening with my leg, but I tried to concentrate on the sweet beautiful warmth that I felt lying against my heart. I basked in the touch, the heat it offered, and its comfort. And the smell, God, it smelled like *home.* I tried to breathe it in deeper, but my chest, just wouldn't let me. The pain was too hot, too real.

Suddenly, a *tightening* wrapped around my thigh and a sharp explosion of agony surged through my body. Someone was trying to put on a tourniquet. Someone found me.

Someone found me.

*That means David was...*

Oh, God, please let the police find him. Please don't let him loose on any other human beings. *Please.*

My hands grabbed and slipped out of someone's hold. I fought a war with my eyelids to get them to open. Lumps of thick saliva caught in the back of my throat, and I coughed, wheezed, and gagged back the metallic taste of blood.

"Sam, don't move, baby," a deep tremulous voice mumbled. Hot breath against my skin, arms held around me in a vice grip.

*Kade?*

Kade!

Kade. Tears stung at my eyes. They burned to open, but no matter how hard I tried, they would not budge.

His strong chest inhaled a deep breath and I heard the harsh exhale of a choked sob. My Kade was crying for me. "Don't move, please. I got you now. I found you. Just feel me, Sam. Feel *me*. I'm wrapped around you, baby. Feel me. Hold on to me and *don't you bloody let me go.*"

*Oh, Kade, don't look at me like this. Just go, Kade, don't remember me like this, leave me here. Let me die. He's going to kill me one day. David will never let me be. I'll never be free from the hole he dug for me and tossed me in.*

"Don't give up on me, Sam."

*I got nothing left Kade, nothing left in me.*

"You can't let that piece of filth take away who you are, baby."

*You did, Kade, you let Thomas take everything from you.*

"Yeah, but then I met you and I took everything back. You got me, Sam. You own my soul, baby. You got me...and you healed me. Just hold on for me, *please*." His sobs shattered my heart. Through a choked mumble, his warm lips whispered against my cheek, "I won't do this without you."

"That's it, Kade, keep her talking," Jen's voice uttered from somewhere in the darkness.

*Jen was there? Did she wrap the tourniquet around my thigh?*

*David! I tried to scream. Kade. David's in the forest!*

Silence answered me. Then, a low deep breath of heat came near my ear. "He's dead. I killed him."

My body felt brittle and dry, and pain and heat engulfed me, pulling me under. My limbs would not respond. My lips would not move, and my beaten eyes could not open. I was powerless against it.

Now, because of me, Kade was a killer. How heavy was that going to weigh on his soul in the end? I let the pain yank me further down, waiting for the numbness, picturing myself standing in front of the fiery landscape, clutching my hands to my chest while yellow crime scene tape fluttered like party ribbons in the wind. Would this be our life, everything around us wrapped up in pleasant little yellow crime scene bows? *My God, how will Kade live through this? How will Kade be, if I never wake? I've lost a lot of blood. I know the tourniquet is not tight enough. I know he's going to lose himself, lose himself completely because              of              me.*

## Chapter 19

# Kade

Through the clink and hiss of the automatic doors, I carried Samantha's limp body in my arms. I screamed for help as Jen ran ahead of me and grabbed a clean white gurney that sat vacant in the hallway. I followed her, running at full speed, until my eyes dropped down. Until I saw Sam, and I mean *really saw Sam*, in the bright lighting of the hospital emergency entrance, and I stumbled, falling to my knees.

My God. In the light...in the light, she was broken, ravaged, dying in my arms. The cut on her leg ripped out my heart, shattered me. Spectacular hues of bruises marred her skin, her eyes and lips swollen a deep angry red. *My baby*. He fucking tortured her. My tears fell like rain against her chin, but she didn't move, she didn't feel a thing. She didn't feel me dying with her.

The doorway to the trauma unit exploded with panic and chaos. Doctors, nurses, and paramedics, ran towards me and emptied my arms, leaving me there alone and broken on the ground. My clothes were drenched with her blood.

I watched helplessly. Defeated.

Another trauma team was assembled for George, who had been dragged in by Dylan, but I saw none of it. I was just focused on Samantha, on a metal gurney in the next room getting tubes shoved up her nose and down her throat. I heard them page the neurosurgeon, and my throat closed up as I began to sob. They yelled for things, medical terms were screamed, drugs were called for, and her clothing was ripped off her body and flung onto a tray for evidence. Then the doors closed and the sun of my world just blinked out of existence.

"Kade?" Jen's voice spoke softly beside me. "Kade, before this place gets over run with the sheriff's office, let's go give blood. It's the only thing we can do to help her right now."

I think I might have nodded at her.

My eyes were still focused on the closed doors. Jen gently placed her hand on my shoulder and spoke once more, "Kade? Come on. She's going to need blood."

I blinked up at her, "She's going to need a lot more than blood, isn't she?"

Jen's chin quivered and her eyes welled with tears, "Yeah, Kade. A whole hell of a lot more than blood, but it's what we can do now to help her, so let's go."

I squeezed my eyes closed and hung my head, "How bad is she, Jen? I want the bloody truth."

"I don't know...," she mumbled.

Dylan was beside me in the next instant, hand held out helping me to stand. He grabbed me by the back of the shoulders and walked me to the triage station where we could give blood. Everything seemed so surreal.

You know, I gave so much damn blood that I passed the fuck out, and got a bloody cookie and a shot of orange juice shoved down my throat. Then it was just a waiting game. She needed surgery, immediately. There was too much brain swelling.

The three of us sat silently on the pale green leather benches of the waiting room. I spent hours staring down at my hands, clenching and knotting them trying to control the panic bubbling inside my chest. Each time I glanced up and out over the waiting area, the stench of utter despair and hopelessness was overwhelming. In the far corner, a television played the breaking news of the forest fire and the shootings in low, barely audible sounds. No one seemed to know the bloody facts, yet they made sure to blast their idiotic opinions. All I drank was burnt flavored hospital coffee, which somehow was always ironically cold by the time it reached my lips.

Shadows of people rushed and moved around me. The Sheriff asked his questions. My head fogged up with questions, accusations, words, and answers. Truth vomited past my lips, but I didn't care. I didn't care if I was arrested for what I did, because in my eyes, I did nothing wrong. I was protecting what was mine.

*What is your relationship to the victim? Mine.*

*How do you know Deputy George Tatum? Friend.*

*How do you know David Stanton? Sam's ex.*

*Why were you there? To look for her.*

*You just happened to be on the same road as the deputy? Yep.*

*Do you have a license for your firearms? Yes.*

*Did you go there with the intent on using your firearm? Yes. They were in trouble. I have a license. I saved your cop. Leave me the bloody fuck ALONE.*

Whispered voices, hushed cries, and I held them all at an arm's distance. Nothing penetrated me. I allowed nothing to come in. The only thing that stood center stage in my brain was the sound of Samantha's voice the last time I slept next to her. My lips on her skin. *"You know when I was younger, I used to lick anything I didn't want taken from me."* My lips were always on her skin. Our bodies tangled in sheets, her breath in my ear, soft sighs, and wet lips.

"Mr. Grayson? Hello? Mr. Grayson?" a deep voice broke into my thoughts. A heavy hand clutched onto my shoulder and squeezed, dragging me from my daydreams.

"Mr. Grayson? I'm Doctor Barns. I'd like to gather Samantha's family members to go over her condition and where we can go from here. I know how devastating this is for everyone here. Samantha was a cherished part of this hospital." The voice spoke to the air; the words floated around in my head aimlessly, and then dropped off into the darkness. I blinked my eyes until the doctor came into focus, and I concentrated on the dreadful grim twist of his mouth. He waited for me to speak, to acknowledge him in someway, with an unnatural stillness about him.

My brother's arms were on me next, helping me to stand and steer me into a room that was somehow starker and whiter than the waiting area. My eyes zoned in on the small colorful dots of the impressionistic painting that hung on the wall directly across from me. It was slightly askew, making me want to rip it off the wall and smash over the twisted lipped doctor's head. "Right now, Samantha is in ICU in critical condition. You'll be able to visit her for a short time when we're finished discussing my initial evaluation. As you are well aware, she sustained a massive amount of injuries, one a severed femoral artery, the large artery in the thigh. We were able to save her leg and deal with the damage because of your quick thinking, and the type of tourniquet that was used. And you did a tremendous job in protecting her neck and keeping her immobilized on the way to the ER. *However,* what we are most worried about is the blunt force trauma to her head and the swelling of her brain." The doctor used his clipboard and hands to speak, obsessively clicking the end of a pen throughout his conversation. CLICK. CLICK. "Right now, she seems to be in a vegetative state." CLICK. CLICK. "We attempted to lessen the swelling of the brain, and now we will monitor her closely. It's too early to say what we are dealing with." CLICK. CLICK. "Over the next few days, we will give careful clinical examinations and additional tests such as brain scans, a CT, MRI, most likely a perfusion scan, brain wave tests, an EEG – electroencephalogram, spinal taps among others to assist us in making a diagnosis." CLICK-FUCKING-CLICKY-CLICK.

"Is she going to be okay? Just tell me if I get to take her home. Just bloody tell me if I get her back," I asked, the words dribbled out of my mouth before I could stop them.

"The chance of her recovery is dependent on a number of factors, including the cause of the brain injury, and how it heals, Samantha's age and her associated medical conditions. From what we could see, there is a closed wound and a fracture to her skull from a direct trauma."

"I don't understand..."

"A direct trauma is any force that penetrates the skull, one that has the possibility to cause severe brain injury, as destructive shock waves travel through the brain matter."

I blinked rapidly. I knew what he was saying, but my emotions were too high, my face was on fire, and my damn chest ached with loss.

"Uh...Direct trauma occurs when it's struck with something, for example, the floor when a person falls, or a steering wheel in an accident. In this case, we believe a, uh...a rock was used to strike the head. The strike fractured part of her skull and caused the brain to collide against the inside of her skull. This violent movement may cause a contusion of the brain, which means bruising and hemorrhage. Samantha was also showing signs of edema, which is a swelling of the brain, as I explained before her surgery. We had to drain the fluids."

*He hit her in the head with a rock. Contusions. Hemorrhage. Swelling.* My head pounded and it felt hard to breathe.

"When the swelling causes a rise in intracranial pressure, it becomes very dangerous to a patient. It prevents blood from entering the skull and stops the delivery of glucose and oxygen to the brain. The only ways to relieve the pressure is through medication, or draining some of the high-pressure cerebrospinal fluid. She's going to need around-the clock observation in our intensive care unit. It's necessary right now to control her breathing by a respirator. She's been given very strong medications to temporarily paralyze her, and make her as comfortable as possible.

He leaned forward in his chair and spoke more solemnly, "The truth is, we don't know how this will affect her. We can't say whether she will wake up or not. We need to run many tests and monitor her brain functions. A young healthy patient like Samantha, although they also will typically have little chance of recovery from a vegetative state, may be kept alive for decades as she is right now, or she could wake up tomorrow. She may have to learn to walk and talk again. Or she might stay as she is for the rest of her life. We're not fully sure. We'll do the tests, take it hour by hour, and see the best plan of action. However, I do think it's always best to prepare for a loved one to..."

"Don't finish that motherfucking sentence," I growled, slamming my hands down.

The wanker looked at me as if he were terrified, like I was about to snap his neck, and he was so damn right. So I wanted his mouth closed before I could lose complete control. This shit was making me spiral out of it faster than I'd ever been. I needed Sam. I needed her, and I wasn't making any plans for anything but taking her the bloody hell home.

"Yes, well," he cleared his throat, "I'll just give you some time to yourselves, and if you have any questions, our team is here to answer them for you."

*Dickbag.*

*Giant emotionless hole of limp dicks, motherfucking little bitch.*

Then the dickbag walked out of the door like his life depended on it.

"Kade," Jen spoke softly, "we're going to need to listen to what those doctor's say, because..."

"No." I shook my head at her vehemently. "No, I'm not listening to them tell me to make plans for her dying," I said, rubbing my hands over the back of my neck. My eyes blurred, and thousands of rainbows reflected across my vision. "I don't want to say goodbye to her. I don't want to let her go. I can't breathe without her." I walked out of the small office, ready to see her, ready to do whatever was needed to have her come back to me.

Doctor Barns was standing out in the hallway surrounded by two other rigid looking men dressed in scrubs. "Mr. Grayson, I understand how hard this is for you..."

"Do you?" I snapped. Hell, I was going to lose it right there in the corridor of the hospital, and they'd have to take me out in handcuffs. Again. "So, you have a woman that you were going to propose to, get kidnapped and tortured for over a week, and then got told you should make plans for her to..." Yeah. I couldn't even get the word out. I sucked my lips in between my teeth so the sobs wouldn't escape, and inhaled deeply through my nose. "No, I don't think you have a goddamn clue what I'm going through. However, I know if you are half as good a surgeon as Samantha said you were, you will do everything you bloody can to get her back to me."

He smiled tightly and nodded, "Yes, Kade, I will." He walked closer to me and held an arm out in front of him, "Come, why don't we see how she's doing right now."

The walk to the Intensive Care Unit was silent. Dylan and Jen followed closely behind us, hands clasped tightly between them.

Nurses spoke in low whispers, flipping through charts at the foot of her bed. The low hum and whoosh of the life support machines serenaded me like my own funeral procession. I had to hold on to the bedrails to keep myself vertical. Bandages covered the majority of her head, and tubes were just *everywhere*. A thick one ran out of the corner of her mouth, thin ones jammed up her nose, medium sized ones inserted into the veins of her hands. Perfect white bed sheets tucked up around her chest. Under the bruises and wounds, her skin was a frightening shade of white to match the sheets encasing her tiny broken body. Her beautiful green eyes were closed, and all I wanted to do was take her in my arms and hold her.

I stood at the foot of the bed and swallowed the hard knot in my throat. As the whoosh-beep-*hiss* of the machines hummed their soul shattering song to me, I broke into tears.

"Is she ever going to wake up from this?" I whispered.

"Like I said, there's no way to tell right now. We can only wait and see. We'll be reevaluating her condition often, looking for signs. People with head injuries rarely wake up all at once. Full recovery of consciousness is a gradual process. In the mildest of cases, it may take a few hours, and in the worst cases, it may take months or even sometimes years. And, Mr. Grayson, some patients only improve to a certain point, and never fully regain awareness."

I wiped the tears off my face with an angry vengeance. "Is there any possibility that she will recover completely? Any bloody hope at all? Have you seen other cases where people recover?"

"Sure, I have. I've seen many patients with severe head injuries end up with no noticeable problems, but I've also seen the same amount require constant care for the rest of their life."

"So," I cleared my throat, tears choking me, "what is the worst possible outcome for her?"

"The best possible outcome we could hope for, of course, is Samantha to wake up and have a complete recovery. The worst case would be no recovery beyond opening her eyes, or what's called a persistent vegetative state. Those are the two ends of the spectrum, though with an extremely wide ranges of variants to the outcomes in between. We just have to wait and see. There's so much damage to assess and other problems may arise, and Mr. Grayson, we don't know the level of traumatic brain injury she has suffered. Even if she wakes up, she might need lifelong care because of long-term disabilities. We just don't know."

I nodded blankly.

"I'll give you some time alone with her, and then you should really get some rest and food in you. I don't think you realize how long you've been here."

I nodded blankly, again.

The shuffle of his feet and footfalls down the hall told me we were alone. Slowly, I walked to the side of her bed. My knees touched down on the cold tiled floor, and I prayed for the first time since I was sixteen. "Don't give up on us yet. Don't give up on this life yet, fight for me, fight for us." I leaned over her, and kissed her forehead. Wet kisses filled with my tears, *wept into her hair as I bruised myself against the iron arms of her bed. I'll take her pain, give me it, leave her be.* Just bloody fucking give it to me instead.

"Just *say* something," I cried against her skin. "Open your eyes. God, *please*. Give me your voice. Call me an egotistical asshole again. Tell me you love me. Talk through my favorite TV shows, tease me while I'm trying to write, shove your ice cold feet between my legs in your sleep, sing off key in the shower again, just *fucking wake up and talk to me*. Okay, Sam? Okay? Because, I won't do this shitty life without you. Okay? We stay here together, or we go together, got it? Do you hear me, Sam? *I won't do this life without you*, so come back to me. Let's finish it together."

Choking on my sobs, Jen and Dylan had to pull me off her. I KNOW, it was a dick move and I could have hurt her more, but I wasn't thinking clearly, okay? I don't how to be away from her. I don't know how to wake up with her not next to me. Dylan had to shove me out of the room, hard, with both hands, to get me to leave. Then I was *escorted* to the truck and Dylan drove me home to shower, change, and eat.

*Like I could have eaten anything.*

I gagged back half a sandwich my mother had made when they told me how long we had been at the hospital. Twenty-nine hours. My mum pleaded with me to take a sleeping aid, but all I wanted to do was go right back to the hospital. I felt more comfortable sleeping there, near Sam. Not that I could do anything more for her, but I wanted her to know I wouldn't leave her to die alone. I was never going to leave her side.

Mum found me the next morning asleep in the chair sitting next to her bed. As the sun rose over the horizon, and the smells of hospital breakfast foods drifted through the halls, Mum grasped me by the shoulders. "Dear Lord, what this poor girl has been through, love. Even if she lives, how will she heal? That was her husband and her father who did all this to her, how will she heal?"

My mum was right, but the question was all wrong. It should have been, *how will I help her heal.*

Because she was going to live.

There was no other option. I couldn't begin to think of a world that didn't have Samantha in it. I just couldn't. If there was one thing the woman lying in that hospital bed taught me, it was to *hope.*

*How had she helped me? How had she let me feel like I could trust again?*

I was forced home again that night for clean clothes and a shower. There was no way I would be staying in my house while she was alone in a hospital room, so I packed a bag, I'd live there if it came down to it.

Jen found me in the bathroom carefully packing Sam's favorite smelly soaps, "Why don't you take some of her favorite books too. She loves reading, so maybe your voice reading to her would help. We could take turns, and when you leave, I could take over."

"I'm not leaving her, but you just gave me a bloody brilliant idea." Quickly shoving all the toiletries into a bag, I ran into my office, grabbed my laptop, and yanked the cord out of the wall. The wire hurled across the room and into my hands.

"Oookay then, glad I can help. Come on, tell me the idea," she called after me.

Bundling up my laptop and bag, without even a whisper to anyone else, I climbed into my truck and drove back to the hospital.

Dropping my coat and bags on the floor near the door, I hesitantly walked in to the private ICU. She still hadn't moved. Her cheeks were still so pale compared to the bright colorful arrays of bruises and cuts. Lifeless on the white tubed-up bed, the only motion was the rise and fall of her chest because of the ventilator.

Rise. Fall.

*Hiss*. Clink.

Rise. Fall.

*Hiss*. Clink.

Somewhere inside that broken body, was my girl. I needed to pull her out, bring her back to the surface, because I knew she was drowning. Pulling up the chair as close as I could to her bed, I sat down.

The room was dark, save for the anemic yellow light that glowed from the long tubed drawstring bulb that hung against the wall. As I opened my laptop, the room brightened, shadows danced and deepened.

I cleared my throat so my voice wouldn't crack. She needed to hear it strong. "Hey, Doc, it's just me again. It's the second day of your coma. The doctor just told me that the swelling has gone down considerably, and so far, there are no infections. I don't know what the bloody hell that means, but it sounds good. I...uh, brought my laptop with me and I thought maybe I'd read my journal to you. You know the one my head doctor told me I needed to write in everyday while I did my psychoanalysis. I thought that maybe it would help you see how bloody much you need to be here. I wanted to read to you my thoughts about Thomas, about us, and about how I've changed, but more so, how much I want you to come back to me. Because I know, you're in there somewhere, Sam. Come on, Doc, open your eyes for me. You spoke with me that night I found you, so I know you're okay, just get back to me." I leaned forward and kissed her forehead, "Okay here goes...here is everything I thought about for the last six months, Samantha. I'm going to give it all to you, so you bloody know." My stupid voice cracked, and I sniffed back a man tear. I inhaled deeply and exhaled slow as not to have her hearing anymore of my bloody man whining. All she needed to hear was that I was waiting for her. "Just so you bloody know how much you are loved."

I clicked open the file folder to my journal and opened it. "And just a little word of caution, Doc. It's sort of bloody crazy in my thoughts, but anytime you want to let me know to piss off, just open those green doors of yours and tell me."

# CHAPTER 20
## Samantha

...

# CHAPTER 21

## *Kade*

"Okay, love. Listen to how much I bloody need you..."

*Saturday*

*The bloody cockfucking wanker therapist wants me to write my bloody thoughts about all the tragedy in my bloody life. It'll be therapeutic, he says. It'll be closure, he cheers. I'd bloody well like to push him over the ledge of his window, I think back. Hang my head over the sill and tinkle my bloody fingers in a wave. Watch him flail his arms about trying to bloody fly as he plummets, then splashes across the sidewalk. Maybe one of his dead brown eyeballs will explode from his skull and bounce and roll down the street. Bloody entertaining.*

*Monday*

*The bloody cockfucking wanker therapist read my journal entry and made some girlie high school air sucking sound with his lips. I believe this to be disapproval. He would like me to try to visualize less violent ways to deal with my anger and anxiety.*

*Therefore, I sit here and think on this a bit, and come to the visualization that I very politely tell my therapist I do not like his approach to said behaviors and hand him a bunch of flowers that I have pleasantly picked for him in some fictional soft colored meadow on the way to his office. THEN I'd bloody push him over the ledge of his window. Hang my head over the sill and tinkle my bloody fingers in a wave. Watch him flail his arms about trying to bloody fly as he plummets, then splashes across the sidewalk. Maybe one of his dead brown eyeballs will explode from his skull and bounce and roll down the street. But it's pleasant because the flowers land beautifully around his corpse in the shape of a bloody heart.*

Monday night

*Okay, I'll bloody try it for real. Thoughts. Keyboard. Go.*

*"Write clear and hard about what hurts." Ernest Hemingway*

*Do you know what heartbreak teaches you?*

*When it tears at you for years?*

*That you're strong.*

*Solid. Real.*

*Thomas, I know you're in Hell, not giving a fuck, probably took over the damn place. But guess what? I found something beautiful, someone so beautiful inside that she erases everything that you are and what you've done. She pours herself inside me and I drink her in greedily.*

*I've been stupidly thinking today of what my life would have been like if I'd never met the waitress with the beautiful green eyes. Numbing darkness. She is not my past; she's my future. Something pure and good to hold onto after the cold grasp of your claws left me for dead.*

Tuesday

*Today I stared in the mirror for far too fucking long. The eyes that she says she loves are only dull gray*

English skies to me. I'm pale and broken and I wonder how it is that she could ever find any worth inside of me. How could she be able to crawl into my arms every night and find solace in their flawed strength? The mirror shatters, of course by my hand, my reflection splinters into thousand of tiny parts, and I linger in their pieces. I shift them about with my hands to find the broken pieces that belong and those that I should discard. And the only thing that remains are the cold gray eyes that look at her.

Wednesday

She has this little cluster of freckles on the back of her thigh.

She probably doesn't know it but that's my favorite place on her body.

Today I watched her hand out hot cocoa to an entire floor of children in the children's ward. For no reason, other than she had the time. She didn't see me, standing in the background, as she lit up the world with her special sort of shine. She laughed full open mouth laughs surrounded by kids with eyes that sparkled with delight yet bodies riddled with sickness. But she saw in them beauty and hope to heal. She met me in her office, smile across her lips, not a stitch of makeup on and all I could do was grab her and kiss her, devour the lips that smiled so hard despite watching the suffering. And when I touched her, I can see it so clearly, our future. Fingers entwined. Both of us sitting on the stone patio, the summer breeze smelling of barbeque and suntan lotion, a gaggle of children and dogs running in circles past our *lounging feet. I see with her a life I never thought I would ever have.*

Thursday

*Today felt like England.*

*Gray stormy skies and the forever drizzle of icy rain.*

*A melancholy wave of sadness filtered in instead of the warm rays of the sun. Shrink says I'm depending too much on Samantha for my stability. But isn't that how it should be? Should we not depend on the ones we love to find our strength? No, he said, you need to do this on your own. Fuck the fuck off, I said back. Politely, I might add. What does he know of us? We've spent too much time apart already while the sheriff's office set up her new life, I don't want to miss another minute more. Those two months were silent for me, the only thing I did was talk with him and have insane fucked up fictitious conversations with a dead sixteen-year-old boy who once tried to kill me. There's nothing left to say to him. Dead is Dead. Life is for the living and I want to start living.*

Friday

*I fell in love with her even more today. Just this morning. Walking into the kitchen, tired itchy eyes, yawn splitting open my face. She was in front of the stove. Back to me. One of my long buttoned up shirts fell to the middle of her thighs, the collar slung casually over a soft shoulder. A spatula in one hand, coffee in the other, her delicate feet wrapped in those heavy furry socks. The bloody brilliant ones with the zombie eyeballs all over them. Turning to face me, she wore a streak of pancake batter across her* cheek, and a bit of the powdered mix on the tip of her nose. 'Pancakes?' she asked. I answered her with 'forever,' because I was thinking of how long I wanted to keep her. She somehow knew what I meant. She knew what I needed. Slowly she shut the stove and pulled me to the table, I followed her sexy smile and those sage green eyes. She lifted herself on the edge of the table and wrapped those perfect legs around me. The cold granite beneath my palms and her thighs, the clanking of dishes and her whispered moans. Arching her back across the table, taking me in.

Sunday

I used to find solace at the bottom of a bottle.
Yet it never lasted long, in a blink it would be gone.
Now I find it in the strangest of places.
Places I never thought it would be.
The crock of her eyes when she laughs.
The curl of her lips when she smiles.
The curve of her thighs as they embrace me.
The heat of her flesh when I crawl inside.

Tuesday

Sixteen years is far too long to be angry.
If I could have met her then.
Two teens with angst you could feel.
I'd be more of a force.
And no one would have ever touched her.
But me.

Wednesday

She's strolling through the woods,

*Breath in icy mists.*
*Snow crunching beneath her boots,*
*Crimson streaked on her winter cheeks.*
*She laughs and looks up.*
*The sun blinds her eyes.*
*The way she blinds mine.*
*And I borrow her smile for a moment.*
*Try it on for size.*
*And find, to my surprise,*
*It's a bloody perfect fit.*

After two hours of reading aloud to her, I noticed a small twitch of her fingers. It made me breathless. Heat tingled across my chest, and my body felt light, weightless. "Jen! Jen! I just saw her bloody twitch her fingers," I yelped.

"Really?" Jen asked, moving closer to the bed. "It could be something or nothing, though. You have to keep this up though, because this is good for the both of you. But, let me read some stuff to her and talk to her, take a break. Get coffee, your voice is getting weird."

I knew Jen wanted to read to her also, so for once, I didn't put up a fight, and went down for coffee and let them spend a few moments together. When I met the doctor on call in the hallway and told him about the finger movement, he just offered me a tight-lipped smile. "Yes, yes," he chirped, "could be an involuntary movement. We'll be taking her for a CT scan in an hour."

Doctor Douche and Doom. Bloody wanker. I crushed my coffee cup in my hand, spilling it all over the floor. My thoughts weren't straight. They were muddled and thick, just tipping over the borderline to rage. Yet, my own thoughts stopped me from plunging headfirst into viciousness. All I thought about, all I wanted to do was run in and tell Sam about the coffee. Crushing it and spilling it all over the floor. She would have reprimanded me for wasting the nectar of the gods. Then she would have laughed at me and told me some crazy story about what it might be like for a surgeon to have to tell a family their loved one was not waking up. How that surgeon's brain was churning and spinning a thousand thoughts in his head to try to help his patient, all while dealing with his own bloody problems and not having a meal for twelve hours straight. I could hear her voice say the words in my head, the ones that calmed me down, and let me breathe. God, how she changed me so that I could do it myself.

Dragging myself back to the cafeteria, I ordered two coffees. One was for me, and the other was a caramel flavored one so I could stick it near her nose and oxygen. I know inside there, somewhere, she was bloody dying to have a coffee.

Jen was singing some crazy boy band song when I walked back into the ICU. "You are seriously going to crack the equipment in here if you keep that high-pitched wailing up," I said. *I had never heard such bloody wailing.*

"Yeah, well I was hoping to hear her complain about it, not you," she replied. "What have you been reading to her in here anyway?"

"Just a few entries from my journal. They're mostly about her. I figured if she knew I couldn't live without her, she'd fight harder to wake up."

Jen's lips moved to speak, then stopped.

"Don't. Jen. Don't tell me she's not going to wake up from this, okay? Because if she's doesn't, you can bury us together. I go where she goes."

"Oh, Kade…"

"Sod off," I snapped.    My fingers clenched together tightly and just as I was about to start a tirade, the neurosurgeon strolled in.   Ignoring us both, he walked past and pushed his glasses up the long thin bridge of his nose.   From out of his pocket, he pulled a thin medical flashlight, yanked open Samantha's eyelids and shined the light right on them.   Those emerald green irises just about blinded me, but what made my heart stop was watching her pupils shrink and react to the light.

Jen's voice whispered into my ear, "He's checking her pupillary reflex to see if her pupils constrict.   Before, when you went out for coffee, they checked her gag reflex, she gagged and coughed."

The surgeon wrote a bunch of unidentifiable scratches and crap on her chart, clickety-clicked his pen and left. Jen slumped down in a seat and hung her head in her hands. Fuck everybody. I was going to read to her my words, everything she'd ever made me feel until she woke the fuck up.

And I did, everyday for seven straight days. I read to her as her bruises slowly faded, her hair became shiny with oil and she lost so much weight that her cheeks looked sunken in. I read to her for hours at a time. For days, until my throat turned dry and my voice rotted into a hoarse raspy shadow of what it once was. I wasn't ever going to stop. Ever.

Tuesday

*My thoughts, my feeling, my fucking heart is tied to the posts of my bed.*

*Captured and imprisoned.*

*By her.*

*I've never wanted to be held against my will until now.*

*She tears me down and rips me raw.*

*Flings the flesh of my chest open and gently lays her lips to my heart.*

*It beats for her.*

*It bleeds for her.*

*She made it feel again.*

*Made it all mean something again.*

*She found me under all the rubble.*

*Beneath the waste and the debris that was piled atop of me.*

*And she grabbed my hand and helped me stand up again.*

*Helped me live again.*

Wednesday

*I sat on the stiff grass; sharp spikes of icy green and I dug my fingertips into the frozen earth. I'm in the yard, my house, my tomb stands high above me. Her soft voice drifts through an open window, she is singing in the shower. I could almost hear the beads of water falling against her skin. Almost taste the salt as she washes it away to lather with apple and cinnamon. My hands* tighten their hold of the earth not to rush in their with her. But the soil just crumbled through my fingers and broke along the cold ground. Suddenly, I'm up, running. Over the frost, crunching my boots in the snow. Through the door and straight into the bathroom. The door is never locked, because she knows. She knows I'd always need her and she would never lock herself away from me. Then I'm standing, fully clothed in the steam, drops of water soaking my shirt, my pants, and my boots. Mud and snow twirling and spinning over the drain and she laughs. Her beautiful, perfect laugh. Her hands cup my face, warm and wet. Her lips meet mine and I'm hers. She's mine. Up against the cold stone tiles, sopping wet pants around my ankles, she's mine.

On day four, I saw a small wiggle of her toe. I continued to read to her. My notes. My thoughts. My feelings. Everything.

Saturday

Doctor Headshrinker, he bloody hates the name I've chosen for him, keeps repeating that I need to spend more time on my Post Traumatic Stress Disorder and not my obsession with Samantha. Why the fuck would I want to do that? He mentioned to me this journal was supposed to be an ongoing way to communicate with Thomas, the dead kid who left me to die in a classroom.

Really, I have nothing more to say to him.

Fuck you, I won.

I lived, you little bloody bitch.

And know I can feel the sun shine on my face. I can feel the warmth on my skin, because my sun, she sleeps *besides me. Every night. Fuck you Thomas. And fuck you Mr. Psychotherapist. I don't need pills; all I need is Sam.*

On day five, I watched as she made a full fist with her right hand, and then her left. I read more. I read faster. The doctor's said it might be all we could hope for, that she may never do anything more. *No. Fuck them.* I will deal with whatever she gives me. If she stays like this, she'll come home like this, and I will read to her every day. If she opens her eyes and has to learn to eat and walk again, then I'll be right by her side teaching and helping her. I will not give up on her.

"I'll read you one from this week, love."

*Will I speak her eulogy before a crowd? Will the words stick to my tongue and tangle in tears? Will her apparition crawl into bed with me each night? Haunting me with scents and fluttery caresses. Meet me in my bed around midnight okay? Just run right in, full-speed, and send me into complete shock, or make my heart burst. Just take me with you, if you decide to leave.*

*I thought you just left me. I didn't trust you at all. I had no faith in what we were starting and us. I doubted everything. If you wake up with no memory, I'll help you to remember. We'll start again. I'll take you to everyplace we've been and make you feel everything we created. If you can't walk, I swear love, I will carry you wherever you want to go, everyday for the rest of our lives. Whatever you wake up with, we'll be fine. Just wake up. Just open those green doors for me and fight. It's not my job to change or fix you...my job is to love you with no expectations of you ever being anything more than what you are. If you change at all, I will love what you become, whatever it may be.*

*Just don't leave me, Sam.*

# CHAPTER 22

## Samantha

I *did* die.

Flatlined with all the bells and whistles just before the neurosurgeon was to drain the pressure on my brain. They had to take the paddles to me. I must seriously hold the record for *most resuscitated* for such an ordinarily healthy person. I've had a damn defibrillator used on me at least a half a dozen times just that last year. I'll have to check Guinness about that.

Clinically, I was dead for nine seconds, which wasn't *too* horrible. Anything longer than that, and I would have been *really* pissed off.

Yes, I know the questions that you may have. No, there was no tunnel with light or long lost dead relatives to welcome me to the other side. Nothing of the sort. Just the gnawing need to tell the idiotic trauma team what the hell to do correctly so I could walk the hell out of this hospital and start celebrating the rest of my life. Most of it was nothingness. Heavy sleep. One minute, I felt Kade's arms surrounding me, and then a powerful feeling of *nothing*.

Consciousness came in bits and pieces. Sounds, low and soft at first, like I was far under the water, then clear and distinctive. Light and movement came slowly, along with the feel of the cold sheets under my palms and the itchy needle of the IV in my hand. All these medical thoughts muddled like fog in my brain, thousands of questions I knew I wanted to ask, yet the only thing to come from my mouth was a thin stream of drool, and the thoughts of still needing to sleep because I was so utterly exhausted. *I listened to what my body needed and I slept. I heard Kade's voice at a constant rate, but I could not get to it. I just slept and listened to him. Slept and listened. Slept and listened. His voice was my music.*

Okay, now hold onto something for a moment, because I'm just about to pull the pin on an awesome grenade. On day seven of listening to Kade Grayson's heart-wrenching words, I gave him a present.

I opened my eyes.

His reaction was brilliant, and I couldn't have chosen a better moment if I wanted to. You see, he'd been sitting in the chair facing my bed, watching my face and trying to read from his journal at the same time. He only stopped for a second to adjust his position, and when he did, I saw him for the first time. His laptop slid off his leg and onto to the ground. I heard the metallic slap of it on the floor, its clink and clank. His sad grey eyes widened with an incredulous dazed stare. Slowly, his hands clamped onto the hospital bed rails and his broad stiff body moved closer and closer to mine. I tried my best to follow him with my eyes, but I was still so tired.

"Sam?" he croaked, tears filling those stormy grey eyes.

"ICU?" I croaked. It sort of sounded more like *iiiisluuuuue.*

His face exploded in tears and laughter, "Oh, God, baby. Oh, God. Oh, God, Sam, I thought I lost you." He swiped at his tears and pressed the nurses call button like a lunatic, then jumped up over me and brushed wet teary kisses all over my face. "Don't you ever leave me again. Oh, God, Sam, I love you so bloody much."

Doctors and nurses swarmed in, shoving Kade away, but of course, he wouldn't budge. He hovered over them, listening to everything that was said, nodding his smiling crying face, and calling Jen on his cell. The doctors yelled at him to move and to shut down his phone, and in perfect Kade style, he told everyone to *sod the fuck off*. When I knew he was okay, I eyed the doctor who was repeatedly asking me the year and the name of the president.

*"What's the damage?"* I asked, softly. *"I remember the wound on my leg. I can feel the bandage on my head and it's throbbing."* However, they couldn't understand me, because my words were slurred, slow, and unintelligible.

The doctors and nurses poked and prodded me, asked me questions and did the normal routines of assessment. I answered as best I could, but my mind fogged up quickly when I began thinking of what I've seen happen to my own patients when the neural pathways in the brain were damaged, and wondered what severity of damage I was to endure. They were simple thoughts, rudimentary. I had suffered a brain injury. How would this affect my behavior and personality? My thinking and ability to solve problems? Will this change who I was forever? Then my thoughts shifted gears, my training and schooling came through, and relief flooded in. The brain communicates and deciphers our physical and mental performance. I was having straight concerned thoughts, about lost information and function. I was aware of things around me and hoped that the doctors agreed. This couldn't be as severe as I feared, right?

*Right?*

I drifted back to sleep while a crowd of doctors and nurses dressed in whites and greens spoke over me. People walked in with carts, someone spilled a tray of noisy metal objects and my nose was assaulted with the familiar smells of a hospital. The scents that most people cringed at when it hit their senses considering what most people's prior experiences were with hospitals. I tried to stay awake to speak with everyone, and to answer and ask all the questions my brain could process. The one nagging at me the most, left me wondering what had happened, wondering where David was, if he was really dead. My last conscious thought was: *I hoped he was in Hell.*

As I drifted off, my hands clutched the cool blankets with the same vehemence I clutched the idea that I would be a surgeon again, and that whatever injuries were sustained would fall to waste and leave me whole.

Life doesn't quite work the way you want it to, though, does it?

Although my waking up was awe inspiring and hopeful...my recovery *sucked*. Each morning, I would wake to a classical piece of music that to me sounded like the equivalent of scratching my nails down a chalkboard. My eyes would snap open fiercely and my teeth would automatically grind. Nails down the chalkboard, *slow* and *screechy*. *Long screeching brittle freaking nails*. The noise always made the front of my teeth tingle, and I'd get the sensation of peeling my gums away from my teeth. And even though my hatred and disdain for it was well known, the music was continuously put on to wake me. Every. Single. Day.

Kade *fucking* Grayson. He did it purposely.

The second after hearing the calamity, I'd struggle to sit upright, reach out and slam shut the culprit that played the atrocity. Some mornings, it was a CD player. Other mornings, it was his phone or an iPod, but every time, it would be hidden in a different place, causing me to *have* to get up and search for the offensive noisemaker to get it to silence. Somewhere in the hospital room, Kade's face would appear in mine with an uncharacteristically cheerful smile. "Good morning, Doc," he'd whisper. Each morning was the same. The first words I'd try to say slurred like warm ooze from my lips and dripped down my chin. Then I'd cry.

Kade just smiled. "Come on, Beautiful. Try it again. Goooood. Moorrr-nnninnng," he said.

I really wanted to smack him.

"Fuuuuuuckkk. Youuuuuuu."

"Brilliant. Your speech is getting much better. How about a stroll around the hospital today? Maybe a shower?" He asked.

*God, he was infuriating.*

"Sam, love, you need to get up and walk. You need to talk."

"Hurrtsss," I slurred.

"I know, baby, trust me, I *know* this pain. But, I'm right here beside you and I'll help you with every step. I won't let you fall, Sam, and I sure as hell won't let you lie there and waste away either."

He helped me shower, which was humiliating beyond anything I could ever know. My body was a colorful array of bruises and wounds, which made Kade's lips tighten, and fists clench. Yet, he washed me gently with my favorite flavored soaps and dried me with soft towels he'd brought from home. Something seemed to have changed in Kade after I woke up, something I could only match to the word *beautiful*. It was as if he'd found some sort of inner peace, because it shined in him, rolled off him in calm cool waves. He'd speak in arousing whispers as he helped me dress, and plant soft kisses against my neck as he brushed my hair. He dragged my IV behind him as he helped me walk and do my physical therapy, always somehow touching me, always watching me – with those intense serious eyes. I noticed too, when he thought I wasn't watching, how he'd care for the other patients around me. Little things, insignificant things, which Kade would have never had the patience for before, I found him smiling through now. A glass of ice chips for Mrs. Williams in the room across the hallway, *fill the water only a quarter of the way up and a red straw* she'd say, and instead of throwing the water in her face, he'd wink and get her exactly what she wished. A newspaper for Mr.

Rilles in the next room, wrapped tightly with a small piece of chocolate inside.

For weeks after I woke, he'd challenge me. To walk. To talk. To eat. To run. To think. To fight. He brought puzzles in for me to do and brain teasers for me to solve. He loaded up his iPad with over one hundred different apps that summoned me to use cognitive thoughts, reasoning, and problem solving. I knew what he was doing. I knew he was trying to prove to me that I would be fine, and I was so grateful for everything he pushed at me. I was also more in love with him than I could have ever thought imaginable.

He was there at night when I awoke screaming from the harsh nightmares of David's hands on me, teaching me how to overcome terror. To talk through it, write it all down, release it instead of letting it take hold of me. Teaching me to face the fears and become bigger and more important than they were. Kade Grayson taught me to live again. What man do you know would do this? I've seen, God, I have seen in my line of work, men watch over their wives for a week and then slowly start living their lives again, planning time without the person who is stuck in a hospital bed. He never once became impatient with me when I refused to move, or when I was too tired or just not able. The last sound I heard each night was the sound of Kade's voice as he read through his stories and poetry to me. And, he was there every morning when I woke. With that *fucking horrible* music. Then he'd push me to move, walk through the pain, and survive it. Who better a teacher, right?

"Let's go, Doc, focus. Time to get dressed. Personally, I fancy the open-back gown look on you, but I bloody hate to share my view of your perfect arse with the rest of the patients. Especially that old wanker, Mr. Timmins," his voice shifted through my thoughts.

Kade had laid out my clothes on the bed while I had my attention on the scenery out the window. Tall evergreens masked in a thick morning fog. Such a different view than that of my office downstairs. I slowly slid my slippered feet along the cool floor. My movements measured and precise, and well thought out. The least amount of movement for the least amount of pain. I intentionally opted out of accepting pain medications. My body was so strung out from what David had injected me with, so I wanted everything out of my system. I wanted personally to diagnose my cognitive reasoning, if I was able. And I sure as shit wasn't able to do so with an ongoing stream of happy pills being shoved down my throat. I just wanted the fog to lift from my thoughts, my memories. I wasn't used to living in the darkness of my own mind. I was a creature of the sun and its warm bright rays.

A sound rustling noise brushed past my shoulder. Kade's soft touch, tucking the loose strands of my hair behind my ear. "Hey, love. Pants first, then slippers," his low voice whispered.

Glancing down, I found myself dressed only in a shirt, cute white lacy underwear and my freaking zombie slippers. "I knew that."

"Uh huh," he smiled, and then softly slid the tips of his fingers over the sheer lace of my underwear. "Nice, panties," he breathed into my ear.

"Stop, Kade. I look and feel like I lived through a horror movie, so don't talk all sexy to me," I snapped, stepping out of my slippers. Zombie eyeballs jiggled past my toes.

The stupid ass, smirked. "Love, your eyes are wide open and you're talking back to me. You, Samantha are the strongest, kickass, most breathtaking woman I have ever bloody seen." Kade shifted his body in front of mine, muscles tight, heat radiating off his skin. His eyes, so grey, so full of hope, made me just melt into him and I slipped my feet back inside my slippers.

"Love, you still haven't put your pants on. Pants before slippers."

"I knew that," I lied in frustration. "You just made me lose focus."

"Uh huh," he chuckled. "It's okay, Sam. You know there's going to bloody be confusion and disorientation after your TBI. Loss of attention and agitation, I'm here to remind you of stuff, help you find some consistency. Hey, love? Guess what today is?"

"Smack Kade in the fucking face day?" I cringed, painfully stepping into my oversized sweatpants and slowly sliding them over my wounds. TBI. I hated those initials. Because of David, the filthy piece of monkey scum, I had a TBI. A traumatic brain injury. Not a severe one, thank God, but still...I just wanted to get back to being *me* again. And I was going to, I so was. Then I was going to piss on his grave.

"Oh, you're bloody brilliant, love. No that only happens on Sundays. Today is Tuesday, which means it's COUNSELING day." He then stuck his freaking tongue out at me.

*Shit on me.* Going to therapy with Kade was not fun. The first week, I was able to speak well enough to talk through the incident. Kade went with me for support, and when he listened to *everything* David did, he almost lost it. Then it promptly became Kade's therapy session, where it ended with him hurling a lamp across the room, screaming he should have shot him in the dick first, *then the head.* Security escorted him out of the building, and he wasn't allowed back inside until the next day after he signed a code of hospital conduct affidavit. It was the first day he was away from me since I came to the hospital, and I know he spent the night with his doctor, talking through his rage. But, I wouldn't be surprised if someone told me he offered them money to help him dig up David's grave and mount his head on his office wall. Nope, I wouldn't have been surprised at all, and I wouldn't have minded either.

That Tuesday, as always, he helped me walk the hospital corridors to make our way to therapy. Our first visit was always to Deputy George Tatum's room, where he was recuperating nicely from his gunshot wound to the stomach. Right below the bottom of his bulletproof vest. "Hey, look at this beautiful little lady, looking good, champ, looking good," he laughed from his bed. His wife

Margie, jumped up from her bedside vigil and gently hugged me.

"How are you feeling today, hun?" she whispered.

"Everyday a little better," I smiled. Then I gave my attention to George, "How about you, George, when you busting out of this joint, huh?"

"They say probably tomorrow, and I can't wait, because the food here sucks."

After a few more pleasantries, Kade and I made our way slowly around the hospital to the dreaded therapy room. I gingerly sat down, careful not to lean too heavily on my right thigh. My puncture wound was still swollen and painful, but I knew it would heal.

"So how are we feeling today, Samantha?" Doctor Ross asked as she handed me a bottle of water.

"I miss being myself. Doing things for myself. I hate having to depend on people. I hate the pain." I looked over to Kade, who was sitting across from me, watching me. "I feel guilty as hell that Kade is here all the time and not working and I know what he did to David is weighing..."

"Don't." Kade's eyebrows pulled together in one of his menacing scowls. "That sentence is going to end real ugly if you continue with those thoughts, so just bloody stop. *You*, Sam. You saved me from drowning in my own misery...now it's my turn. And nothing I did to David is weighing on any bloody part of my body."

"How are we going to get through this, Kade? You are going to crush yourself with what you did, you will regret..."

"No, I will never regret protecting you. I will never regret taking the life of someone who didn't deserve to live. I won't. I'm not Thomas. I'm not a psychopath or a sociopath, I don't take pleasure out of physically hurting people like your sadist of a husband did, and I'm not a unloving greedy fuck like your father. But I will stand proud and say that I stopped evil. I put a bullet into a man who killed a woman, shot a cop, and tortured the woman I love more than my own life. So no, I will never regret what I did. Now piss off about me and start talking about what YOU went through. Instead of healing every-bloody-body else, heal Sam!"

Kade was right. And I never talked so much about myself in my life. All the while with Kade's hand in mine, always touching me, watching me, as if he feared he would lose me if he turned the other way.

After three months in trauma rehabilitation, complete daily physical therapy, occupational therapy, speech therapy, and a hefty hand basket full of other therapies, Kade took me home.

"Up to the attic first, love."

"Why? I want to jump in bed with you," I laughed.

He stood in the doorway with a sheen of pure lust in his eyes, and then promptly shook it out. "Up to the attic, now."

"Fine," I huffed and walked up the stairs, which made me have to sit at the top and take a breath. "Sheesh, almost dying, really kills you."

Wrapping his arms around my body, he lifted me up and walked with me the rest of the way into the attic.

My eyes widened when I saw the entire room rearranged into an exact replica of the physical therapy gym in the hospital. That wasn't the only thing he did for me either. No, Kade fucking Grayson took weekly trips to a farm for fresh organic foods, and he cooked them for me. Do you understand the depth of this? Kade Grayson, King of the burnt-microwave-dinner-I'll-just-have-a-bag-of-pretzels instead. I watched him Google recipes, healthy ones, and coffee, my God, he bought me a brand new Keurig with a closet JUST FOR COFFEE. So many flavors.

Kade made what happened to me easier to deal with. He made learning to walk correctly again *easier,* learning to speak right again easier, but none of it was *easy.* Not at all. What David did was sick and twisted, and made me feel weak and small, but Kade made me realize, little by little, I was never weak, and I was never small. The monster was weak and small, *not the survivor.* Kade, the one they used to call the devil, showed me that it's okay to be scared as long as you're brave. To be strong when all you feel is weak, and to believe that I can survive and live after being touched by violence.

Six months after my abduction and torture, my father stood in front of the media, lawyers, and the federal court sentence for sentencing. The night of his arrest, he had been indicted and held without bail, and he pled guilty on all charges. It gave me a small amount of pleasure to know he admitted to everything, clearing my name and spending the rest of his pathetic life behind bars. Within the last eight years of him as head neurosurgeon, and then president of one of the prestigious New York City Hospitals, my father, Dr. Michael Matthews, along side his business partner, Dr. David Stanton, spread their venom into the white walls of the foundation, wiping out everyone in their path of destruction. A total of twenty-seven other doctors, pharmacists, lab technicians, and other medical workers were also arrested for knowledge, and helping with their fraudulent criminal actions.

It began as it always did, with big hospitals and greedy little doctors. My father and David billed Medicare for services NOT rendered, and began distributing controlled substances outside the course of routine medical practice, and for no legitimate purposes, except to make extra money. In the first year alone, they billed Medicare for approximately $567,000 in claims, yet this monetary value was not high enough for them, they wanted more. So they created their own Pharmaceutical Company, SamMatt, with me as the President. I guess that was easy for them, since I was gone to another world overseas, and my father really believed my achievements to be so little and insignificant that I would not return without the cover of a body bag.

The first action SamMatt did was misbrand painkillers and promote the drug to treat acute pain at dosages the FDA had previously found to be dangerously high. When they got away with that, they began using fillers and gave free units of the new drug to encourage doctors to buy their products. They inflated the prices from government programs and submitted false price reports. The criminal actions from my father and David went on and on, identity theft, pharmaceutical fraud, CME fraud, and off-label marketing, and so, so much more. The biggest one to me was helping to premeditate my murder, and the forced drug overdose of my brother. They charged my father with knowledge of everything that David Stanton did, because it was true. He knew of it all, and was fucking okay with every last detail. He was charged with criminally negligent homicide, which just means that he didn't intend any deaths to happen. They were just a consequence of all the other offenses. A means to an end. That's what my brother, Dr. Michael Matthews, Jr.'s, murder was; just a means to an end. It sickened me.

My father pleaded guilty to *everything*. I attended his sentencing. I went as a witness and stared that motherfucker in the face as Kade growled next to me. George stood on the other side of me, his arms clamped around my body, holding back Kade.

I was allowed to speak at the sentencing. I specifically asked to, because hell, I wasn't going to let him go without a word from me, *the last words from me* that he'd ever hear. My father, in his nifty orange jumper, sat stoic, staring forward. His eyes never diverted. His head never moved. He just sat still and motionless, as if he were a statue that nothing, and no one, could break.

Until me.

The judge called me up. Kade escorted me toward the front, but we did not move towards the podium. Oh, hell no. Kade and I walked right in front of my father's face, three feet in front of him, and made him look at me.

I had a speech eloquently written out folded deep in my pocket, but I left it there, not needing it any longer. Kade's fingers wrapped around mine, anger and rage simmering just under his skin, but he kept it in check, held it in. "You'll look right at her until she's done with you," Kade hissed. Even though it was said threateningly and menacingly, nobody moved to stop him from speaking. In fact, the bailiff just chuckled.

"I had *wanted* to ask to you *why*. I wanted to scream, shout, cry, and ask *how you could do what you did, but* I'm not going to do any of these things. Not ever. What I am going to do is forget you," I stated. My father's eyes filled with tears. They dripped down his pale face like rain. His tears gave me strength.

"There will not be a day I will live from now until my end, which a thought of you will be allowed to enter my mind. But *every* day, I will think of my *brother*, who was a great man, who touched people's lives with his strength and his courage, with his love for medicine, his knowledge and talents. He saved lives. He was and will always be my hero."

His tears fell faster. His breathing became harder, but I didn't care.

"But *I will not think of you*. I will not think about the pathetic man who allowed someone to torture me, use me, and abuse for his own monetary gain. Where's that money now? Gone. Just. Like. You. You're a coward and a thief. A weak poor excuse for a man. And I survived. I survived you, and I survived David. I thought I would hate you and want to claw your eyes out, but I don't, because you don't affect me at all. You're nothing. And you know what?" I took a deep breath and smiled up at Kade. "I'm done with you. Let's go, Kade. I feel like having a slice of pizza."

Dr. Michael Matthew's chin trembled. His eyes poured out tears that I wondered if they left his body just to escape his horrid pathetic soul. "I'm so sorry. Please find it your heart one day to..."

"STOP!" I yelled. Kade's grip on me tightened, and I squeezed his fingers back a strong reply of my own strength. "That's just a pathetic confrontational plea designed to draw an emotional response from me, and Mr. Matthews, you don't deserve anything I have to offer you anymore. Enjoy prison." *Rub that in like a lotion, bitch. Let it penetrate the skin, sink in real deep, you can't hurt me again. Ever.*

The courtroom erupted in applause and cheers, Jen's voice over all of the others. Yet, as I walked away, I heard my Kade rumble deep and low, "Watch your arse in prison, old man. I have friends in low places, and karma? Karma can bloody bite you right in that arse, literally."

Kade and I exited that courtroom with an army of people behind me, and my heart thundering like a battlefield. Running down the stone stairs, Jen stood on the lowest step and held her arms out wide as Dylan danced around her. "I say we ce-le-freaking-brate. Let's go dance on David's grave," she pointed her finger at me and narrowed her eyes. "Don't say I'm being horrible, because I've heard you say you've wanted to do it for months." *Yes, that was my best friend, always and forever my comic relief.*

Kade's hand slid up my back to the nape of my neck and all I wanted was to go home. Just go home and spend the rest of my life with that man. My eyes traveled up to his, clear gray skies, only the small whisper of a storm within, and I sighed, "Take me home, Kade."

Without a sound, he walked me to the truck, lips in my hair, hands digging into the flesh of my neck. He helped me climb in and skimmed his hands over my back, my ass, and my thighs. It made me shiver. *He always makes me shiver.*

Kade walked around the truck, eyes locked on mine as he passed in front of the dirty windshield. Kade was still mysterious, dark, and intense. And *mine*, he was all mine. He climbed inside the truck in silence, pulled the keys from his pocket, the muscles of his hands and his jaw tense, rigid, and so damn strong.

Heavy silence hung in the icy air between us, the mist of our breaths, mingling and spreading. We drive without heat, since we have enough inside us to keep us warm. We drive without music, because each other's breath was all the music we needed. We were all we ever needed.

Foot heavy on the pedal, green blur of wintery trees pass the sides of my vision, but I see nothing, nothing but Kade.

Then we're home. Time is tangible. I can feel it still around us, letting us live in the moment, and hell, and we both deserved it.

Without a word, he exits the car and quickly moves around his truck, warm hand against the small of my back, just where my coat meets my waist. His fingers touch skin, and they're like fire. Singeing and scarring, his touch burns into my flesh, rewriting, rewiring, reviving, and relentlessly, redefining everything I ever knew that was violent, savage, and vicious. Turning all my bruises to blushes, and all my scars to strength.

# EPILOGUE

February – Two years later.

*Samantha*

I scanned the crowded room and sighed happily as I eyed my husband sitting next to me in his tuxedo. Kade and I sat in Los Angeles's Dolby Theatre, surrounded by the most profound and talented artists in Hollywood. Kade's book about my abduction and torture, *Savage Heart*, was turned into a movie for which he wrote the screenplay. It was the hardest thing he'd ever written, his labor of love, but we did it together, side-by-side, with our therapist on call. There were days that it felt like we were tearing each other's hearts out, a pure and primal pain. Sometimes, we fought frantically, blamed each other, cried, and vomited out everything dark and evil. Other times, our sadness took control and left us empty and full of despair. Yet, we wrote, together. We healed together. We were intense, raw and passionate, twisted, dark and *forever*.

To no one's surprise, but Kade's, his screenplay was nominated for *The Academy Award for Best Adapted Screenplay* at the awards ceremony. He clutched the armrests, still uncomfortable in a big crowd, but we were there together, facing everyone, and that was all that mattered.

"I wonder if we could find any empty closets in this place. I bet I could make you stop choking the seats if

I could get you alone for a few minutes," I whispered, seductively into his ear.

His stormy eyes locked on mine and his hands let go of the chair and reached for mine. Interlocking our fingers together, he softly caressed the dark tattoo I had gotten encircled around my left ring finger. My tattooed wedding band that was the identical twin to his. We forwent the flimsy, easily discarded golden ones once we were married. What we had was intense and permanent, painful and beautiful all at once.

Will we ever fully heal from what we both endured in our pasts? Who is to say? Living one day at a time and doing the best you can is all that you could ever be in control of. Kade still has nightmares sometimes, as do I. Some featuring Thomas, others with David, and I'm still the calm in his storm, and he's turned out to be mine.

As they called his name for his award, he smiled. Muscles tight, jaw flexing, his strength and courage showing through as he faced a fear and ignored its taunt. I *knew* he would win. After all, the movie was brilliant, the writing perfect. There was never a doubt in my mind. Kade Grayson was not a man ever to be doubted. Yet, I was surprised when he walked up to the stage, long sexy masculine strides, accepted the award, then the microphone, *and* began to speak.

Kade *speaking* in front of an audience, and not thrusting his middle finger at the crowd of people cheering him on? *Un-freaking-believable.* And boy, did they cheer him on; they *stood up and cheered him on*, all of them. *All* the big names in Hollywood stood up for him and applauded, every single one of them. In my heart, I knew it wasn't just because he wrote that screenplay. God no, it was because of what he'd been through, what I'd been through, and how we saved each other. They were applauding our courage, our strength, our *fuck you to the haters*, and our love.

As the crowd slowly quieted down and the hush of heart pounding, nerve-wracking anticipation filled the large room, the dark brooding expression he always wore on his face transformed into a smile. He stood at the podium for a moment and took it all in, and then he glanced over the crowd quickly and found my eyes, and I watched him let out a breath of relief. He astonished me. It was breathtaking to see how this man had grown, how the both of us had.

Then his deep voice filled the speakers, echoing across the great sea of people, and grabbed hold of my heart. As always, he grabbed hold of my heart.

"Thank you. Thank you all so bloody much. However, there's truly only one person who deserves my utmost respect and gratitude. My beautiful wife, Samantha." His eyes were on mine. Sparkling. Shining. Heating. Coiling.

"People think that compared to men, women are the more vulnerable of the sexes. I think that's a huge bloody fallacy. When men become damaged, they usually stay broken and beaten, and they wait for someone else to put them back together. Women are the ones that pick up all the pieces, set them all up and seal up the holes. They heal. And, my God, did she build me up whole again.

I would not be up here today, if it wasn't for her, I don't even think I'd be breathing today, if it wasn't for her. So, thank you, Sam, for loving me, staying here and bloody fighting for me, and believing that I could be *more*. Thank you for showing me what courage and strength look like, and what compassion and love feel like." He held up the award and nodded to the crowd, but I knew I was still the only face he saw. "And, thank you Academy for this award. It's a pittance though, compared to who I have waking up next to me every morning. She's all the reward I'd ever need in this life."

He motioned for me to walk up on stage with him and I did. Of course, I did. Kade and I were a team, so I'd be by his side everywhere. When I reached him, he leaned into me, both hands grasping hold of my face, thumbs pressed hotly into my cheeks, and kissed me. His body unraveled and loosened, and he breathed me in deeply. The crowd erupted in mayhem. Cheers, whistles, screams, and a standing ovation. He waved blindly to the crowd and pulled me off stage in caveman Kade style.

The night continued with after parties that, of course, Kade declined. Right after we stepped foot backstage, he whisked me out of the back door to a waiting car headed to the airport. He just wanted to be on the next flight home. So did I, because tonight, with Dylan and Jen's help, I planned a huge celebration for him at the bar, which included a private performance from my favorite band, just for this occasion.

"There's a really *pretty guy* singing on my brother's stage," he eyed me suspiciously, as we walked inside the bar. A round of cheers and clapping exploded when everybody noticed we had walked in, and an explosion of streamers and confetti were thrown in Kade's direction. "Ah, yes. This looks like just as much fun as bloody root canal, yeah? We're staying fifteen minutes, and then we leave. I have another party planned."

"Oh, do you now? Who will be in attendance at this party of yours?"

"Me, you, and an empty house. I'm going to fuck you in every damn room."

"Let's make it ten minutes and you got yourself a deal," I said as I leaned on my tippy toes and kissed his lips. He growled against my lips.

Jen and Dylan call us over to the bar and give us a beer each, as the band's song ends. The tattooed lead singer taps on the microphone, and I swear the entire audience of women sigh, as he chuckled into it.

"That man is just so...I mean just look..." Jen stuttered.

"Yeah, love, he's almost as good looking as me, yeah?" Dylan teased next to her.

Before the singer began to speak, a pair of red lacy panties flew across the room, landing at his feet.

Kade laughed next to me, "What the bloody hell? He's not that bloody good looking, is he? How do you know this band, Sam? You know them personally?"

"The two singers were once patients in my trauma unit. They were in a motorcycle collision."

His eyes narrowed.

"Hey, how's everybody doing tonight? We're here tonight for a very special woman, Doctor Samantha Grayson, who once saved both me and my wife's life. We're here to celebrate Kade Grayson's award! Let's motherfucking party!"

"Babe, I'm having that specifically violent jealousy fantasy where I'm killing him with my bare hands. Are you sure he was just your patient."

Jen giggled as I winked at Kade and walked away. A slow rock ballad started, and I went to start my rounds of hello *and goodbye*, because we seriously only had like three more minutes. I wanted to leave just as quickly as Kade. Nights alone were far and few between for us.

I listened to the music, the beat and heavy rhythm of the sounds and I felt Kade's eyes watch me. *I should go around and just thank everyone for coming and then we could... All my thoughts* completely faded when I looked up and noticed Kade's dark stare. I heard myself gasp when I saw him. The air just sort of sucked itself right out of my lungs. No one ever watched me like Kade did. It was personal. Intimate. My cheeks heated, when his lips curled into a sexy smirk of a smile. It was animalistic and primal. Hot-as-hell; it made me tingle with a damp warmth between my thighs and against the silken material of my panties. I started to fan myself a bit with one of the bar's laminated menus. I loved this game we played. Every night, like the first night we met. I never knew...I never knew what it felt like to be truly loved and desired, until I met Kade. I felt *wanted*. Desired. Hungered for. *Lusted*. Preyed on. I fanned myself faster.

He was leaning back against the red velvet of the booth chair, dressed in his tuxedo. His inky black hair wildly arranged on his head. His *face*...all hard angles. A jaw carved out of stone, strong cheekbones and full perfect lips. He wore his strength on his expression, dark, passionate, and profound.

I stared back at him too, holding his gaze, which made my senses, all of them, kick into overdrive. The exchange was maddening and arousing, and like nothing I'd ever felt before Kade, primal and visceral in texture. It was purely mouthwatering.

"Hey, Sam? Mum still watching the kids tonight?" Dylan's voice broke through the beginning sequence of my pornographic thoughts.

"Huh? Oh, yes. Your mother said she'd look after them, take them for ice cream and stuff. Give me and Kade some time alone to celebrate."

Jen and Dylan laughed as they both looked back and forth between Kade and I. "Looks like you two are starting your staring foreplay right now. So, yeah, we'll see you guys tomorrow, huh?"

My eyes were still locked on Kade's. "Uh huh."

And the music softy drifted to my ears.

*What have we found*
*A diamond in the rough*
*What have we lived*
*To know we've had enough*
*You're what I craved*
*When the loneliness takes hold*
*You're what I need*

*To waken up my soul*
*You're what makes it all beautiful*
*You're the one that makes it worth the fight*
*You're the one that took my wrong*
*And make them all turn right*
*Side by Side*
*Don't wanna do it on my own*
*Together, together*
*With you I'll never be alone*
*You make it all beautiful*
*You make it worth the fight*
*You make it all beautiful*
*You make it worth the fight*

# Kade

The bloody song fades into background noise. I was sitting at my usual table, texting Mum to see if the kids were behaving. Yes, bloody hell, I'm a dad. It's the best bloody thing I ever did. As soon as we were married and I was cleared of any suspicions concerning the *self-defense* killing of that monster, Samantha and I adopted three children, who also suffered abuse at the hands of the ones they loved. The first of our little ones was Sophia, who was seven, and she came to us neglected and so undernourished, she only weighted forty-eight pounds. Our second was five-year old Toby, who was witness to the bloody murder of his sisters and mother by the hands of his father. And lastly, there's my little Sunshine, with hair as bright as the blazing sun. She's three, but was abandoned and left at a hospital when she was only a few days old. Because of what David did to Sam, doctor's told her she'd never be able to have children of her own, to which she laughed at the man and said, "Oh, I'll be a mom, and I will have children of my own, maybe just not through birthing them." I think my wife plans to save all the children she can find who suffered as we have, and show them what love and family truly is. And, you bloody know what? I love her more for that, so much more. My mum texts back that all the children are tucked away in bed at her new house, a few miles away from ours, and to enjoy our night alone, when a small fluid movement caught my eye. Backlit as she stood in front of the illuminated bar, I had a perfect view of her silhouette. Deep cinnamon hair tumbled wildly over her creamy white neck, falling to her tiny waist as if it were liquid silk. Petite, yet voluptuous, with soft curves that had me instantly thinking about sinking inside deeply, and riding her hard. On one side of her face, her long hair was pinned back with a soft lilac ribbon that made her look indecently innocent. Shiny waves were cascading down from the little clip and fell around her face, framing soft porcelain features. She wore a familiar emotion on her face that I knew all too well, *haunted*. The plain raw intelligence of her face was utterly breathtaking, and for the first time in my life, I couldn't find the correct adjectives to describe something. No mere words would have done her natural beauty justice, or could have described the way she moved.

It was like...*liquid*.

That's the only word I had for her.

Flowing, fluid, melting into everything with a precision that seemed naturally calculated. I felt like Adam looking at Eve for the first time, having never seen another woman before her. *Just like the first night I saw her*. I get up and stalk towards her, devouring the distance of the room between us in long strides. I can't stand to be away from her any longer. I can't stand not being inside her for a minute more.

I don't know what will happen to our love, or to our family, does anyone? I hope that we will always be as strong as we are, and never know more heartache. All I do know is that people can heal. They can go on. The can survive and not only *live though it, but beyond*. Especially if you open up your heart and let people in.

In the middle of the bar, in the crowd of people, which being stuck in the middle of always makes me on edge, I grab her cheeks and crush my lips to hers. She opens her mouth greedily, my Samantha. My everything.

"Kade, are you okay?" she says, green eyes staring up. "What are you thinking about?"

"Our future," I whispered against her lips. Gently pushing her with my body, hands clasped around the soft skin of her neck. She lets me lead her, walking her backwards down the back hallway and straight into Dylan's office. My hands twist and tangle tightly in her hair, and I press her into the wall. Her lips part with mine, her hands slid up my sides, digging fingers and nails into my muscles. "I wouldn't be here if it weren't for you, baby."

"And what do you see of this future, Mr. *Academy Award*?" She murmurs, as her fingers swiftly skim down to my belt. Buckle yanked, teeth of my zipper scraped, hot hands fisting and pulsing around me.

I lean my head back. Green, green eyes. The eyes that are my redemption. "You want me to write our epilogue?" My hands tighten in her hair, pulling down, her face...her green eyes burn out in heat.

"Yeah, what would it be?"

"We make love every single morning, and we fuck every single night. You are in every character I write. You're the strength in my hero, the courage in my victims, you're the face of every fierce woman I write... And we'll have as big a family as we can." I watch her swallow back tears and smile. "You'll go back to the hospital but you won't go back to trauma. You find living with me is all the adrenaline rush you need. But you help so many people that have been touched by trauma, by violence. By evil. You bloody fucking heal them all. And you are an amazing mother to our children, and you center me, and sit beside me until my last breath."

"Sounds perfect."

"It will be."

"How do you know for sure?"

"Because our future is anything we can make it. Anything you bloody want it to be, love. I'll write that epilogue for you."

# ACKNOWLEDGEMENTS

There is a huge stack of teetering people I should be thanking and acknowledging publicly in this book, yet I feel I should just whisper thank you, quietly to each of you.

*Pssst.*

Thanks.

# COLD-BLOODED BEAUTIFUL PLAYLIST

*Whiskey In The Jar* – Metallica

*Leaving Earth* – Clint Mansell
(Mass Effect 3)

*Simple Man* – Shinedown

*Paint It Black* – The Rolling Stones

*Raise Your Glass* – Pink

*Just Give Me a Reason* - Pink

*Radioactive* – Imagine Dragons

*So Far Away* – Avenged Sevenfold

*Down With the Sickness* – Disturbed

# BOOKS BY CHRISTINE ZOLENDZ

*Mad World Series (Paranormal Romance)*
Fall From Grace
Saving Grace
Scars and Songs

*The Beautiful Series (Suspense and Romance)*
Brutally Beautiful
Cold-Blooded Beautiful

**For more information about Christine Zolendz, please visit:**

https://www.facebook.com/ChristineZol?ref=hl

https://www.facebook.com/christine.zolendz

http://christinezolendz.blogspot.com

https://twitter.com/ChristineZo

https://www.goodreads.com/author/show/6448939.Christine_Zolendz

Made in the USA
Lexington, KY
23 February 2014